BLIND
FALL

A NOVEL

CHRISTOPHER RICE

SCRIBNER

NEW YORK   LONDON   TORONTO   SYDNEY

SCRIBNER
A Division of Simon & Schuster, Inc.
1230 Avenue of the Americas
New York, NY 10020

First Scribner hardcover edition March 2008

SCRIBNER and design are trademarks of
Macmillan Library Reference USA, Inc., used under license
by Simon & Schuster, the publisher of this work.

For information about special discounts for bulk purchases,
please contact Simon & Schuster Special Sales:
1-800-456-6798 or business@simonandschuster.com.

Designed by Kyoko Watanabe
Text set in Garamond 3

Manufactured in the United States of America

1   3   5   7   9   10   8   6   4   2

Library of Congress Cataloging-in-Publication Data

ISBN-13: 978-0-7432-9399-0
ISBN-10: 0-7432-9399-1

For Eric Shaw Quinn,
with great love and admiration.

Listen to me, boy. Only gods and heroes can be brave in isolation.

—STEVEN PRESSFIELD,
Gates of Fire

BLIND
FALL

PROLOGUE

The dog was sprawled under the rear bumper of an abandoned Opel sedan, its left leg bent at an impossible angle. There was no gore to suggest that it had been run down by the car that now concealed its forequarters, so Sergeant John Houck moved in for a closer look. Then he heard the slap of bare feet hitting pavement and looked up to see someone strangely familiar running toward him down the sidewalk. His younger brother looked just as he had when he was sixteen years old, back when he and John still lived under the same roof—bright freckles and narrow blue eyes crowding the bridge of his button nose, a thick cap of nappy red hair that moved like cake icing under even the toughest hairbrush. Dean Houck ran past the other men in John's recon team, past Captain Mike Bowers, who was scanning the empty door-ways on the other side of the street.

Only later would John come to realize that the true definition of a ghost was a hallucination so powerful it could distract you from a task of monumental importance.

Within seconds, John became oblivious to the flies swarming the dog's carcass several yards away. He also forgot about the M-4 he held in a two-handed grip, and he no longer felt the biting snakes of sweat that slithered down his body, tracing the edges of his Kevlar vest and looking for tender spots in his groin to sink their tiny fangs into. His brother wore one of those sack dresses the boys in Iraq always wore. There was an Arabic term for them, but it was Lance Corporal Dickinson who called them "'raqi sacks." The men in his unit called him Panama Dick because he informed any Marine who would listen that his hometown of Panama City had the "prettiest goddamn motherfuckin' beaches in the whole U.S. of A." Panama Dick was walking point, as their team pro-ceeded on foot toward a location at the town's northern border, where they had been ordered to establish a guard station, a station that the Army wusses who controlled this area were too damn lazy and disorganized to set up themselves.

Panama Dick and Lightning Mike Bowers both seemed miles away suddenly as John Houck watched his younger brother turn into a break between buildings that held an abandoned well. His brother turned his back to him, reached up, and unwound the length of rope that held the cracked bucket to the singed metal frame that arched over the well's mouth. Whip-fast, he let out the bucket's rope between both hands, bending forward to watch the bucket's progress, rising up onto the balls of his feet, which John could now see were dark brown, not the freckled, milk white shade of his dead brother's skin.

A deep clang echoed up from the well, followed by another.

The boy was swinging the bucket deliberately, playing it like a bell inside the well's shaft. John felt a presence behind him suddenly; then he heard the familiar voice of Lightning Mike Bowers say his last name in a terse whisper. Bowers went silent for a few seconds as he assessed the scene in front of them.

"*Shit!*" Bowers hissed. Bowers realized how badly John had fucked up before John did.

The dog's impossibly bent carcass positioned conspicuously with its lower half exposed . . .

The boy's dark skin and tight cap of ink black hair, nothing like his younger brother's . . .

The expectant look in the boy's pale eyes when he looked back at them over one shoulder, his arms splayed over the opening of the well, rope clasped in his hands as the bell rang out its death knell . . .

And then the dog's carcass vanished in a blinding flash.

The back end of the Opel sedan rose into the air on a bed of jagged white flame. At the precise second when he expected the shrapnel to tear into him, John ate dust and felt the weight of Mike Bowers come down onto him. The blast deafened him, but he could feel Bowers's breath against his right ear, could even feel the guy's lips moving. Mike was trying to tell him something, but it had been lost to the initial explosion. Then the weight pressing down on John got heavier.

Once Bowers was pulled off him, John still found himself unable to move and deafened by the blast. Thick black smoke blinded him. In a vague way, he knew that he had no sense of time, that he was fading in and out without losing consciousness.

Something hot flowed down the back of both of his legs. Blood? Still flowing with too much force to have come off Bowers, and Bowers had been lifted off him . . . who knew how long ago? He could feel a deep pounding in his chest and suddenly the smoke around him started to clear. The medevac. Another side-step into the darkness that hovers at the edges of every reality, and then he was back, pushing himself up onto his knees, struggling to his feet.

Convinced blood was pouring down his back, he grabbed furiously at his pack, pulled it down his right arm, and hurled it to the dirt at his feet. Not blood. Water! Leaking all over the place. He tore open his pack, which had searing holes all through its skin. The torn remnants of what had once been eight water bottles tumbled to the dirt, shredded by shrapnel.

Jesus, he screamed silently. *Jesus Christ. Bowers was lying on my pack, for fuck's sake. If that's what happened to my pack, then what the hell happened to Bowers?*

Something hot and wet filled his left eye and his vision was all but blocked. A field medic raced toward him, bandage already out. The medic pressed the bandage to the left side of John's face with one hand and forced him back down into a seated position with the other. Unable to hear his own pleas for Bowers or whatever the medic said to stave him off, he felt helpless and childlike as the medic swabbed the blood from his left eye and dressed the wound.

Then he saw the stretcher, the stretcher that carried Bowers toward the Black Hawk helicopter twenty yards away. When he rose to his feet and followed Bowers, the medic followed right beside him. John knew his own injuries weren't serious enough to merit a trip to Balad, but the medic didn't stop him, and that was good, because it meant no other injured needed the space. Inside the Black Hawk, it was just John, his medic, and the two medics cutting away the front of Bowers's blood-soaked uniform, wrapping Bowers's bloodied head in bandages.

John looked out the window, saw the other men in his team returning to the street. Some of them had fanned out in search of the triggerman, but others had stayed behind. He watched them watch the chopper take off, and he could feel the accusations in their stares.

×

Fifty miles north of Baghdad, the U.S. Air Force Theater Hospital occupied three dozen tents and three trailers set up on the sands of a former Iraqi Air Force base in Balad. As soon as they set down, Bowers was rushed to surgery, and the flight medic ushered John through a controlled chaos of doctors and nurses that seemed to have the professionalism and urgency of an ER at a top-flight hospital back in the States.

The doctor found two pieces of shrapnel in John's side and dug them out in no time. Unlike the medic who allowed him on the Black Hawk, he wasn't happy to be spending time on the kind of minor injuries that could have easily been dealt with at an aid station closer to the scene of the blast. John's hearing was back by then, so he asked a lot of questions about Bowers, but no one saw fit to answer any of them. Then he realized that no one at Balad knew Bowers by his last name, only by the last four digits of his Social Security number, which one of the flight medics had written in Sharpie marker on the flesh of Bowers's right arm after reading them off his dog tags.

A hefty blond nurse, probably Army by the look of her, told him patient 9260 was in surgery and would stay there for some time. A neurosurgeon had been called in—and an ophthalmologist. "An *eye* doctor," she said when she saw the dazed expression on his face. Then she moved on, past the spot where a doctor and several nurses were trying in vain to resuscitate a young Iraqi boy who barely had any flesh left on his legs. Only blood hid the bones.

Not the kid who had alerted the triggerman for the IED that had almost taken them both out, but it could have been. Here in Balad, Americans and Iraqis were treated side by side; soldiers and insurgents alike received the same care. A day earlier, this lack of a division would have infuriated him. But given how badly he had fucked up that day, given that they were now trying to save Mike Bowers's eyes because of it, harsh judgments eluded him.

Outside, he wandered the perimeter and watched Black Hawks rise into the fading light of dusk, tried to fend off some attempts at conversation from a battered PFC in a wheelchair. The kid couldn't hide his excitement over the fact that he was leaving Iraq that night in one of the C-17 transport planes that routinely ferried the hopelessly wounded to Germany and beyond. And he had smokes, so John bummed one and pretended to listen to him talk, trying to keep his mind off the e-mail that started it all, the e-mail he read before leaving on patrol, the e-mail that had placed his little brother in the middle of Ramadi.

Mike, he thought. *Make Mike the priority here. Make Mike the focus.* And, of course, it was Lightning Mike Bowers's voice he heard as he thought these words. Lightning Mike, who had reached out to John, had seen a guy hanging on the periphery, doubting their mission, and had brought him into the fold. It was Lightning Mike who had explained to him, "We fight the wars presidents tell us to fight because to do otherwise would be to turn America into a Third-World nation in which rulers are casually unseated by militaries without any genuine loyalty to the countries they are formed to protect." It was Lightning Mike who had given John his dog-eared, underlined copy of *Gates of Fire* by Stephen Pressfield, the novel about the Spartans' last stand at Thermopylae. Every man in their unit had read the book at least twice. Bowers had memorized it.

In six short months John and Mike had become something close to brothers: two Marines who had gone for the elite Force Recon Company because it had once offered the toughest-of-the-tough a kind of independence, trained them to slip behind enemy lines far from the overbearing presence of a commanding officer. All that had changed with the invasion, when Rumsfeld had decided to surprise the Marine Corps by placing their most elite units at the very tip of the spear. Recon Marines who had been trained to be invisible found themselves manning lumbering convoys, placed at the wheel of vehicles they had never been trained to drive. Bowers had responded to this change by reaching out to the guys who had become alienated and moved to the fringes, guys like John.

After hours of pacing, John parked himself on a bench a stone's throw from the outdoor toilets, where he was lulled to sleep by the occasional hum of an armed reconnaissance drone and the footfalls of overly caffeinated doctors on break making their frequent pit stops. When he awoke there was a bright glow in the eastern sky, the kind of clear first light of dawn that reminded him of his teenage years in Southern California. He was staring up into the pale face of the blond nurse who had finally given him news of Bowers the night before. Dark circles around her eyes and flyaway hairs suggested she had worked through the night.

"Your buddy's awake," she said. She spoke to him in a ragged voice as he followed her inside. "Took a couple hours, but they removed four pieces of shrapnel from the left side of his face."

"The optha—" His dry mouth was still sticky from sleep.

"The eye surgeon, you mean?"

"Yeah."

"Yeah," she said. "His left one"—for a second he thought she was mocking him, then he realized she was genuinely hesitating, considering how to deliver the blow—"he lost it."

He paused where he stood but the nurse didn't notice and took a few steps before she realized he wasn't following her. She stopped and did a bad job of hiding her impatience. "Worse things have been lost here," she said. When he didn't respond, she softened. "This guy your captain?"

He wanted to tell her that Mike was more than that, much more, probably the greatest Marine John had ever met, but he could already see that she would roll her eyes, dismiss it as just some battlefield sentiment that would be forgotten as soon as they were home again, just another example of the Marine brotherhood bullshit the Army boys and girls seemed so sick of here at Balad. John started walking again, without saying anything, and she led him into a patient ward where ten occupied hospital beds ran the length of the tent. Generators hummed on the other side of the flaps, and the pull curtain had been drawn around the bed for patient 9260. John drew it back, and the nurse left him.

Bandages wrapped Mike's entire head and covered the left side of his face. A mound of what John assumed was gauze lifted the area underneath the bandages where Mike's left eye should have been. More bandage strips covered the traces of stitches along his right cheek, forehead, and jaw.

The nurse had left out that both of his legs had been broken.

There was so much attached to Bowers that was not Bowers that John almost forgot he was staring at a human being until he saw his buddy's right eye roll toward him. John prepared himself for rage, but instead Bowers did his best attempt at a smile and in a drowsy voice slurred, "They tell me I'm not a candidate for transplant surgery. Maybe if I was into collecting coins or something I'd be moved up the list. Guess it's 'cause I like to live life on the edge, you know? Kind of takes me out of the game."

In the silence that followed, John felt like shit for not having rehearsed what he needed to say. The least he could have done was laugh at this joke because that would have been polite, and given that he was to blame for the scene before him, polite would have been a nice fucking change of pace. Polite was the way Bowers effected a mild Southern accent with John so he wouldn't feel like white trash sitting next to a superior officer with a degree in classics from the University of Arizona.

Finally Mike said, "They're taking me to Germany soon, Houck. You want me to get you something? Piece of the wall, maybe?"

"Something I need to say," John whispered.

"Germany, Houck. Lots of fine gift opportunities. Speak now or forever—"

"You're not getting me a fucking *gift*!" Humiliation flooded him when he realized he had snapped at Bowers as if he were a bad dog. But Lightning Mike just stared at the ceiling with his good eye while he tongued his chapped blood-blistered lips.

"There's something I need to say," John tried again, enunciating this time.

"No, there isn't," Bowers said. If he hadn't been bandaged and restrained, he'd probably be leaning toward John, tapping the side of his left hand into his right palm for emphasis, cleft appearing in his chin. Bowers continued, "No after-action report's going to come out of this. It was just the two of us and that boy, and if anybody asks, you just tell 'em there was still some part of you that didn't want to think they'd use kids for spotters. Maybe you knew different, but you wanted to *believe* different. Sound good?"

John said nothing. He felt a kind of childish anger, as if by letting him off the hook, Mike was preventing him from experiencing some crucial rite of passage, like a parent who wants his child to stay a virgin forever. But his anger wasn't enough to force him to give voice to what had truly gone down out there. There had been an e-mail, but if Mike didn't want to know about it, why should John say a word?

So he didn't tell him that barely an hour before they had left on their mission, John had read an e-mail informing him that his younger brother had committed suicide, an e-mail written by an older sister he had not spoken to in ten years. John didn't apologize for not telling Bowers this before they had geared up, before John had seen a ghost in the middle of a city already so crowded with ghosts it barely had any room to accommodate his.

But after only a few seconds the silence between them grew unbearable and John heard himself say, "Something happened back home. . . . I should have told you before we left on patrol. We were going through a hostile area. I should have told you I wasn't . . . I wasn't going to be at my best." No reaction. "My brother . . . he killed himself." He looked up and saw that Bowers's right eye had drifted shut. His lips were slightly parted. His chest was rising and falling with deep breaths.

His confession spoiled, John had no choice but to see the words of his sister's e-mail as they had appeared on the cracked, fingerprinted computer screen.

> John, I wish there was a better way for me to do this but there
> doesn't seem to be. Our brother Dean took his own life on the
> third of this month. Is there any way for you to come home for
> the funeral? I will wait for as long as I can to hear back from
> you before I bury him. . . . I love you, Patsy.

John Houck wondered how long these words would have to roll back and forth in his head before they would collect enough grit and blood to seem as significant as the loss all around him.

✕

John was asleep in the chair when they came to start preparing Bowers for his flight, and he felt a kind of dread when their motions finally forced him from the small halo of space between the curtain and the bed.

Once they were in motion, John followed close behind the flight medics, trying to see if Bowers was conscious enough to hear him, trying to see if Bowers was searching for John with his one good eye. Then they were being crowded by other traveling gurneys being pushed by other teams of flight medics, all of them filing toward the entrance to the airfield and the dull roar of jet engines. Outside, the medics pushed the gurneys past the chain-link fence at the edge of the tarmac, and one of the medics turned and held John back with an open palm.

John had hoped for a better good-bye than this.

Panic seized him, and because he could think of nothing better to say, he shouted, "Don't get me a damn thing, Mike! No gifts! Soon as we're back home, I'm going to have something for *you*! All right, buddy? Deal?"

Suddenly Bowers gave him a thumbs-up. John gave him a thumbs-up right back. Even though there was no way for Mike to turn around and see it, John kept his hand high as Bowers and the other patients were rolled in single file up the ramp and into the massive belly of the C-17 transport plane, its wings extending 170 feet on either side, the four jet engines attached to them powering to life.

It was the last time John Houck saw Mike Bowers alive.

1

Nine Months Later

John Houck was on his way back from the mailboxes at the front of the Devore Meadows trailer park when he saw Little Dan sitting on the bright redwood steps of his mother's trailer. The nine-year-old boy was staring down at his feet as he traced a pattern in the dust with the tip of his right sneaker. The kid's apple-cheeked pout could have melted the heart of a serial killer, but when he saw John approaching, the boy pulled his backpack up onto his lap and began carefully unzipping it, as if he had suddenly remembered he had some important bookkeeping to do. John figured the whole display was for his benefit, and he was happy to play along. The kid was sharp, but unlike a lot of the other kids being raised in Devore Meadows, he didn't have the kind of smart mouth and bad attitude that suggested a future relationship with the California prison system.

"What's up, Li'l D?" John asked him.

The boy squinted at this nickname, probably because it was a few days old and he had heard it only once or twice before. A few nights earlier, after John and the boy's mother had watched the kid drift off to sleep in front of one of the *Matrix* movies, John had allowed her to pull him into the back bedroom of her trailer, where they spent an hour working their way to a finish so explosive she sank her teeth into John's forearm to stifle her cry. Now the kid was giving him a smug expression that suggested John wasn't the only guy in Devore Meadows to have used movie night as an excuse to hit the sack with his mom.

"What's that?" the boy asked quietly.

For a fearful few seconds, John thought Li'l D was talking about the bite mark his mother had left on John's arm. Then he realized the kid was gesturing to the stack of mail he held under one arm. John sat down on the steps next to him, tore open the large white envelope, and pulled out an Applicant Study Guide for the California Highway Patrol that he had requested several weeks before. After a few months working a construction job renovating a big resort up on Lake Arrowhead, John now had enough cash saved to get him through cadet training.

The boy said, "Mom said you were already a cop."

"Sheesh. You can read already?"

"I read all the time. I'm *nine*. So you're not a cop yet? How come you have to study?"

"CHP's the best darn law enforcement agency in the country," he said. "There's a lot a man has to know." Of course, John thought he knew most of it already, and he probably did, given his ten years in the Marine Corps, three of those as a sergeant with First Force Reconnaissance Company out of Camp Pendleton.

Recon was the closest the Marines had to a special forces unit, even though most Marines would balk at the idea that one Marine was more special than another. CHP offered him a different uniform from the one he had been wearing when Mike Bowers lost his left eye for him, but still, John didn't know if he had what it took to wear any uniform proudly again.

As if he could sense this stream of doubt running through John, Li'l D watched John intently as he put the study guide back inside its envelope.

"What you doing out on the steps, Li'l D?" John asked. "Waiting for a lady friend?"

Without a smile the kid said, "My dad took me today. He was supposed to keep me until six but he said he dropped me off early. We were supposed to go get pizza but instead we had McDonald's and went to some stupid park that didn't have any ducks or swings or anything. Then he said he had to bring me back. He said he'd tell my mom but I guess he didn't, 'cause she's not here."

"Let's give her a call. Where's she at?"

"Work."

"Where's work?"

The boy tilted his head, squinted against the bright sunlight but managed to focus on John's face. "You have sleepovers with my mom but you don't know where she works?"

John shot to his feet, tugged the boy down the steps by one shoulder, and started them toward his own trailer, several plots away. "Is that what your mom called it? A sleepover?"

"Yeah. I told her I thought only kids got to have sleepovers."

"And here we are!" John opened the door to his trailer and showed the kid inside. That morning, the harsh winds that regularly tore through Cajon Pass had buffeted the walls of his trailer like they were canvas, but they had died down now. He opened the freezer just to see the mess inside. A bottle of Corona had exploded inside it at six in the morning, and John awakened to find himself down on all fours next to the bed, sighting an invisible M-4 at the tiny television in the corner of his bedroom. He forgot he stashed the bottle in there the night before to get it cold. He wasn't sure what to be more afraid of: his forgetfulness or his predawn acrobatics.

Most civilians thought post-traumatic stress disorder caused murderous flights from reality. For John, it came up as a split-second failure of perspective that to the outside observer might appear as embarrassing as a loose bladder. You had to have spent most of your life being trained to react to every situation with immediate and decisive action to comprehend how demoralizing it was, like going to draw on an enemy and finding a banana in your gun holster. Maybe he was lucky. He knew some guys who checked out and stopped returning phone calls and e-mails and postcards. Guys like Lightning Mike Bowers. Or at least that's what John thought was going on with the man. But it was also possible that Bowers had given some serious consideration to the cost of having saved John's life in Ramadi and decided that postcards and phone calls from John just weren't going to work for him. This thought bathed the pit of John's stomach in ice.

John was about to offer the kid a cold drink when he saw Li'l D standing at the foot of his bed. He drew the kid backward out of the bedroom by one shoulder and shut the door gently. "Off-limits, okay?"

"Why?"

Because there's a Sig Sauer P-220 in a holster behind the headboard, he thought. *It's a .45-caliber handgun and I'll go to my grave before I let you or any other child get your hands on it.* As John groped for a response, Li'l D moved to the kitchenette's tiny table and said, "I guess you have sleepovers, too."

"Your mom got a cell phone?"

"It got turned off."

"So, back to place of employment . . ." The kid wrinkled his nose at this strange adult phrase. "Her job. Where does she work?"

"A gas station."

"Which gas station?"

"I don't know. She won't tell me. She says there's no way in hell she's going to work at a gas station long enough for no kid of hers to know where it is."

"Watch the language."

"It's what *she* said!" There was pain in the kid's voice, more pain than the embarrassment of being chastised for bad language by a man who was for all intents and purposes a stranger. John wanted to ask the kid how long he had been sitting on the front steps, but he figured that would only make him feel worse.

The most he knew about Li'l D's mother was that she was a regular at karaoke nights at a bar down in Highland called The Lantern—she had asked him to go with her next Thursday and he'd said he'd get back to her—and like every other girl he had been to bed with since returning home from Iraq, she had a dream of auditioning for *American Idol* someday. He also knew that she loved cats but was allergic to them, so she had to settle for two-dimensional versions of them on all her dishrags and in the pages of the calendar hanging over her kitchen counter.

She also pretended to be interested in the Marine Corps, listened attentively as he described the Battle of Belleau Wood to her while he traced designs on her bare stomach, but that could have just been the boxed wine they had been drinking or an after-effect of the orgasm she might have played up for effect. What he knew was that she was a short, big-boned, apple-cheeked blonde who came on as bossy and assertive and flirty all at the same time, and that was a package that had been making him weak with desire ever since he was a teenager. What he didn't know was why she was currently unreachable and why she didn't have enough cash to pay her cell phone bill.

John had been raised by his older sister, Patsy, who had sacrificed everything to make sure that he and his brother didn't end up in the custody of a drunken aunt after their parents were killed in a car accident. And Mandy, cat-lover and *American Idol* wannabe, was not living up to Patsy Houck's stellar example. But there was no need for the kid to know this, so he rose to his feet and said, "You wait right here. When I get back, we're going to get you some pizza."

The kid raised his eyebrows but didn't crack a smile: he had already learned not to get too excited about any promise an adult might make to him. "Pizza Hut or Domino's?" John asked him.

"Golden Door."

"What the hell is the Golden Door?"

"Um . . . *language*."

"Where is it?"

"Loma Linda." John tried not to curse. It was a good twenty-minute drive south and they were sure to hit bumper-to-bumper traffic on the way back. The kid continued, "And it's not just pizza. They have everything—an arcade, a play area, live music—"

"I got it. I got it. The Golden Door it is."

Live music. The only term that struck greater fear in his heart was *enfilading fire.* But he was a good kid and he didn't deserve to spend the afternoon being ignored, even if it meant John might have to put up with a mariachi band in his face.

Just as he had expected, John found his neighbor Emilio working on his truck in a makeshift garage he had built next to his trailer out of two-by-fours and canvas tarps that were so wind-battered they looked like they had been shot through with bullets.

The truck's hood was up, but Emilio was in the front seat, surfing stations on the radio. The forty-seven-year-old Mexican man-aged an auto body shop in Highland, and a few weeks earlier a cousin of his had brought some friends in who had needed serious fender work done at a serious discount. When the guys decided not to pay even the reduced price, Emilio's cousin caved and told him the guys were all gangbangers who wouldn't take kindly to multiple invoices, this after Emilio had called one of the *cholos* in question a no-account thug. His pants wet, Emilio had shown up on John's doorstep one night and told him the whole story. John spent the entire next day teaching him basic defensive moves. Ever since then Emilio had been strutting through Devore Meadows like a rooster on steroids.

When he saw John through the windshield, Emilio shot from the front seat and threw his arms around him. John gave him a pat on the back until he was released, and said, "If you see Mandy, tell her I took her kid to get some pizza."

"*Mandy.*" Emilio winced. "Aw, tell me you're not gonna hit that shit, man."

John whacked Emilio across the back of the head, just as his own sister had whacked him across the back of the head every time he'd referred to a female by any term besides *lady* or *woman* or *ma'am*. "That's no way to talk about a lady, Emilio."

"Dude, you're a fuckin' Marine. You could walk into any bar, have any woman you want. You just throw her right over your shoulder, walk out. Ace in *every* hole, man."

"I don't just want any woman. I want Jessica Biel," he said, turning from the truck. "When Mandy comes back you tell her that her kid's dad dropped him off early and he asked me to take him to some pizza place in Loma Linda that sounds like a whore-house."

"*What?*" Emilio called after him.

"The Golden Door! Loma Linda!"

"Got it," Emilio called after him. John was almost back to his own trailer when he heard Emilio shout after him, "Hey man, you be careful of that kid's stomach. One time I gave my sister's kid some pizza—it was like a horror movie, man!"

✕

The Golden Door had everything Li'l D had promised and more, including a birthday party made up entirely of shrieking little girls, seated at the table right next to them. To keep himself from losing his mind, John kept his attention on the boy sitting across from him. A band played onstage, a band made up of giant animatronic animals who belted out the lyrics *It's time to be happy to-daaaay! It's time to be happy to-daaaay!* Their heads jerked from side to side. Their giant furry eyelids rose and fell in time to the music. A giant puppy played drums—he had big floppy ears that shot up into the air on the high notes and a long mouth lined with rounded white teeth that made him look like a barracuda. Li'l D was transfixed by this display, his eyes wide and glassy as he slowly chewed each bite of cheese pizza.

If John had known how loud the place was going to be, he might have begged off. But he had learned since coming home that it wasn't a series of loud noises that got to him. It was a single unexpected one: a car backfiring, the deafening crash an empty automobile carrier truck made when it hit a bump in the highway. Sounds like these reminded him of the first gunshot, the first explosion, the first sign that your life was about to be altered irrevocably. These were the hardest for him. These were the sounds that reminded him that he'd had a life before Iraq, a life that had been altered by events not of his choosing, events not on anyone's battle plan.

Li'l D pushed his empty plate back without taking his eyes off the monsters onstage. He scanned them nervously, as if he thought they were about to jump down onto the floor and start for the table. John said, "How you doing there, big guy?"

"I don't like that dog," he said, a low tremor of fear in his voice.

"Me neither. What do you say we hit the play area?"

Li'l D nodded emphatically, put their plates in the nearby trash can just as John instructed him to, and then led John right into the arcade, where John felt his wallet tense up in his back pocket. He handed the kid a dollar and told him to make it last as long as he could, then he found a spot in the corner of the room where it would be almost impossible for the kid to leave his sight.

A little while later a hand came to rest on his shoulder, gently, as if whoever it was knew how he might react to a sudden touch. At first he didn't recognize the woman standing next to him. She had gained almost twenty pounds, and her once shoulder-length brown hair had been chopped off. There were bags under her eyes and a fresh sunburn on her pale skin. The last time he had laid eyes on Trina Miller had been at a BBQ in Oceanside, after he came back from Fallujah and before he had made the indoc for First Recon, where she had cried a river as she thanked him for saving her husband's life. Now she threw her arms around him with the same level of emotion, even though her fatigued appearance didn't match up with this gesture.

John hugged her right back. He assumed it was a coincidence, running into the wife of a Marine whose life he had saved, and his heart did a jump he hadn't thought it to be capable of doing. Surely this was some sort of sign from an otherwise cruel universe that he was on the right path—that just bringing this kid to this pizza place was a good act. How many hours did he spend replaying what Bowers had done for him nine months earlier? And he spent almost no time acknowledging himself for the life he had saved.

"What are you doing here?" John asked.

"Looking for you," she said. "We stopped by your . . . place, talked to some guy named Emilio."

"You and Charlie? Where is he?"

"Outside. He needs to see you, John."

"How is he?"

She nodded and looked at some spot over his shoulder, then glanced down at her feet as if she might find her next words there. But all she could manage was, "I don't know. He just says he needs to see you." John had no trouble believing it, given that they had driven all the way up to his trailer park, and then another twenty minutes south to find him.

After he had introduced Li'l D to the woman who would be watching him for the next few minutes, John headed for the patio where Trina had told him he could find Charlie. *It's Bowers,* he thought. *Charlie knows why Bowers isn't calling me back. Something's happened to him and he's here to tell me.*

After taking a couple of deep breaths, John realized how absurd this thought truly was. For all he knew, Bowers and Charlie Miller had never even met each other. The two men came from separate halves of John's Marine Corps career—he'd met Charlie in boot camp, only to end up fighting next to him during the Battle of Fallujah years later. Bowers, on the other hand, had been the first captain John had ended up under after officially becoming a "Reconnaissance Man," a title that had been assigned to him only after he completed twelve weeks of backbreaking training that made boot camp look like summer camp.

In some ways, Charlie Miller was from a former life, a life in which John had been a hero, pure and simple, a life in which no one had been forced to give up an eye to save his life.

During the Battle of Fallujah in the fall of 2004, John had been part of a four-man sniper team doing sweeps for IEDs in

Ramadi. The team went inside a seemingly abandoned house, when a grenade was tossed into the room by an insurgent cowering on the floor of the hallway. Charlie Miller was blasted out onto the balcony, where he was hit by insurgent sniper fire the minute he got to his feet. The grenade took out half of the insurgent's head, so John crabwalked out onto the balcony to cover Charlie while another member of their team went to call the Quick Reaction Force. For three hours, he and Charlie lay together, John counting his blessings that the concrete spines of the balcony railing were too thick to allow a bullet to pass through. But mother of God, those sons of bitches tried. Volley after volley of AK-47 fire splintered against the concrete railing while John told Charlie dirty jokes and tried to keep him talking, because checking Charlie's wounds or trying to carry him back inside would expose them both to sniper fire.

Outside the Golden Door, he found Charlie sitting at a concrete patio table, a pair of metal crutches leaning against the bench seat next to him. His long legs were sticking out almost straight in front of him as he rested his back against the edge of the table. He almost looked relaxed, but John knew the reason for his extended posture was that he couldn't move his left leg thanks to the bullet that had felled him on the balcony that day. His brown hair was now a shaggy mess, and John thought he resembled the pimply-faced Tennessee hick John had met long ago in boot camp, the kid who could barely suck down an entire cigarette and who held a rifle like it was a cottonmouth that might sink its fangs into him, not the Marine he had grown into by the time they went to Iraq.

Charlie sat up as straight as he could to receive John's one-armed embrace, and John emitted a high, barking laugh that sounded surprised and relieved at the same time. "You look good," John said before he could think twice.

Charlie lit a Marlboro Red and blew a thin stream of smoke from pursed lips. "I look like shit, man. I didn't come all this way for you to blow smoke up my ass."

"Good," he said. "'Cause I don't smoke." Charlie's laugh was tense and almost silent—it worked his shoulders and eyes more than it did his mouth.

"What you gonna say next, John? Trina look good, too? Shit—she's gained like twenty fucking pounds since I got back, and she walks around the house like I beat her with a stick." He sucked a quick drag off his cigarette. "She wants to move close to her parents in Kentucky, but I can't get the same kind of care out there, so the answer's no. But she keeps bringing it up and the answer keeps bein' no." Charlie's eyes caught on John's, as if he had suddenly heard himself. "Shit, man, I'm sorry. I didn't want to start off this way. And I don't mean to rain on your little pizza party, but sometimes when you can't move your legs so good, you just gotta sit in it, you know what I mean?"

He didn't know what Charlie meant, so he just nodded gravely for a few seconds. Then he asked, "What are you *starting off* here, buddy?"

Charlie's eyes focused on some point in the distance; then he started digging in the plastic drugstore bag on the bench next to him. As he pulled out a large manila envelope and handed it to John, he said, "Did I ever tell you I've got a cousin who's a PI over in Murietta? He owed me a favor, so . . ."

John opened the envelope and extracted a manila file folder. In the series of eight-by-ten photographs that slid onto the stone table, the man who had raped John's younger brother walked his dog through a grassy neighborhood of one-story tract homes. The dog was a healthy adult boxer with an alert expression. As for the man himself, not much had changed about Danny Oster in the ten years since John had almost beaten him to death outside of their house in Yucca Valley. Oster still had the same shaggy blond hair that made him look like an eighties rock star; the same long, fat-lipped mouth; the same flabby arms and freckled shoulders.

As he studied the photographs, John tried to focus on the sound of his own breathing. He groped for some memory of when he had shared this dark chapter of his life with Charlie. After a few minutes, he remembered—the same BBQ in Oceanside where Charlie's wife wept and thanked him for saving her husband's life. Considering he had never shared the story with any other Marine, he had to have been seriously overserved, so overserved he could barely remember doing it.

Charlie said, "The reason you couldn't find him is that he left the country for a while. Came back about a year and a half ago and changed his name to Charles Keaton. He's got a job at the IT department at the University of Redlands. Computers and some shit." That made sense, considering Oster had been a computer freak back when everyone in Yucca Valley was willing to sell their soul for a dial-up connection.

"I told you I tried to find him?" John asked.

"Yeah. You don't remember?"

"Barely, Charlie."

This answer and the sluggish tone with which John delivered it made Charlie shift against the bench and run one hand down his paralyzed left thigh. "You saved my life. I sat up nights thinking about how I could repay you." Charlie looked his way. When he saw that John's attention was on him and not on the photographs, he bit his lower lip a few times and said, "Did I do the right thing? Tell me I did the right thing, John."

As his father had liked to say, Charlie had opened up a can of snakes, each of which had nine lives. Yes, he had tried to find Danny Oster, but that had been years ago, back when his little brother was still alive and John was convinced that some final reckoning with Oster might lift Dean Houck out of the life of a heroin junkie. Back then finding Oster had been a desperate, last-ditch effort to bring his brother back from the land of the living dead, one he had turned to only after all his attempts to reconnect with Dean had failed. And ultimately, another deployment to the Middle East had driven out all thoughts of his broken family and derailed his search.

Now John was confident he had only mentioned this pursuit to Charlie because he had wanted to come off as the protective older brother. But he couldn't fault Charlie for trying to pay John back for what he had done for him that day, even if he believed Charlie would have done the same for him in a heartbeat.

He had become so lost in his thoughts that he had failed to notice the transformation Charlie had undergone. His eyes were wide and fearful and he was leaning forward slightly, as if it were helping him to breathe. He had raised one crutch on the pavement next to him, as if at any moment he might try to push himself to his feet.

"I thought it might be good for you to have the information," Charlie whispered. "That's all." He sounded like a man whose marriage proposal had just been rejected.

"I appreciate that, Charlie. I really do." But it sounded pathetic, and all John could think about was that tonight he would have to put his head to his pillow knowing that the man who had ruined his brother's life was also turning in for the night about twenty miles south of him.

Charlie looked to the crowded parking lot, placed both hands atop his crutch, and said, "Whatever you go and do, John. It's all right with me. . . . And your brother—well, I bet wherever he is, he's proud to have a brother like you."

He didn't tell him that his brother had been in the ground for going on a year. He didn't say anything at all, because the words were all tangled up and Charlie seemed to be headed to some far-off place that didn't have a lick to do with John Houck. John was searching for some way to close out their meeting when Charlie said, "Mine was a teacher."

John didn't ask him to elaborate. He didn't need to. But what struck him was the phrasing Charlie had used, the way he had taken possession of the man who had violated him. And oddly enough, there was something about this confession that made John feel exonerated, as if it revealed Charlie's reasons for finding Danny Oster had everything to do with Charlie and barely anything to do with John.

Maybe because he was relieved by this, or maybe because it felt like the right thing to do, John reached out and laid a hand on the man's shoulder. For a few minutes Charlie didn't pull away, but then he sucked in a breath through his nostrils and stamped out his cigarette under his good foot. "Sorry. Like I said, when one of your leg's busted, sometimes you just have to sit in it. Whatever the fuck *it* is."

John went to help him to his feet, but Charlie pulled away and bowed his head, refusing to meet John's eyes, then pulling away farther when he found himself staring down at the spread of photographs on the stone table. *He knows it was a bad move,* John thought. *He knows he screwed up, but he was trying his hardest, and who are you to not let him have his moment? He's got more balls than you do, driving all this way to find you when you've written Lightning Mike out of your life because he won't respond to a goddamn postcard.*

"Let's find Trina," John said.

"It's cool, John. I've got it," Charlie said, putting both crutches to the ground and starting for the entrance. "You just do what you need to do."

John was about to follow him when he looked back and realized the photos were still spread out all over the table. He collected them hurriedly, shoved them back inside the envelope without bothering with the folder that had held them. He was about to throw the folder away when he saw that there was a sheet of paper stapled to the inside flap—a list of relevant details about Charles Keaton, aka Daniel Oster.

For what felt like hours, he stared at the second detail on the list.

An address.

2

Li'l D nodded off as soon as they pulled out of the parking lot, which gave John a chance to consider taking the on-ramp to I-10 East and heading for Redlands. Instead he joined the Vegas-bound motorists who turned the 15 North into a chromium river every weekend.

Even though he was now stuck in gridlock traffic on a freeway headed in a different direction, John managed to pull a map from the glove compartment without waking Li'l D. He opened it against the steering wheel and found the street Oster lived on; it was on the north side of Redlands, a block away from where the city dissolved into vacant lots and a cluster of gravel pits. Something about those gravel pits, which were marked on the map with the same dotted lines used to delineate dry lakebeds, seemed like an invitation to John. The proximity of so much empty space so close to where Oster rested his head each night—it could be a kill site or a dumping ground or just God's way of saying that even though he'd traded up from the high desert, Danny Oster was still living right next door to purgatory.

The last half of John's teenage years had been spent an hour's drive east, and to him, Redlands had always been the first piece of Southern California civilization that sprang up on the drive to Los Angeles, its canopy of palm trees and healthy oaks looking out of place against the parched lower flanks of the San Bernardino Mountains, the entrance to a world his big sister had only been able to bring them to the edge of in her struggle to give them a better life

"John?"

Even though he was moving only about five miles an hour, he was about to roll into the back of an eighteen-wheeler idling in front of him. But the kid hadn't noticed—he seemed more upset by whatever expression was on John's face.

He folded up the map, without taking his eyes off the road, and asked Li'l D to put it away for him. Another few minutes and their trailer park would come into view, carved out of the mountainside and set high above the 15, like a landing pad for a UFO. But John knew the silence before they reached home would be too full of dark possibilities for him, possibilities that involved the Sig currently resting in a holster behind his headboard.

John said, "You tell your mother everything we did today, okay? Whenever you go anywhere, meet anyone, I want you to tell your mom about it. Make sure she knows who you're with and all that stuff. Are you listening?" The kid nodded, but John barely noticed, because he was seeing in his head the sequence of images that always slugged him when he thought about how he had failed his brother and sister that day—Oster's fleshy ass, the rumpled green comforter riding up over the foot of the bed as he thrust himself forward into Dean's prone body, the matching green curtains pulled so hastily shut over the window most of the rings were crooked. "You want a good mom? Well, you've got to give her a chance to be one, okay?"

"Okay," Li'l D mumbled.

John held his tongue so he wouldn't say anything more. The last thing he wanted to do was frighten the kid. And it wasn't like he and Patsy hadn't known about Danny Oster—John had just assumed the guy was a harmless computer geek interested in helping Dean with his homework. Knowledge was one thing. What he had lacked was an accurate perception of who Oster really was, and it wasn't Dean's job to give that to him. John had been the big brother; it had been an unwritten rule that he had to look out for the guy while his sister worked herself to the bone to keep them in school, to keep them fed, to keep the AC running.

"John?"

"Yeah."

"I don't feel so good."

×

The kid stopped throwing up by the time they reached Devore Meadows, but only after John had been forced to pull over to the shoulder of the freeway, where they had drawn the attention of a highly amused CHP officer, who couldn't stop laughing into one fist long enough for John to tell him he was about to start cadet training in a few weeks.

Now Li'l D was practically hanging on to John's right leg for support as they walked toward his mother's trailer. The door popped open when they were just a few feet away and Mandy flew down the steps, still dressed in the burgundy polo shirt and khaki slacks that he figured were her gas station uniform. John had barely managed a greeting when she took Li'l D by his free arm and escorted him back inside the trailer as if he had been caught trying to set fire to something small and defenseless. She shut the door behind her, and when he heard her blessing out her son, John fought the urge to intervene. Instead, he held his ground, because she was clearly pissed and he wasn't going to hang the kid out to dry by himself.

After what felt like ten minutes, Mandy opened the front door. "You two had quite a field trip today."

"We tried calling you. Did you talk to Emilio?" She responded by lighting a cigarette. "You know, if you're mad about it, yell at me, not the kid. I was ju—"

"You couldn't have watched him here? You had to take him halfway across the Inland Empire?"

He realized she was embarrassed, not frightened, and this made his tolerance for her foul mood lessen by a third. "You know what? I apologize. Next time I'll just leave him with Emilio so by the time you come home he can be covered in auto grease and smoking a doobie."

"How many more weekends you going to have for my son John? How many more little field trips you all going to take before you become a cop, huh?"

"Oh, for Christ's sake, Mandy."

"I'm just saying—I don't need any grand gestures from you, okay? And he doesn't either."

"Fine. Tell your son where you work and I'll drop him off with you next time."

"Should you really be acting like we're married when you've got other lady friends dropping by?"

"Trina Miller?"

"Tall, thin, too much makeup," Mandy said. "Older. Long brown hair with some kind of crazy white streak running through it." John's heart thudded at this description of a woman he had not stood face-to-face with in almost ten years. "She tried to leave a note, I think." At this, John turned on his heel and headed back for his trailer. His heart fell when he didn't see anything on the doorstep, so he threw open the front door and stepped into the kitchen and spun in place, his eyes on the floor as if he were looking for a mouse.

"It was *yesterday*!" Mandy said. She had followed him but was standing at the bottom of the steps, as if she thought a prowler might be waiting for John in his bedroom. When she saw John's desperate expression, she grimaced and rolled her eyes. "Jesus, John. If I'd known trailer trash was your taste I would have knocked out a few of my front teeth before you came over the other night."

"My sister doesn't live in a trailer. You do."

Her cheeks flushed at her own misperception, but she wasn't about to relent. "Yeah, well so do you."

"Which is why I think twice before I call people I don't know trailer trash."

"You've got an answer for everything, don't you?"

"My father was a minister. So—yeah, I do."

"Fine. You want to do something nice for my son? Try spending an entire night with his mom, instead of sneaking out at three in the morning like she's some five-dollar whore."

He wanted to suggest that her son might be better off if her bedroom were a little less active, but he knew this was a low blow, and a cover for the fact that he didn't want to tell her the real reason for his predawn departure.

The last time he had tried to spend an entire night with a woman, she had awakened him at four in the morning for another go-around, and before he was even conscious, he had hurled her halfway across the room into a dresser. Thank God he hadn't injured the woman physically, but he had so frightened her that she could only react to his attempts at comfort by nodding her head and staring at him wide-eyed, like a woman being held captive by a solicitous lunatic. When he finally volunteered to leave, the light came back into the woman's eyes and she had happily showed him to the door, as if her life had been given back to her.

"There's no envelope here. Did she give it to you?"

"No," Mandy said. "It was big. It looked like it wouldn't fit under the door. Call her."

"Thanks, Mandy. I'm glad we could light up each other's lives today."

"You practically jump up and down like a little kid when you find out she's paid you a visit, but you can't pick up the phone and call her?"

"Good night, Mandy," he said firmly.

The disappointment in her eyes surprised him. She had attacked him suddenly and forcefully, and now she seemed to want him to come back across the line she had been so angry at him for crossing. Maybe she had just needed to vent her jealousy.

She was halfway back to her trailer before he could ask her. But, of course, that wasn't the question that came out of him. Instead he said, "I'm sorry I got him sick. If you need me to run out and get something for his stomach, I will. I don't have to give it to him myself. I could just pass it to you through a window or something."

"That's nice of you, John," she said quietly.

"I'm sorry I left, Mandy. Nights . . . they aren't so good for me."

She turned to face him, but she didn't move to close the distance between them. "You're sweet, John. But come on—it's not like you're going to *stay* here." She gestured to the park all around him. "I mean, you're a friggin' war hero, for Christ's sake, and you'll probably be the best damn cop in the state." The qualifications for being a war hero were a lot higher in the Marine Corps than they were in Devore Meadows, but he didn't rush to disabuse her of this notion. This was her version of the comment Emilio had made to him that afternoon about being able to have any woman he wanted based on his time in Iraq. But she didn't finish the thought; she seemed embarrassed by her sudden candor and hurried back to her trailer, shaking her head at the ground.

As usual it seemed like the people around him were expecting a lot more out of him than he expected out of himself. But the message from Mandy was clear; it was the same message that had been telegraphed to him day after day in Iraq: go help someone who wants it. And the sadness that rose in him as he watched Mandy slip inside her trailer sidelined him; he wasn't sad because he had seen a bright future for the two of them. Her departure meant he'd probably spend the night alone with the file Charlie Miller had delivered to him that day, pondering all the ways to get revenge on Danny Oster. But with his brother almost a year in the ground, John couldn't see how that would help anyone at all. So Mandy's challenge remained: go help someone who wants it.

A few hours later he had used a putty knife to scrape all the frozen blotches of Corona from the inside of his freezer, and had downed a few good bottles in the interim. He spent another hour cleaning his gun, telling himself for the hundredth time that he didn't keep the gun in his bedroom because he had nightmares; he was afraid of other men whose nightmares were as bad as his. Then, before he could think twice about it, as if it were just another task in his long evening ritual, he went to the phone and dialed his sister's number in Yucca Valley. He had looked up the number months before, but he usually never made it through the first four digits before he hung up. This time he made it all the way to the machine.

The sound of her voice, the faint traces of her Southern accent that put the emphasis on the last syllable of every other word, greased his palm with sweat against the receiver.

In the second before the beep, he hung up and spoke his message to his empty trailer: "I'm sorry, Patsy."

3

The phone woke him at a little after 9:00 A.M. A few extra bottles of Corona the night before, three more than his nightly allotment, had left him with a dull headache. As soon as the man on the other end identified himself as Kyle Marsh, John remembered the website he had found four months earlier, a website with photos of middle-aged, middle-management types marching across empty baseball fields in full Spartan regalia. On his site, Marsh claimed that he could locate high-quality replicas of most ancient Greek weapons "for the serious collector only."

"It's finally in, buddy," Marsh said. "Last time we spoke, you seemed pretty eager to get this to your friend, so I had my guy put a rush on it. I know four months may not seem like a rush, but in this business . . . anyway, it's here and it's a real beauty."

"When can I come see it?"

Marsh gave him directions to an address in Hesperia, and a shower and three strong cups of coffee later, John was in his Toyota Tacoma, heading north on the 15 toward the desert. Kyle Marsh was watering his parched front lawn when John pulled up. Most of the homes in his subdivision were still under construction— John had to navigate among Dumpsters and pallets of sandbags just to get down Marsh's street—but all the lots boasted views of the San Bernardino Mountains and the miles of empty desert that lead up to them.

Marsh gave John a handshake that was almost as firm as his own, then led John into a garage where a dusty green minivan sat parked with its nose flush against a mannequin outfitted in a Corinthian helmet and crimson tunic. John was so distracted by the intricate uniform that he almost missed it when Marsh drew the weapon he had come for.

"It's probably a lot shorter than you were expecting," Marsh said. "Thing is, the Spartans liked to use their swords as a weapon of last resort. Lots of close-quarters fighting with this baby—after the spears broke, that is."

"Right. And the swelling of the blade created a weak point at the blade's neck—near the hilt." John indicated the spot on the sword Marsh was holding almost protectively to his chest. "After a while, even the best of them would eventually shear."

"You certainly know your stuff," Marsh said. Then, as if in recognition of this fact, he handed John the sword. John gave him a respectful nod and took the sword gently by the handle. "My friend—my *captain*, I mean—he's the one who taught me."

"He the one you're getting it for?"

"Yep."

"Well, he should be real pleased. Now, unfortunately, none of the original Laconian swords have survived, but this one's modeled after a bronze sword they found on Crete in the late 1800s that they think is probably the same shape. To get the rest of the details right they used old vase paintings."

John turned to face Marsh head-on, tried to put as much desperation into his gaze as he could. "How much?" he asked quietly.

The look on John's face made Marsh laugh nervously. "Starting price for this guy is four hundred, or it should be, at least. Now, you could probably find another one at a major retailer online for around one hundred and fifty, but the blade's going to be stainless steel, and I doubt you'll have the same attention to detail."

"Four hundred's just a bit out of my range."

"Yeah, I figured, given that you're young enough to be my son." He rested his elbow against a shelf and stared down at his feet, his cheeks puffed out. "Three hundred fifty going to do it?"

"Three hundred fifty's tough. Now, three hundred would mean I'll be doing Tyson's frozen dinners for a couple weeks instead of Applebee's. But it'll be worth it."

"Fine. Well, after I add on my discount in honor of your fine service to this country, that would bring us to about two hundred seventy-five. How's that sound?"

"Perfect. Cash okay?"

"If you got it."

John returned the sword to him as the man gave him directions to a nearby ATM. He was almost out the door when Marsh said, "Let me guess. Marine?"

"How could you tell?"

"You look like you could break me in half."

"Yeah. Then I could just take the sword and leave a few dollar bills on the table."

Marsh laughed, but it was nervous and high-pitched, as if he thought Marines rarely kidded around about breaking people in half.

John was almost back to Devore Meadows, the sword rattling in the backseat of his truck, when he realized that his having a nice gift for him didn't change the fact that Mike Bowers had acted like a man with no interest in seeing John again. But then he thought of Charlie Miller driving all that way to deliver a gift that may well have implicated him in an act of violence against a man he had never met. It didn't exactly fit with the accepted translation of *Semper Fidelis,* but it was closer than anything John had done for Bowers in the past nine months.

No, he had no choice but to sit down face-to-face with Bowers, whether Bowers was looking forward to the meeting or not. He couldn't see himself putting on another uniform and swearing an oath to uphold the law if he didn't make some attempt to turn his gratitude into action. And maybe then Bowers would be able to hear the truth about why John had fucked up so badly that day.

✕

Emilio was the one who suggested that Bowers might have moved. He let John use his laptop to Google the address in San Clemente where John had sent two unacknowledged postcards four months earlier. A little while later John was on the phone with the building's manager, who didn't need to hear much of John's sad story about two war vets separated by too much time and distance before he told him that Mike Bowers had moved two months ago. Not long enough to prove that John's postcards hadn't reached him, but he had left a forwarding address behind—a P.O. box in some town called Owensville.

"Where's that?" John asked.

"North, I think."

The map he had used to find Danny Oster's new home the day before told him that Owensville was nestled in the low north-south mountain range that bridged the distance between the southern terminus of the Sierra Nevadas and the mountains circling the L.A. basin. Another Google search took him to a professional-looking webpage for the Owensville chamber of commerce, which featured pictures of rolling green hills dappled with wildflowers. It was a nice town, nice enough to dispel images that Bowers had gone there to hide out in some shack while he picked at his scabs and saw hajjis peeking in every window.

By three o'clock he had driven out of the northern mouth of Cajon Pass for the second time that day, then west into Antelope Valley, where Joshua trees studded the landscape and the towns looked like scattered assemblages of corrugated tin. Fear and hunger forced him to pull over in Palmdale, where he chewed KFC chicken and stared out at the parking lot as he rehearsed the apology speech he hadn't been allowed to make in Balad.

The straightest shot to the mountain highway that would take him to Owensville was a two-lane blacktop, which meant hours of trying to pass lumbering flatbed trucks hauling chickens, vegetables, and who knew what else. The heavy storm clouds that had piled on the northwestern horizon winked lightning at him—not a warning so much as a taunt. Given how long he had waited to make this journey, a rough drive was the least he should have to endure.

At eight o'clock he was barely a quarter of the way up the mountain when rain started sheeting across the road and he hit a traffic jam at two thousand feet. A long red chain of winking brake lights snaked through the grass-flecked mountains. He only traveled several feet in an hour. Some of the other drivers got as fed up with it as he was and started pulling off onto the shoulder and speeding toward a Valero gas station that sat on a small plateau above the road. The place had no snack bar, but some motorists were sitting in the aisles, and one of the clerks was passing out cups of coffee. People were saying there was a mudslide ten miles up the road that had covered one of the up-mountain lanes. No injuries, but it would be another few hours before the cleanup crews were finished and traffic was back to normal.

He asked for a phone book from the clerk and got a slender volume with a photograph of a grassy wildflower-dappled hillside that said it covered the entire Hanrock County, including the towns of Briffel, Gallardo, and Boswell. What it didn't have was a listing for Mike Bowers.

He handed the phone book back to the cashier without thanking her, walked outside, and stood under the fluorescent-lit overhang. He didn't like that Mike wasn't listed—it brought back the nightmare images of a PTS-demolished vet cowering in the corner of an abandoned shed. But he knew he wouldn't have bothered to call ahead even if his name had appeared in the phone book. Given that he had no idea how Mike would receive him, John knew surprise was his best approach. The late hour would certainly give him that. And if it was too late to bother Mike, at least John could get some kind of glimpse into the life Mike had been able to build for himself in the wake of his great sacrifice.

✕

Owensville sat in a narrow valley between the rounded flanks of the mountains that cradled it. At one in the morning, the town was a small grid of weak amber light. The main street was called Graham Road, and it was lined with fussy log-cabin-style buildings, some of which had plastic replicas of animals out front. A bear reared up on its hind legs in front of The Hunter's Outpost, and a mother deer delicately sniffed her doe's neck by the locked entrance to a gift shop with a front window full of ceramic animals conducting their own petrified tea party.

He was about to leave the town center when he saw a gas station that was closing up for the night. The attendant was an older woman with a long mane of gray-streaked black hair and the gaunt facial features of a lifelong smoker. She tensed when she saw John moving toward her across the parking lot. He lifted both hands and decided to cut right to the chase.

"I'm looking for Mike Bowers," he called to her. "Do you know him?"

She took a step toward him, then peered at him as if he were out of focus. She hadn't asked him to repeat Mike's name but he said, "He was injured in combat. He's missing his—"

"I know who he is," the woman said. A light rain had started to fall, and she didn't seem to mind that she was safe under the overhang while he was exposed and hesitant to come any closer lest she make a break for it. "You're a friend of his?" she asked with evident suspicion. John felt his face flush. He had never had to work very hard with women, but everything about this chick said she could smell the twin stink of Louisiana coon ass and desert trash. The town was nice, but it was no Lake Arrowhead for Christ's sake, and even there, the rich weekenders from L.A. had been nice enough to nod and smile as they passed the construction site where John had worked.

Because he was getting rained on, John said, "We served together in Iraq. It's been a long time and it's late, I know, but I went through hell trying to get up this mountain."

She uncrossed her arms and rubbed her hands together, as if he had gotten something sticky on them in the past minute. "It's been a while, huh?" she asked. There was hesitancy in her tone. "Well, I guess . . ." She shook her head, as if ridding herself of some fear. A fear of contamination by outside elements, John guessed. "About five miles west, over the next rise, you'll come to Graham Valley. It's smaller than it sounds. I'm not sure of the address, but it's on Nesbit Road, which runs right along Nesbit Creek."

"Thank you," he said, but he stayed where he was, trying to get her to look him in the eye. He wanted to tell her: *I didn't go to Iraq to fight for the rights of women like you to judge men with battle scars on their faces and distant looks in their eyes. While you were safe in your little mountain town with all your fake little prancing animals, I was meeting children with no skin on their legs and no compassion in their hearts.*

But he said none of this, and it left him with a feeling of helplessness and dissatisfaction.

Just as she had told him, he crossed over a rise and came to Nesbit Road, which curved along the base of a mountainside. His headlights revealed cottonwood trees crowding the sides of the road, hiding whatever was on the other side of the stake fences. Some of the houses had placards next to their mailboxes announcing their names, but John couldn't see Mike living in a place called Rabbit's Warren and Shelia or with a family who called themselves the Fussy Fawns. The size of the lots made John wonder if Mike's parents were wealthier than he had let on. The most he had ever said about them was that they were Bible-thumpers, which Mike hated, but he had taken care to explain to John that it wasn't the essence of their faith that Mike couldn't abide. Their fundamentalism prevented the kind of cool-eyed inquiry Bowers felt was required to move through the world as a complete man.

Finally, he reached the end of the road, was about to turn around when his headlights flashed off a tiny decal posted to the fence. John only got a glimpse of it, but it was familiar. The insignia of Force Recon, not the Marine Corps globe and anchor most civilians were familiar with, but a skull and crossbones girded by the words *Celer, Silens, Mortalis*—Latin for "Swift, Silent, Deadly." Against his will, John looked back at his truck, at a patch of shredded adhesive paper stuck to the lower right-hand corner of the rear window. A few months after returning home, and after a few too many beers, he had pulled a Recon decal from his junk drawer and stuck it on the truck. The next morning, after the beers had faded, he had scraped it off with the same putty knife he had used to clean out the freezer the night before. Yes, he was proud to call himself a former Marine. But he couldn't deny that his fuckup with Bowers had called his status as a Reconnaissance Man into question.

The fence was locked. He jumped it, then made his way beneath dripping cottonwood branches and up a muddy pathway that appeared to be the driveway. He passed a small woodshed off to his right, then followed muddy tire tracks. He'd taken a Maglite out of his truck but he didn't use it because he wanted his eyes to adjust to the dark, didn't want his field of vision to shrink to a bright halo at his feet. He'd also tucked the Sig into the back of his jeans.

After about twenty yards, the trees broke, revealing a massive two-story, imitation log cabin at the crest of a grassy slope that ran down toward a rushing creek. The cabin had an expansive wraparound porch on the first floor and a massive stone chimney. There was a large garage in back and a manicured set of stone steps leading down to the creek. It was the kind of place that was designed to look rustic but probably had every modern amenity inside you could think of.

And the front door was open. The rain was coming down hard, the house was entirely dark, and the front door was standing open by several feet. He flicked on his Maglite, shined it on the front door as he approached. The place was being robbed surely. As he pulled his Sig from the back of his jeans with his right hand and switched the flashlight to his left one, he saw the scene play out. Mike was away. Robbers had broken in, not expecting to have their asses kicked by a former Recon Marine—a far better gift than the Spartan sword still sitting in his truck. He was elated suddenly, a level of adrenaline coursing through him that he hadn't felt since combat. He stepped inside the front door.

The front room was almost dark except for the dying embers in the massive stone fireplace. He saw the back of a large, modern-looking sofa, glimpsed framed prints of wilderness scenes hanging on the walls. A set of carpeted stairs led to the second floor. The white carpet was thick under his feet. At first he thought the rain had soaked it. Then, he heard movement: a quick scrape on the carpet from the second floor. He would have kept his mouth shut and gone after the guy full bore, but his flashlight had given him away, so he said, "This is John Houck. I'm looking for Mike Bowers!"

John raised the flashlight. At the top of the stairs, the beam hit an open door, flashed across a doorknob. John almost passed it over before he noticed something on the knob. A dark V-shaped stain. Blood. Almost silently, he mounted the stairs, gun raised. When he reached the open door at the top, he lost all composure, left himself exposed to whoever might have been behind him when he saw what was waiting for him in the bedroom.

Mike Bowers had been tied to the metal bed frame by both arms, his legs splayed in front of him on the bloodstained sheets: a seated crucifixion. He was shirtless, and the gashes in his chest—several of them straight through the area over his heart—had spilled what looked like ink down his abdomen and onto his crotch and thighs. As his eyes adjusted to the darkness, John saw that there were twice the number of stab wounds in Mike's chest than he had first thought. He remained in a crouch in the doorway, listening to himself whisper a stream of curses with snippets of prayers jammed between them. Every frail border he had imposed between himself and his recent bloody past had been ripped away from him.

In an instant, he became convinced that what really tied the universe together was not the bright light and airy-fairy bullshit that spiritual people were always trying to sell. It was blood spilled in violence; it was split-second rage exacting eternal consequences, and it could happen just as easily in Owensville, California, as in the streets of Ramadi. The horror in front of him made perfect sense in a way he would spend the rest of his life trying to forget, as if Mike had been torn apart from the inside by the same horrors that lived within John, horrors that carved themselves into a different part of his brain every time he remembered them.

He was about to go to Mike and check his pulse when he heard floorboards creak. He raised the Sig on one of the dark, half-open doorways on the other side of the banister, felt every inch of skin on his body constrict, a full body reaction he hadn't felt since Iraq. He was positive there was someone on the second floor with him, but then there came a shuffling sound from below, the first floor. A tall, slender shadow appeared at the foot of the stairs. John couldn't make out its facial features, but the shadow saw him, went stock still.

"Don't you fucking move," John said.

For a split second it seemed like the guy would comply. Then he was out the front door of the house, long legs pumping, a flash of pajama bottoms before he sprinted off the front porch. The muzzle flare lit up the staircase, and John realized he had fired— a stupid move but he didn't stop to beat himself up over it. He pursued the figure out the front door, glimpsed him running down the slope, paralleling the steps that led to the rushing creek, leaping through bushes. John followed the guy's path, almost lost his footing in the mud, came to the bottom of the slope. The creek in front of him was rock-strewn, about eight feet wide, ripping against its banks from the force of the rainfall. He swept it with the Sig while he eyed the opposite bank, almost a forty-five-degree incline, densely packed with cottonwoods and untamed oaks but full of possible escape routes.

What looked like a man-made bridge of stepping-stones crossed the creek, but they weren't stable. He took to them, eyes on the far shore, gun raised. He was almost halfway across when the water exploded all around him. A ghostly, soaking-wet figure rose out of the miniature rapids, leaping to its feet in what turned out to be only three feet of water. John realized too late that the guy had been lying flat on his back under the surface to conceal himself. The rock the guy held in both hands slammed into John's right knee. The blow sent him into a half spiral. His back hit the water, and he felt the Sig slip from his hands. The pain had paralyzed him and the flow of the river carried him along, into a deepening channel. He felt the sand under his back fall away, and enough panic filled him to overcome the throb of white-hot pain in his right knee.

His head broke the surface and he stood up in waist-deep water, saw the guy clawing at branches and pumping his long legs as he made his way up the opposite bank. John gripped at rocks, pulled himself to the far bank, and hoisted himself out of the water on a low-hanging oak branch. He ignored the pain and summoned every muscle he had to pursue the guy. It worked. The rain must have muffled the sound of his footsteps, because he overtook the guy just as he was heading sideways along the slope. John seized the back of the man's neck in one grip and slammed his forehead into the trunk of a cottonwood. Immediately the guy fell to his knees, a long, agonized groan issuing from him. There was enough of a tremor to it that John thought for a second he might have fractured the guy's skull, fucked up the speech centers in his brain. But he didn't release his grip on the back of the man's neck, gave him only a few seconds before he yanked him to his feet. The guy was still groaning, but now John could hear the sound for what it was. Defeat, a terrible defeat at having been apprehended in the midst of his horrendous crime.

"I should just kill you right now," John said. "I should just fucking kill you right now!"

At this, the guy went limp and silent. The tree trunk was still just three short feet away from his forehead. John had lost the gun, but the guy didn't know that. "We're going to walk back toward the house. Nice and slow. Turn around and I'll kill you, got it?" More sobs. More rain. *Got it?* The guy nodded furiously, and John backed up to allow the guy to get his footing. John told him to raise his hands over his head, and he complied. Carefully, they began their descent. The guy kept his hands raised over his head and his legs bent as he tried to move down the steep slope without falling head over heels. A few times the guy had to reach out and grip a branch to keep from falling, but he did so briefly, releasing it as soon as he was done, never once looking back. It took them twenty minutes to descend thirty yards. Along the way John managed to snap off the end of a thick branch. They reached the edge of the creek. The Sig hadn't washed to shore, but now that they were both on level ground, John pressed the butt of the branch he had broken off against the small of the guy's back. He jerked and lifted his hands higher.

The grassy slope on the other side of the creek concealed most of the cabin, except for its roof and chimney. The stepping-stones were in front of them. John said, "Cross. No bullshit this time."

"What are you going to do to me?" the guy whimpered.

"Cross!"

John knew better than to engage this fuck. He was shirtless, scratched up from his climb through the cottonwoods, but John was confident some of the blood on the guy's body belonged to Mike. Was the sick fuck jerking off over his corpse after he stabbed him through the heart? Given the determination with which the guy had tried to flee, John saw no other choice but to get him back to the house and restrain him before he called the police. His cell phone had been doused, so that meant he would have to use the landline.

But as they neared the front steps of the cabin, the guy started to hyperventilate. "Where's Mike?" he asked, gasping.

John used the branch to keep the guy moving up the front steps and onto the front porch, all without responding to the guy's query.

"Where is he?" the guy screamed.

It was the possessiveness in the guy's voice that enraged John. Did all monsters feel that way about their victims? Had Danny Oster cried out for his brother in the same way? Fine. He would show him Mike. He drove the guy into the foyer, then up the carpeted stairs and toward the yawning master bedroom door. "What—what are you going to do to me?" the guy spat.

"Nothing. You want to see Mike again, you get to see Mike again, you sick fuck!"

At the top of the stairs, he gripped the back of the guy's neck as he shoved him into the master bedroom doorway. He heard a siren wailing in the distance, probably responding to the shot he had fired. Before John could stop him, the guy reached up and hit the light switch on the wall just beside the doorway.

The light from the hallway fell across the empty bed, which had been freshly made, the waffle-print comforter drawn up to the four king-sized pillows. John heard the breath go out of him, was so shocked by the scene in front of him that he ignored the feeling of the guy turning slightly in his grip, just enough so he could look back at John with one big blue eye.

"John Houck," he whispered.

John hurled him against the wall. "How do you know my fucking name?"

The guy went silent, raised his palms in a gesture of surrender as he slid down the doorframe. His blue eyes were wide and unblinking. His soaked bangs draped his forehead. His skin was pale, smooth, like he had never worked a day outside in his entire life. "How do you know my name?" John screamed.

"I live here," the guy whispered.

"Bullshit. There was someone else. Someone else moved the body!"

"Turn around, John."

At first he thought it was a threat, but he knew there was nothing behind him except for a wall. "Who are you?"

"I'm trying to tell you who I am. Turn around and look! I'm not going to do anything. I don't feel like getting my head blown off."

John turned. The wall behind him was hung with framed eight-by-ten photographs. The first one his eyes landed on featured Mike and the guy sitting behind him standing shoulder-to-shoulder, smiling at the camera. There was a large metal pole behind them, and behind it, through plate glass windows, was a boulder-strewn, pine-studded mountain slope—the rotating tram car that carried tourists to the top of Mount San Jacinto, high above Palm Springs.

Then another photo: Mike was the center of this one. He sat on a bar stool, beaming, as he received a big wet one on the cheek from the guy John had almost killed. A neon sign above the bar spelled out the word *Budweiser* in all the colors of the rainbow, and the chunky little bartender serving a drink behind him wore a green T-shirt that said *The Catch Trap,* a gay bar in San Diego that was the punch line to some of the fag jokes John heard while he was stationed at Camp Pendleton.

John turned. The guy hadn't moved from where he had crumpled to the floor.

"We live here, John. Me and Mike. This is our home."

The stranger's eyes moved to the branch John was still stupidly holding in one hand. He dropped it to the carpet just as two khaki-clad sheriff's deputies came through the front door, their hands on their holsters, calling out to anyone who could hear them. One of them saw the scene at the top of the stairs, and without taking his eyes off John said, "Are you all right, Alex?"

"No, I'm not. This man broke in and tried to kill me."

And before John could put words together to defend himself, let alone make any kind of sense of the pictures he had just laid eyes on, they cuffed him and shoved him facedown onto the wet carpet. He managed to get a look back as they dragged him down the stairs, expecting to see the guy watching this with some kind of satisfaction. But he wasn't there.

He could hear him, though. The stranger named Alex was walking through the house shouting Mike's name, but not with enough fear in his voice to suggest that he believed any real harm had come to the man.

4

The deputies led John to a windowless room with Navajo white walls that looked like it had been turned into an interrogation room five minutes prior to his arrival. The wall behind him was taken up by a chalkboard, and the chair his cuffs were attached to sat in about three feet of space between the wall and the edge of a massive conference table. The exhaustion he could feel deep in his bones couldn't escape to the rest of his body, so when a man he presumed was the sheriff walked in, out of uniform, looking as if he had been roused from bed, John sat up as politely as he could given his restraints and gave the man a deep nod, which seemed to amuse him.

He was movie-star handsome, with thick jet black hair that

still looked perfectly combed even though the man had clearly traveled through the rain, a dimple in his chin, and a jawline that looked like it had been drawn by a comic book artist. He was tall with broad shoulders and the kind of stout body that suggested muscles under his clothes.

For what felt like hours, he just stared at John as if he were growing a second head right there in front of him. Finally he said, "Mr. Houck, I'm just going to throw something out at you and see if you catch it for me. As you told my deputies, you came up here tonight because Mike Bowers saved your life over in Iraq and you wanted to give him a present, which I'm going to presume is the sword we found in the back of your truck." John opened his mouth to answer, but the man didn't give him time. "Now, what you would like us to believe is that you walked in on Mike's corpse and that while you were chasing Alex Martin out into the woods someone *moved* this corpse. Presumably Alex Martin, who not only has the ability to take it up the back end like a champ but also to bend space and time and be in two places at once."

"No," John said.

"No? He doesn't have the ability to be in two places at once?"

"Whoever committed the murder moved the body."

"And you don't believe Alex Martin was responsible for what you saw in that bedroom?"

"You're the sheriff."

He sank down into a padded chair on the other side of the conference table. "Captain Ray Duncan," he said, then extended his hand and made a show of realizing that John was cuffed to the chair. "Sorry, but there's not a chance in hell the sheriff of Hanrock County is going to come up the mountain from Boswell on a night like this. So it's just you and me. And Alex Martin. And one missing Marine who went to a great deal of trouble to

keep you from finding out he was a homo. Personally, I think he's
still trying to hide it, given that he's nowhere around to explain
himself."

John said, "Are you trying to tell me that you didn't find any
trace of Mike Bowers in that house?"

"We found a lot of traces. He lives there. He's lived there for
about four months—with Alex. Can you see why I'm having trouble accepting any story you tell, given how much you don't seem
to know?" When he saw the look on John's face, he flashed him
his palms in a gesture of apology and placed his elbows on the
table. "Look, I know I may seem a little combative here, but it's
late, and I'm actually trying to throw you a bone."

"What does that mean, sir?" John asked.

"I'm giving you an *out*. An out from having to play the role of
crazy, fucked-up Iraq vet with post-traumatic stress syndrome."

He let this sink in, paid no mind to the furious expression
John could feel on his face like a mask. "So here's what I think
happened: I think you came up here with the best of intentions,
and you walked in on something you couldn't quite understand.
Some kind of sex game. It may be the twenty-first century, but
this isn't San Francisco, and I'd prefer not to go into detail. Let's
just say you misread the scene, which is understandable. But it's
not murder."

"Then where the hell is Mike Bowers?"

"Waiting for you to leave, John. Waiting for you to get the
hell out of here so he can go back to his little gay life with his little butt buddy, without any of his old friends poking around in
his business."

"I don't believe that."

"Well, Alex Martin does." When John said nothing, Duncan's
expression grew grave. He clasped his hands on the table as if he
had lost all use for sarcasm and leaned forward. "Brief visual flash-

backs brought on by certain auditory stimuli," he whispered. "Read that online just a few minutes ago. It's a common occurrence among our fighting men and wo—"

"Don't you even try that!" John shouted. "Don't you even *try* that shit on me. I may have a hard time some days, and I may not like hearing a car backfire, but this is not some PTSD bullshit. I don't *see* things! I don't imagine things. And I've never seen Mike Bowers stabbed through the heart before tonight. So tell me how the hell that could be a flashback."

"There's not a drop of blood in that entire house, John. You never gave Alex Martin a chance to see this alleged corpse or crime scene, so he can't verify your story. I don't think you're a bad man, John Houck, but I think you've had quite a shock, and you're responding to it in the way a man who has already been through a helluva lot might respond to it. You get me?"

Maybe it was his years in the Marine Corps, but John could better tolerate being shouted at than being condescended to like this, and he could feel pure anger swelling within him. "I see. So this isn't convenient for you, is that it? I'm just some dumb jarhead who wandered into your town and dropped a pile of shit. I'm too stupid to realize that people only investigate murders around here when it's convenient."

Duncan tried to laugh it off, but the effort left a grimace on his face and a tense set to his jaw. "This isn't *anything,* my friend. It's not a murder, and it's not even a pile of shit. And believe you me, if anyone at this station took you seriously, you wouldn't be talking to me. You'd be talking to two homicide guys out of Boswell. But you're not, John. Now, if Mike Bowers doesn't turn up in forty-eight hours, you're welcome to come back and file a missing-person report. But I'm fairly confident that his *huuusband* will beat you to the chase."

"You're talking like you're already done with me," John said.

"Pretty much am."

"Your deputies informed me I was arrested on suspicion of breaking and entering. Aren't you going to charge me?"

"No," he said quietly. "Alex Martin has decided not to file charges against you."

John was stunned silent by this. Duncan studied his reaction intently. John's wrist tingled, a memory of the secondary impact he had felt when he had slammed Alex Martin's head into a cottonwood trunk. Duncan continued, "He cited your friendship with Mike. Said he thought you were going through a lot because Mike sure is. All you guys are, which I can understand. But he also added that he never wants to lay eyes on you again. Don't take it personal, but I happen to feel the same way. You've got a lot swirling around up in that head of yours, John Houck. Bring it under some kind of control before you come back to Owensville."

"Where is he?" John asked.

"Beats me."

"Not Mike. Alex."

"He's at home. Waiting for Mike."

"He'll be waiting for a long goddamn time."

Duncan groaned and rubbed the bridge of his nose between his thumb and forefinger. He got to his feet and lifted his hand, as if he had spent the past few minutes giving John sound investment advice, only to watch him sink his money into snake oil. Duncan was almost out the door when John said, "He's hiding something. Maybe he said it was because I was a Marine and Mike's friend, but he's not filing charges against me because he wants this over, and that means he's hiding something."

"Are you accusing him of murder?"

"I said he's hiding something. That's all."

Duncan forgot about his planned exit entirely, closed the distance between them slowly. It was the first time since they had met that John saw what the man looked like angry. "You don't believe most people have good intentions, do you, Mr. Houck?"

"I beat the holy hell out of him tonight and he's not filing charges against me. Pardon me if I don't think he was able to *work through that* in less than four hours. I think he wants me out of here as much as you do."

"That's fine. But I need you to remember that you may be a veteran, but in my book, you're a civilian, which means when you have a suspicion about something you report it by phone to an officer of the law. And that's the end of it for you. Got it?"

John didn't answer. Duncan didn't move an inch. Finally he said, "Have I made myself clear, son?"

"Yes, you have."

✕

Bowers lied to me. He repeated these words to himself like a mantra. They carried him home, through the harsh, unfiltered dawn that lit his way back to Cajon Pass and his trailer park, where his neighbors were rising and going to work, making him feel like a gutter drunk returning from a bender. Everything inside his trailer seemed to point an accusing finger at him. The unmade bed suggested the presence of someone else who had not expected him home so early because he was supposed to be out there still, looking for Mike's body, hunting for bloodstains on the floor of his bedroom.

Mike Bowers lied to me. True, he hadn't gone so far as to invent a fake wife, had never mentioned anyone who might be waiting at home for him aside from his Holy Roller parents in Phoenix. But it had been a lie of omission. Wasn't that the worst kind?

John pulled a beer from the fridge, downed it in several swallows, and collapsed at the kitchen table and remained frozen there as if awaiting the arrival of a tax man.

He stopped himself from dozing off by going to the phone. Bowers and his father had the same first name, but when the operator told him there were fifteen different listings for Michael Bowers in the Phoenix area, he groaned and asked the woman to give him a minute. When he took three, he thought the operator might hang up on him. Then, as if a ghost were speaking to him, he could hear the derisive manner in which Bowers had once referred to his parents as *Mike and Suzy*. There was one listing for a Susan and Michael Bowers in the Phoenix area. He dialed the number and got the machine after a few rings. A chipper, high-pitched female voice with a trace of a Midwestern accent told him to leave a message. The sudden beep left him feeling as if he were back up on the high-dive board at Las Pulgas, staring down at a swimming pool full of other potential Recon Marines, the skull and crossbones leering at all of them from the far wall.

He managed to stutter his name, but as soon as the words "friend of Mike" left his mouth, he heard the machine shut off, then the sound of the receiver on the other end brushing against fabric. "Who is this?" a frantic female voice asked him, even though he had just told her.

"My name is John Houck. I served with your son—"

"Mike," she asked, voice accusatory. "You're a friend of Mike's, are you?"

He heard a man enter the room. Words passed between them, but the woman was obviously holding the receiver to her chest. It sounded like the woman was protesting as the receiver was pulled from her hand. Then a man's voice, a slightly weaker version of Mike's commanding baritone, said, "We aren't interested in hearing any more of your *slander* today. Is that clear?" In the background there were louder protests from the woman—Mike's mother. She was probably trying to tell Mike's father that John was not the same man who had called earlier. But Mike Sr. ignored her. "If you are confused as to the whereabouts of our son, perhaps it is the good Lord's intention that you *stay that way*!"

Only after he hung up was John able to assemble the brief sequence of events. Clearly Alex Martin had phoned Mike's parents to find out where he might have gone. In the process, he had let them in on Mike's big secret. John prowled up and down his trailer for about half an hour, telling himself he was giving Bowers Sr. enough time to calm down. But when he tried their number again, an automated voice informed him that his phone number had been blocked.

This time he called information and asked for a listing in Owensville, California. He already knew Mike wasn't listed, but the man he had been living with was. But when John called the number for the house, the phone rang ten times before he was given a voice mail message. In a clear and level voice, Alex Martin told him that no one was available to come to the phone. Neither one of those people was identified by name.

John didn't leave a message.

×

The phone woke him at a little after six in the evening. John's plan had been to drive to Phoenix and try to confront Mike's parents face-to-face, but exhaustion had overtaken him, and he woke up to the orange light of dusk framing the shade over his tiny bedroom window.

As soon as John answered, Alex Martin said, "He said you were a good Marine but you had all kinds of shit in the way."

"Like what?" John asked as he sat up straight.

"Like you drove yourself nuts 'cause you couldn't live up to your sister and you never wanted to admit to any of the other guys that you were living in the shadow of a woman." Alex let this hang. There was a ragged edge to his voice that suggested tears or alcohol or both. John thanked God he hadn't confided in Mike what had been done to his brother; he doubted he could have kept his cool if Alex had thrown that at him in this moment.

"He never said one word about you," John said carefully.

"He didn't need to. He was going to spend the rest of his life with me. You? He only had to lie to you for six months."

He could hear the fear in Alex's voice, the fear that John hadn't been hallucinating the night before, so he ignored his insults and said, "I called the house."

"I'm not staying there," Alex said. "I can't stay there right now. I'm at a motel."

"Has he come back yet?"

A long silence, and then Alex said, "You know he asked me if he should tell you. He thought maybe you would understand. Or try to, at least. He was thinking about inviting you up here."

"And what did you say? When he asked you?"

"I told him based on what he'd said about you I thought you would spit in the one eye he had left."

John's anger got the best of him and he sat up quickly on the side of the bed, as if Alex were standing against the wall in front of him. "Then why the hell are you talking to me right now?"

Alex went so silent John thought the connection between them had broken. Then, in a quiet voice he said, "The flat sheet's gone." John didn't catch his meaning at first, but Alex gave him some time to. "Last night, when I got back to the house, I went to unmake the bed, and the flat sheet was missing. There was just the comforter and the pillows. So I checked the mattress, and there's a stain. It could be any—"

"Have you told Duncan?"

His answer was implicit in his silence. John felt his hand tense around the receiver. "Something else was going on in that house last night that you don't want Duncan to know about."

"We ass-raped some choirboys as soon as we got done designing a nice dress for your sister. Fuck you, asshole. It was our *home*. You want to get to me? Then go back to treating me like a killer."

"No."

"Something changed your mind?"

"Yeah. You're not strong enough to do what I saw." Only after he hung up did John feel a startling urge to apologize. Sure, he didn't like being called an asshole, but he had not intended the words to wound, even though he was sure they were God's truth.

5

After he hung up on Alex, John wrote out a list of possible courses of action, all of which seemed insane as soon as he put them to paper. Contacting some of the men who had served with him and Bowers on their last tour so they might put some heat on the Hanrock County Sheriff's Department would require him to try to convince each one that he hadn't gone off the rails, had truly seen Bowers with his chest cut open. The idea made his palms sweat. Maybe it didn't matter—the guys who hadn't been deployed again were scattered to the four winds.

There was no other choice but to drive to Phoenix himself and confront Mike's parents face-to-face, and he was getting ready to pack an overnight bag when something slammed into the side wall of his trailer, right below his window. Having forgotten that he had lost the Sig the night before, he reached for the holster behind the headboard and broke into a cold sweat when his fingers grazed empty leather.

When John opened the front door of his trailer a crack, Alex Martin stepped forward into the security light's near-blinding halo. No strange car parked nearby. Obviously he'd been trying to sneak up on him. But he wasn't dressed to do harm. He wore a dark green polo shirt with an alligator label, jeans that showed off his time at the gym, and a heavy black waffle-print coat with a faux fur collar. A branch had clawed him during their race through the rain, leaving a long scratch on his left cheek that was starting to scab over. John didn't remember him being so tall, probably because he wasn't hunched over sobbing or running like hell to get away from him. The muscles he had were vanity muscles, the kind he'd lose in a few weeks if you got him away from whatever protein powder he was devouring every morning.

With a wave of his right hand, John invited him inside. Alex followed, reaching into the flaps of his coat. As soon as John took a seat, Alex gently set his Sig on the tiny table in front of him, then backed away from it as if it were radioactive. "I found it a few yards from the house," Alex said.

"Thank you."

Alex nodded, gave his full attention to the floor. He stood with his back to the fridge, his arms crossed, and if John hadn't known how much time it had taken him to get there, he probably would have assumed he didn't intend to stay for more than a few minutes.

"Tell me what you saw," Alex finally said.

The tone of his voice was gentle, not the lisping parody of homosexuals John had acted out and laughed at all his life, but something strangely close. His lips were parted slightly; John thought it looked almost like he was anticipating a kiss. *I'm not a homophobe,* John thought, wondering why this word had entered his vocabulary so easily. *But he better make it clear he's not expecting anything out of me that requires me to drop my drawers.* Telling Alex what he had seen the night before would be equivalent to signing some sort of pact that wasn't quite clear to him. Nevertheless, he needed to be believed.

So John told him, starting with his decision to deliver the gift in person and his long drive through the rain. He described how he had been forced to ask for directions from a gas station attendant who had treated him as if he were dirt—now he could see that this woman had known Mike's secret and had been afraid of what a reunion with John might bring. He told Alex about how he saw the Force Recon decal through the rain and debated going back to town for a room before he headed up the driveway, entered the house, and found Mike lassoed to the bed's headboard, his chest hacked open, and his blood the color of ink in the dark.

Then he remembered the detail about the V-shaped bloodstain on the doorknob. When he mentioned this, Alex blinked and straightened against the counter he had been leaning against.

"You saw it, too?" John asked, hating the desperate note in his voice.

Alex nodded. "On the front door, when I started running."

In the silence that followed, John expected the guy to break down in front of him, to sob like he had done in the woods. Instead, Alex appeared to be in a daze, as if he were straining to visualize the scene John had just described.

"He never told me that you had a way with words," Alex said.

John almost asked Alex if he were being sarcastic, but he could tell he was sincere from the way he was standing, still dazed, staring away from John now, as if his image were too bright to look directly into. "Right," John said. "He was too busy telling you about how I wasn't a real man because I . . . how did he put it? Because I live in my sister's shadow?"

Alex seemed surprised to hear his own cruel words repeated back to him. It looked as if he had forgotten about making the comment just hours earlier, and John realized that given the events of the past forty-eight hours, that was probably the case. Then Alex lowered his eyes, shamefully. "He said all kinds of things about you depending on what kind of mood he was in. Picking one over the other . . . that was unfair of me."

John felt a tightening in the center of his chest, but he wasn't sure which small revelation had caused it. Mike, whom he had been too ashamed to face for months after their return home, had respected him enough to say all manner of things about him. And now someone he had almost killed the night before was apologizing to him. The sound of his sudden deep breath startled them both. Embarrassed, John got to his feet and brushed past Alex, pulling a beer from the fridge and blaming the four he'd already had for the change that had just come over him. It was easier than entertaining the idea that Alex Martin's gentleness was responsible for the knot in the center of his chest.

"I was high," Alex said. "I hadn't planned on it, but I was."

John was too startled by this admission at first to realize that Alex was coming clean about what he was covering up about the night before.

"You didn't plan to be? What does that mean?"

"I think Mike spiked my drink with a drug called GHB. Because we'd been fighting. Because he wanted me to loosen up. I'd told him you weren't supposed to mix it with alcohol, but I guess he thought he had the right dose. He didn't. I passed out downstairs." In the silence that followed, Alex must have seen confusion on John's face because he said, "A few months ago we went down to San Diego to hit the bars. A friend of mine gave

Mike some to try, said it was for people who wanted to get buzzed but didn't like to drink."

John said, "It's the date rape drug."

"I know that," Alex said, an edge to his voice. "I didn't exactly sign off on this habit, okay? I thought it was a one-time thing. Just that night, you know? Going out to the bars. It was hard for him."

"Because he didn't want anyone to know he was gay."

"No. Because he had one eye. Gay guys aren't exactly charitable when it comes to being overweight, let alone physical deformities."

"What about you?"

"I couldn't have cared less. But it didn't matter how many times I said that to him. He started taking it whenever we had sex. He felt . . . incomplete."

Be cool with this, John told himself. *He's testing you. Don't be the hater he thinks you are.* "He could get it up on that stuff?"

"He didn't need to get it up to do what he liked to do. I did."

In any other circumstance John would have quickly excused himself and beelined to the nearest shower. But instead a bark of laughter escaped him before he could stop it. In the silence that followed, he looked up to find Alex glaring at him. John said, "I'm just waiting for the next big revelation, that's all. Was he going to have a sex change, too?"

"I'm sorry I'm such an oddity to you, John."

"I wasn't talking about you. I was talking about Mike."

Alex rolled his eyes, gave a throaty grunt, and sucked in a deep breath through his nostrils, a series of gestures John found to be so condescending, he tensed his fists against his lap. Maybe Alex sensed his anger because when he spoke again, it was quickly, almost breathlessly. "After I got off the phone with you I went to see Duncan and I told him everything I just told you. I also told him the flat sheet was missing from the bed. Then when I told him about the stain, I figured he would place a call to the sheriff in Boswell. Instead he interrogated me for three hours. Several times he asked me if I wanted a lawyer. I declined."

Alex gave him a chance to respond, but John was too stricken by this information to come up with something to say. Alex said, "Tonight at midnight will be almost twenty-four hours since Mike went missing. Another day and he's officially a missing person and Duncan starts taking all this seriously. And if he starts thinking it's a murder, he's got two primary suspects: a Marine and a faggot. And mark my words, he will pick the faggot, because that's who he is. That's how he was raised and that's how his mommy and daddy were raised and so on and so on."

John said, "Is that really the world you live in?"

"The thought never crossed your mind last night that I could live in that house too, did it?" Shamed by this fact, John broke eye contact with Alex for the first time since they had started talking to each other across barely three feet of space that felt like a gulf. "Then I'd say it's the world you live in too, John."

When John didn't make eye contact, Alex said, "I'm going down to San Diego to stay with a friend. All I ask of you is that if you really believe that I'm not strong enough to do what you saw, that you make that very clear to Captain Ray Duncan before he charges me with murder."

John was positive Alex was overreacting, misreading the situation. How could Duncan have gone from disbelieving the entire tale the night before to being on the scent of blood after being told about nothing more than a set of missing bedsheets? But Alex's request seemed shockingly humble given the situation he believed himself to be in, so John nodded, which seemed to take the wind out of Alex's sails. He looked around the trailer as if he were searching for another conversation topic.

When a knock cracked against the front door, Alex jumped and backed away from the fridge. John peered around the edge of a window shade. His blood went cold when he saw who was outside. When he turned to Alex and mouthed Duncan's name, Alex lifted one hand, as if he thought this simple gesture might put everything on pause. Then he looked to his feet in deep concentration. Another knock. Because he could think of no better option, John pointed to the bedroom door, as if Alex were a cheap mistress. Alex took a step, saw the Sig resting on the table, and picked up the weapon by the handle before moving off into the bedroom and shutting the door behind him.

Duncan was out of uniform, in blue jeans, scuffed cowboy boots, and a blue and red checkered long-sleeved shirt. As he stepped into the space that Alex had occupied just moments earlier, he studied the kitchen with a sad-eyed look, as if everything about it were a great disappointment but he cared about John too deeply to say anything.

"You want something?" John asked him.

"Coffee would be nice," he said.

Duncan took a seat at the table, kept silent, so silent John wondered if he were waiting to be asked just what the hell he was doing there. John made coffee instead. Duncan locked eyes with him as John delivered the steaming mug and apologized for not having anything to put into it.

After blowing into the cup for a few seconds, Duncan said, "I think I owe you an apology, John."

"Is that so?"

"Yes," he said. "I had some conversations earlier this evening. Conversations that have led me to believe you may have walked in on something last night, something you weren't supposed to see." John kept his mouth shut because he thought it was the best way to hide the fact that he wasn't surprised by this information.

"I know you went through a lot last night, and I know I might have come across as flip. But I thought it was in your best interests to—"

"I know what you thought. You thought I was some fucked-up vet having a meltdown."

"I thought you were a decent Marine who had just discovered something very . . . *unpleasant* about a friend of his. Something his friend had obviously kept a secret from him. And to be frank, I happen to sympathize with you."

"How so?"

Duncan lifted his hands to the sky and looked up as if he were asking for divine guidance for his next words. The gesture allowed John to see the Band-Aid around Duncan's right thumb: it was flesh colored and easy to miss, but it explained why Duncan had been holding the handle of the coffee cup almost delicately by hooking it with his forefinger and holding the bottom in his left palm.

Duncan said, "I'm no bigot. But I'm not a fan of the *oppressed,* the *victimized.* This is a good country. As long as a man's sober and in his right mind, you'd be hard pressed to get him to say otherwise. And people need to do certain things to get along and that's the way it is and most people are fine with it. But when an entire group of people come together and try to make some kind of identity out of their *strangeness* . . . well, they usually end up convincing themselves they're allowed to do any damn thing they want. No matter the consequences."

"Alex doesn't strike me as . . . an *activist.*"

"Alex Martin got kicked out of his parents' mansion down in Cathedral Beach for being a fruit. His daddy gave him their vacation cabin as a consolation prize, but the whole deal left Alex with a mighty big chip on his shoulder that I'm tired of dealing with. My concern here is that Mike was tired of dealing with it, too."

John was startled by this kind of admission from an officer of the law, but Duncan seemed unfazed by his reaction. "Look, I know it's a new day and age, but I sure as hell don't know what put a man like Mike in that house with a man like Alex, and I don't think it was very strong, whatever the hell it was. I think it came apart."

"Are you out of uniform so you'll feel more comfortable talking to me like this?"

"I don't follow," Duncan said.

"You're being very candid with me, Captain Duncan. This might be a murder investigation we're talking about here."

"It might be. But I don't investigate murders, even when they happen in my jurisdiction. That's the job of the homicide guys out of Boswell. But it is my job to make sure they are fully apprised of those facts of which I'm aware. And one of those facts is that you walked in on a very bad scene in a manner that is *incredibly* hard to explain, in a manner that makes you look like a suspect. Now, how that gets presented to them is not just up to me. It's up to you, too."

John took a minute to digest this. Duncan lifted his coffee mug to his mouth and sipped without breaking eye contact. "Well then, there's something you should know," John said. Duncan raised his eyebrows. John said, "I killed him."

Duncan jerked, and the motion combined with the strange manner in which he held the mug sent hot coffee spilling down the front of his shirt. He guffawed suddenly, held out his soaked hands, and said, "We seem to have gotten ahead of ourselves, and I've got myself a little mess here."

He made for the bedroom door, and John's heart leaped. "Bathroom's right here," John barked, grabbing Duncan's right shoulder and steering him toward the opposite end of the trailer. Duncan ducked inside, pulled the door shut behind him.

John heard a click and turned to see Alex open the bedroom

door several inches. Their eyes met, and John saw the fear in Alex's eyes, the fear of a man who knew he was a prime suspect in a murder. John shook his head silently, raised a hand, trying to find some gesture that would calm Alex. But then Alex's eyes cut past John, locked on something behind him. The blood drained from Alex's face. He turned and followed the direction Alex was staring in.

On the bathroom doorknob was a V-shaped stain exactly like the one John had seen on the door to the bedroom Mike had been murdered in. This time the twin marks were left by coffee and not blood, but it was the same hand that had left them, the hand of someone with an injured thumb who had been forced to grip the knob by hooking his index and middle finger over the top of it. Next came the same feeling that would strike John in the split second before he was fired on by insurgents: a sudden compression of the air around him and what felt like a brief ability to hear the smallest preparatory movements of your potential assailant but without the ability to see exactly where he was hiding.

The bathroom door opened and Duncan emerged, dabbing wadded-up toilet paper at the long coffee stain down his right thigh. Then John was rocked sideways. Alex shoved past him, the Sig raised in his right hand. Duncan's face went lax when he saw the gun and who was holding it, but then John reached out with one arm and hooked it around Alex's chest.

But Alex kept trying to charge, so John was forced to hurl him backward until his back slammed into the bedroom door with an impact that seemed to rock the entire trailer. To John, the sound that came welling up out of Alex, a growl and a sob in one, was the only appropriate music one could write for the sudden union of the images that had passed between them that evening—the handprint and the bloody crime scene that had vanished into thin air. He was relieved and surprised when he heard the Sig hit the floor. Alex had flown from the bedroom with such determination and force, John assumed he had the physical strength to give him the confidence to do it. He didn't. He had pure rage and all the stupidity it brought with it.

When he looked back at Duncan, he saw the man had weakly raised both hands but was staring down at the coffee-stained door-knob that had given him away. John saw the man's lips move softly with what appeared to be a stream of curses. By then, John had retrieved the gun from the floor, was rising to a standing posi-tion. Duncan saw this and reached in the direction of what John assumed was a side holster.

John said, "Draw on me in my home and I will kill you where you stand."

"Now that's about where you need to stop talking, my friend," Duncan said quietly. "Now I'm not sure what the hell's going on—"

"The hell you aren't," John said. "You know damn well what we just saw." Duncan nodded slowly, as if indulging a madman, and then opened his mouth to speak. But John cut him off with, "I walked in on *you,* didn't I? You drugged Alex's drink so you knew he was passed out downstairs and you were setting the scene. What were you going to do? Frame Alex for Mike's murder?"

Duncan said, "This is not something you can see through, John."

"Get the phone, Alex. Dial nine-one-one. Tell them we have a murderer here."

Duncan let out a throaty laugh and John listened to the shuf-fling sounds coming from behind him as Alex righted himself, tried to get his composure, and went for the phone. "Turn around," John told Duncan. "Put your hands on the wall above your head."

"That's not going to work for me," Duncan said, but now there was a tremor of fury in his voice. So John replied by taking the safety off the Sig.

The small snapping sound forced Duncan to comply. A silence fell and John was about to ask Alex why he hadn't called the police, when he felt the entire phone, cradle and receiver as one, slam into the upper portion of his neck. It wasn't the force of the blow that dropped him to his knees, it was the positioning of it: a near-perfect brachial stun. His vision blurred, then seemed to expand and contract, and when Alex pulled the gun from his hand, it felt like a light tug because his fingers had turned to jelly.

Outside, John saw Alex's shadow disappear around the end of the darkened trailer in pursuit of Duncan. He knew how this would end: with Alex shot dead and John's word against that of an officer of the law. He pursued them, expecting Duncan to turn and fire at any moment, but the man did no such thing. The three of them were moving down a side alleyway that ran along the outer row of trailers and fed into the small parking lot next to the trailer park's business office. And that's when it hit John: Duncan was running for his car. Duncan was trying to get the hell out of there without firing a shot. Alex had no such plan. He came to a sudden halt at the entrance to the parking lot, which told John that he had Duncan in his sights.

Alex raised the gun in both hands. When he was five feet away, John threw himself at Alex, sending them both crashing onto the asphalt as tires squealed and headlights swung over them and past them. For a brief second, John thought Duncan might plow his unmarked Ford Explorer into their tangle of limbs, but instead he raced out of the parking lot. Then he was gone, and John pulled Alex to his feet. But when he saw the anger twisting Alex's face, his own anger got the best of him and he hurled Alex so that the guy practically had to skip and airplane his arms to keep from falling over.

"You stupid *faggot*!" John cursed.

Alex was walking away from him, hands gripping the back of his head, seemingly drawn to the twin pinpricks of light that were the taillights of Duncan's Explorer snaking its way down the service road toward I-15. "You would have blown off the side of your own goddamn face!"

A trailer door popped somewhere in the distance, someone probably drawn by their shouts. Alex heard it, too, and looked over his shoulder at John. There wasn't a chance in hell John was bringing him back to his trailer, and the shattered look in Alex's eyes told him he knew.

Footsteps were approaching, and John could hear mumbled conversation; it sounded like two neighbors had met up and were approaching the parking lot. John said, "Get the hell out of here!"

John expected Alex to protest, but instead he held the same defeated look, as if everything from the revelation that Duncan was Mike's killer to John's current treatment of him were all part of an inevitability he no longer had the energy to fight, or even dread. Then Alex spoke, which surprised John because nothing about the guy's body had indicated he was preparing to say a word. "Stupid faggot? Is that what you called me? You were chasing me out of my own house while that son of a bitch was getting away with Mike's body. I may be the faggot, but you've got *stupid* covered all on your own, *Sergeant*."

The words slugged John in the chest. Now he could see clearly how he had managed to avoid saying them to himself over the past day: some part of him had known how much they were going to hurt. Calmly, as if they had just concluded a discussion about which route to take to Grandma's house, Alex turned and started toward a yellow Nissan Pathfinder parked next to the trailer-park manager's 4Runner.

John turned on his heel and started walking back to his trailer. He heard a voice call out, but he didn't recognize it and assumed it belonged to the neighbors who had spotted Alex. A car engine answered them by starting up. John turned, glimpsed the yellow Pathfinder as it sped out of the gate. John waited, watching to see if Alex headed in the same direction as Duncan. He didn't. Alex took the service road in the opposite direction, toward the interstate on-ramp that would put him in the southbound lanes. He didn't have the courage to follow Duncan. Not without a gun. Not without John.

If any neighbors had come to investigate the shouting in John's trailer, they were gone by the time he got back. Inside, John went to return the Sig to its holster behind the headboard, but as soon as he did, he envisioned Alex's headlights cutting lone swaths through the night. It felt like a valve had opened in his chest, emptying something cold and thick down into his stomach.

John imagined helicopters circling high over the trailer park, saw their searchlights probing the nest of trailers below, looking for Alex. Looking for John.

John was behind the wheel of his Tacoma and bouncing down the rutted mud road that led out of the trailer park before it occurred to him that he might be away from home long enough to merit bringing a few changes of clothes along. By then he was idling just outside the gates of the park, trying to decide which route to take: the one Duncan had used, or the one Alex had used. He was sweating and having trouble breathing because he knew full well that Alex's parting words had been God's truth.

John had made another seriously bad mistake. He had pursued the wrong man and allowed the real killer to escape with all the evidence of his crime. Then, he sent the man who paid most dearly for his mistake out into the night alone.

Thoughts of GHB and crimes against nature and sexualities kept secret all seemed to recede from view, like the black space around an aperture, and he saw clearly the one thing the Marine

Corps had taught him: wherever he had made wrong, he had to make right.

So John headed south, the same direction Alex Martin had taken on the 15, with the same clarity of purpose that had driven him to Owensville the night before. As he drove, he kept seeing the expression on Alex's face before he had left, the defeated look that told John he was just another son of a bitch in a long line of fag haters.

By the time John reached Temecula, a spread of lights covering the hilly inland of Riverside County, he could see Captain Mike Bowers giving him the same expression with his one good eye.

6

John doubted he would find Alex in any of the parts of San Diego he was familiar with. That meant he had one real lead, and he didn't like it.

In Poway, he pulled off the interstate and found a pay phone. Because it was a business, the information operator was happy to give him the street address for The Catch Trap, the notorious gay bar featured in one of the photos hanging on the wall of Mike and Alex's cabin. Next, he purchased a *Thomas Guide* from the nearest gas station and used the index to look up the address and plot a good course there from the 15. The neighborhood was called University Heights, and it was almost midnight by the time John was cruising its streets in his truck.

The Catch Trap was designed to look like a French Quarter brothel, with green shutters framing its blacked-out windows. A short line of pale-skinned boys with gelled hair and high-pitched laughs filled the entrance. John ignored the looks they gave him. Instead he studied the chunky guy with spiky blond hair at the head of the line checking IDs and slapping wristbands on legal drinkers, the same guy who had been standing behind Mike and Alex in the photograph on the wall outside their bedroom. John considered charging the line, but he figured that would draw more attention to him than hovering in the back, his hands shoved in his jeans pockets, the bill of his baseball cap shoved down over his forehead.

On the wall next to John was a poster advertising some special event that happened at the bar every Thursday night called Booted! The poster featured a muscle-bound model wearing cammie pants and a cover and glistening dog tags that hung between his blown-up pecs. For a full minute, John just stared at it. Maybe he was just fighting fatigue, but it was almost as if the man on the wall was a truer version of Lightning Mike Bowers than John had ever been allowed to know.

When John reached the head of the line, Spiky said, "May I help you, sir?" The stiffness and defensiveness of this greeting startled John, made him feel as if he had been pegged as an outsider.

"I'm looking for Alex Martin."

"Let me guess. You heard he gives the best head north of the border?"

Anger surged inside him, and the kid rocked back on his heels at the sight of his expression. "You don't need to be an asshole," John said.

"I give a lot of head a lot of the time. If you want my help, stop acting like I called your mother a whore, *girlfriend*."

"Where is he?" John asked quietly.

"Why do you want to know?" the guy repeated, slowly, drawing out each word as if John were a badly behaved eight-year-old.

"I said some things to him earlier tonight that I'm not proud of. I'm here to apologize." Spiky squinted at him; John figured Alex hadn't confided that much in the little shit-ass, so he decided to keep the details to himself.

"Philip Bloch," the guy said, as if just giving John his full name was some kind of defeat. Then, he summoned a co-worker to take his place, and John followed him into a crowded wood-paneled room that led out onto an equally crowded patio, where two muscular men in thong underwear gyrated on boxes above a largely oblivious crowd. John was busy trying to avert his eyes from the sexualized display of male flesh when he knocked into a drag queen done up like a 1940s cigarette girl, only in a nod to the current age, her cigarette box was filled with candy and breath mints. John smiled against his will and the girl said, "If you ever feel like doing porn, call me."

Philip jerked him forward by one shoulder and pulled him deeper into the crowd. John said, "Alex actually came *here*?"

"He used to work here. Is that a problem for you?" Philip stopped suddenly and turned to face him. Their noses almost touched, and John realized that Philip had deliberately brought them to a halt in the middle of a veritable sea of homosexuals. "This is about Mike, isn't it?" Against his will, John found himself scanning the crowd around him.

The men all around him were more clean-cut and attractive than he would have liked them to be, and the long looks they were giving him were cold, intent, focused—they made him feel as if he had farted in church. This was the cycle he went through with Alex, and now with these men. First came the belief that they weren't truly homosexual because they didn't look like those leather-clad slow dancers at The Blue Oyster Bar in the *Police*

Academy movies he'd loved as a kid. Then came the paralyzing embarrassment, as if their looks meant he had something hanging from his nose. Then, like a lightning bolt, the anger struck—anger that other men he could take in a fight, hands down, could make his cheeks get hot.

"Hiding in plain sight," Philip shouted over the music. "That's all he told me. You want to tell me why he needs to hide *anywhere?*"

"There's been some trouble," John said. Back in his real hometown, Baton Rouge, "trouble" was a polite term used to describe everything from flat tires to wife-beatings, and John couldn't manage a more suitably general term for the gay stranger standing nose-to-nose with him.

Philip sneered and started to lead him through the crowd again. John had barely made it another few steps when a hand sunk into his ass. He seized the guy's wrist and used it to bend his entire arm back over his right shoulder. The perv was about half John's height and twice his weight, but John kept pushing back on the guy's awkwardly bent arm until the man bent at the knees and his mouth became a silent O. He shoved the guy backward and when he saw how much trouble he had regaining his footing, John realized how drunk the stupid son of a bitch was.

John turned around, preparing himself for Philip's anger. But his new guide was standing with his hands on his hips, having watched their brief tussle with what appeared to be boredom.

"Sorry," John said. "Was that a *hate* crime?"

"Not in my book," Philip said. "Nobody has the right to grab my ass unless I invite them to, and I didn't hear you invite him, so you get a pass on that one." They started through the crowd again, toward a door in a small outbuilding that sat at the back of the courtyard. Once they were inside a cramped and darkened hallway, Philip said, "He wanted to stay here until my shift ended and then I was supposed to take him home with me."

They passed a cramped employee lounge, then a messy office where a heavyset woman in a white T-shirt that bore the bar's logo sat behind a desk talking quietly into a phone. She looked like she could hammer the shit out of them both. "And after you took him home? Then what?"

"Then we were going to make sweet, sweet love in the morning light. I don't know what. All I know is that he showed up here a couple hours ago looking like he had run all the way from that hick mountain town he's been living in. He won't tell me what the hell's going on but I have a pretty good guess it's got—"

John cut him off with, "What about his parents?"

"His mother's a fucking bitch. She pretty much cut him off when she found out he was a fag. Hasn't said a word to him since."

"His father? He gave him the house they were living in, right?"

"I'm sorry. Are you actually friends with Alex? His father's been dead for three years. Wait! They *were* living in it? Did they move?" When John didn't answer, Philip went pale and cursed under his breath as he stared at the floor between them. A transformation seemed to take place inside him as he realized that by harboring Alex he had taken part in something more far-reaching than he had previously assumed. He averted his eyes from John, led him to a closed door, opened it, and ushered him inside quickly, which fooled John into thinking they were walking into a real room. Then he knocked into a rolling mop bucket and saw Alex sitting on a bar stool right next to it, looking ghostly under the single hanging bulb. The three of them were wedged inside a crowded janitor's closet.

Philip stood just inside the door. John noticed he was holding the knob with one hand wedged between the door and the small of his back, as if he were trying to keep them both prisoners now that all of three of them were together. Alex studied John with a furrowed brow and a pained look that exhibited his deep fatigue.

Philip broke the silence. "Your new friend here started using the past tense when we were talking about your house. So I guess that means that either your house burned down or—"

John cut him off. "You really thought this was a good place to come?"

"I didn't plan on staying here for very long," Alex said.

"Right. Philip was supposed to take you home. Which puts him in danger."

"You're real helpful all of a sudden."

Philip stepped forward. "I need one of you to tell me what's going on." Neither man answered. "Fine. Then I need one of you to tell me what the fuck happened to Mike."

The mere mention of Mike's name sent a shudder through Alex. Philip noticed this, and as Alex screwed his eyes shut and tried to suck in a breath through his nose, Philip closed the distance between them, tenderly cupped Alex's chin in one hand. "Babe," he whispered gently. John couldn't take his eyes off this display, couldn't decide whether it was their motions that seemed unreal to him or the ease with which they executed them. *They've got to be kidding me with this,* John thought. *They're homos. Not women.*

Alex blinked back tears and tried to meet Philip's gaze, but then he seemed to remember John's presence. He reached up and took Philip's hand away from his chin, shook his head brusquely. It had been a small moment, but it told John that Alex was filtering himself—not lying to him, but showing him a different face than the one he almost displayed to his close friend, a furious and angry one, meant to imply that the guy who wore it was tougher than he actually was. "Can you give us a minute?" John asked Philip.

"I'll start counting right now," Philip said.

He left them alone with bass beats knocking at the walls all around them and rattling the mops in their buckets. Finally John said, "You pull another move like you did in my trailer and you're going to get yourself killed."

"What are you doing here, John?" Alex asked, his voice breathy and distant, his eyes glazed with exhaustion and the kind of numbness that moves in to turn fear into something bearable.

"We're going to go to the authorities. The right authorities."

"Who would that be?"

"The sheriff of Hanrock County."

Alex's silent laughter shook his shoulders, twisted his mouth into a joker's grimace. "Are you shitting me? Hanrock County is one of the most right-wing places in the country. If I'm going to accuse one of their own of murder without a shred of physical evidence, I'll need the entire Marine Corps backing me up. Can you arrange that? Besides, what are we going to accuse him of? Having a weird fucking handprint?"

"Trying to frame you for murder."

"Bullshit. He wanted to kill me."

"Then why did he spend so much time on Mike while you were drugged downstairs?"

"Maybe you stopped him. Maybe I was next."

"So he ties Mike to the bed and leaves you there, passed out, without any restraints?" Alex took a moment to consider this. John checked the door behind them to make sure Philip wasn't eavesdropping. "He wasn't interested in killing you. He wanted you to take the fall for it. If I hadn't shown up, it might have worked. I didn't believe your story about Mike spiking your drink when you first told me. If I hadn't seen Duncan's handprint on the doorknob, I still wouldn't believe it."

Alex took this in, closed his eyes briefly as he seemed to accept it.

"We need to get out of here," John said.

"Where are we going?"

"Someplace where you can think this through. Look at what your options really are."

"You're going to help me? That's one of my options?" John nodded because it was easier than giving voice to his agreement. When Alex stared into his eyes intently, it looked as if he were about to reject an offer John hadn't brought himself to make explicitly. "Because Mike saved your life. Semper Fi and all that?"

There was nothing John hated more than when civilians used Marine Corps expressions with false bravado. But Alex was a few steps closer than your average civilian to knowing the true meaning of expressions like the one he had just used. John just had trouble with what had put Alex in such a place.

"Fine," Alex said, as if the offer on the table were nothing more than a lunch date. "Start by handling Philip."

In the hallway outside the broom closet, Philip leaned against the wall, arms folded over his chest, lips puckered in anger. He stood up straight when he saw the door open. "Did anyone see him come in?" John asked.

"No," Philip said. "He called my cell and asked me to meet him in back."

"Good."

"It is?"

John stared at the guy, hoping to unnerve him. He didn't see any evidence of this taking place so he said, "It's called plausible deniability, my friend."

"Is Mike dead?"

"Yes."

"Murdered?"

"You got any vacation days coming to you, Philip? Because if you keep asking me questions like this, you better take them all, starting tomorrow, so that when the people who are looking for us come here asking questions—"

A door opened behind them, and John turned to see the heavyset lesbian he had spotted earlier emerging from the office down the hallway. Philip gave her a terse nod and a smile, and the woman pointed a finger at them in warning before she shuffled off. Maybe she thought they were trying to sneak a romantic moment together. Once the woman was gone, Philip said, "I've got two weeks of vacation and some sick days. From *both* my jobs."

The color left Philip's face as John told him the entire story. Then, in the silence that followed, it returned until the guy's cheeks were flame red with an outrage John had yet to marshal.

"You're here to help him?" Philip asked.

John had barely addressed the question himself, so he just nodded, hoping Philip would move on.

"How?" Philip asked.

"I don't know."

Philip seemed genuinely affected by this display of vulnerability on John's part, if only because he waited a considerable amount of time before asking his next question.

"Why?"

"Because I have to." When Philip shook his head in confusion, John added, "Mike saved my life."

At the sound of these words, Philip retreated into his anger. "Mike's dead," he said.

"That doesn't change what he did."

"What he did for *you,* maybe. You want to know what he did to Alex? He forced him to give up his entire life. He forced him to move to the middle of fucking nowhere, where this kind of shit can happen and nobody notices. I don't care about Mike Bowers and I don't care what kind of bullshit death-before-dishonor crap you've got all tied up in this. I am asking you: *What are you going to do for Alex?*"

"I'm going to protect him," John snapped. "It's the only thing I know how to do for him, all right? I'm not a lawyer and I'm not a cop. I'm not even a Marine anymore. But I know how to protect him, and that's what I'm going to do, okay?"

Philip seemed to relax, studying John without any sense of anger or urgency. "I swear to God, I watched Alex fuck up his entire life for one Marine. I won't watch him do it for another one. If you so much as make him sniffle . . ."

John thought of Emilio's foul comment about the sex appeal of Marines. *An ace in every hole, man.* Now Philip was basically saying that Alex was no different from the type of woman Emilio had been referring to—the kind of woman who got freaky and stupid for any man in uniform. But what had been in it for Mike? Maybe he just got off on being worshiped.

Philip was about to turn away when John said, "You make it sound like Mike used to beat the shit out of him."

"No!" Philip snapped, taking the bait with a child's petulance. He seemed to sense that he had exposed his own jealousy because he dropped his eyes. "I just can't help but wonder if we would be here right now if Alex could have loved someone like Alex."

"Or like you," John said.

✕

John walked back to his truck but stopped half a block away. For a good while he stood in the entrance to a service alley and scanned the street for any unfamiliar vehicles. A small-town captain like Duncan surely didn't have unmarked cars at his disposal, but there was a chance he might have put out some sort of bogus APB on John and Alex, enlisting other police departments in the hunt. Of course, that wouldn't fit with Duncan's previous behavior, which included running like hell and not calling for backup.

Once he was satisfied he wasn't being watched, John got in his truck and circled the block. He steered through the tiny service alley behind the club, saw Philip waiting for him, the back door open and propped against one shoulder.

As soon as Alex was in the car, John let his foot off the brake.

"I need to go to my car," Alex said. A visit to Alex's vehicle had not been part of the escape plan they had just discussed. John kept his mouth shut, but Alex could sense his anger. "I need something out of the backseat. It'll take two seconds."

"Fine."

Alex gave him directions to a quiet street three blocks from The Catch Trap that was lined with tall, sickly palm trees and unadorned stucco duplexes with barren front lawns. When Alex saw his car, he placed his hand around the door handle and unbuckled his seat belt. But just then, John saw the black Royal Marquis parked across the street and several car lengths away, in a spot that offered a perfect view of Alex's vehicle for the police officer John imagined was sitting behind the heavily tinted windshield.

When John accelerated, Alex cried, "What the hell are you doing?"

"There's a cop back there!"

"Bullshit!"

Alex unlocked the door, cracked it by several inches, so John accelerated more and turned the first corner. "Knock it off!"

"Every piece of evidence I have that Mike ever existed is in the trunk of that car. Now you stop this fucking truck!"

"There is an unmarked cop car waiting for you back there."

"Then shoot him!"

Alex threw open the passenger door and, because he felt he

had no other choice, John slammed on the brakes. He wasn't sure whether the sudden stop threw Alex from the truck, but the next thing John knew, Alex was skittering toward the sidewalk like a circus clown, as he tried to break into a run and get his balance at the same time. He half-succeeded, almost tripping over the curb, then taking off into the shadows between streetlights.

The passenger door stood open. For what felt like a dangerously long moment John just sat there, listening to the hum of his idling engine. Then he reached across the empty seat, pulled the passenger door shut, and hit the accelerator. As he approached the street where Alex's car was parked, he killed his headlights, slowed to about five miles per hour, and nosed slightly around the corner. He saw a single shadow standing in the middle of the street. The Marquis hadn't moved. The shadow started walking toward John. It appeared misshapen at first, and then John realized Alex was carrying a large cardboard box in both arms. Without a word, he dropped it in the truck's cargo bay; then he opened the passenger-side door and got into the cab.

They sat in frosty silence like a married couple that had just argued themselves into exhaustion. Finally John said, "You really expected me to shoot a cop for you?"

"No. I expected you to leave."

"I should have."

"That box is the only evidence I have that Mike Bowers was a part of my life," he said. "You can be sure that if his parents ever get their hands on his body, I will not be invited to the funeral."

John didn't take the bait, nursed his anger for the next few minutes.

"Where are we going?" Alex asked him.

"I've got a stop to make, too."

✕

Almost forty minutes later, they were leaving behind the Pacific Beach neighborhood where John had switched his Tacoma's license plates with those of a Honda Accord parked in front of a Cape Cod–style cottage a few blocks from the ocean.

Alex's hometown had been just a few miles up the coastal road, but he didn't make any remark about it. Instead, he waited until they were heading north on the 5 to say, "Feel like telling me how you learned to change license plates so fast?"

"One of my sister's ex-boyfriends. Only good thing I ever got out of him."

"Jerk?"

Not just a jerk. John thought. *A supposedly recovered drunk who had been full of spiritual wisdom until he fell off the 12-step wagon and broke Patsy's nose right in the middle of the living room.* John said a silent prayer that that guy had, in a blackout, driven into a telephone pole. But he said none of these things to Alex.

Alex seemed to sense the omission because he shifted slightly in his seat and held the shit handle above the window as if the truck had suddenly accelerated to ninety miles an hour. They passed a series of eucalyptus-framed exit signs for Cathedral Beach, but Alex watched them fly by without any discernible reaction.

"That's your hometown, right?"

"Notice I didn't go there for assistance with this predicament I'm in."

"Yeah. I noticed."

John waited for him to elaborate, but he didn't. Another long silence and then Alex said, "My grandmother's sick," and John heard the wet sound of tears in his voice. "Sorry. It just feels like I'm not going to see her again."

You might not, John thought. *If you stay stupid and don't go to the authorities.* But he kept his mouth shut, fought images of he and

Alex living together in a hut in the mountains, all because John had fucked up and Mike had decided to save his life.

How far was he willing to go to repay this debt? Where was the line between honor and guilt? They were questions better answered by a man who was going to get a lot more sleep that night than John could reasonably hope for.

He was pulled from these thoughts when Alex started to speak with a sudden authority, as if the guy were delivering a lecture he had rehearsed for years, and drew John's attention from the road. He didn't check to make sure John was listening, didn't seem remotely interested in the posture or body language John was displaying.

When he realized Alex was telling him the story of the night he met Mike for the first time, John knew he was being tested and resolved to listen to the entire thing in respectful silence.

7

Alex said he could tell the guy was a Marine the minute he sat down at the bar. These days every gay porn star went out in public sporting a set of dog tags, and given that San Diego was the unofficial gay porn capital of America, it was sometimes hard to spot the real servicemen. Starched collared shirts, khaki pants, and rigid poses they managed to hold for the ten minutes it took them to get phenomenally drunk—these were the markers of San Diego's true gay fighting men.

The customer in question wore freshly ironed blue jeans. His broad shoulders stretched a blue and black plaid shirt. The bill of his baseball cap shaded an angular face, with thick black eyebrows and a Roman nose. When he ordered a bourbon and Coke, his eyes roamed Alex's body in a cold and detached manner that suggested he was looking for weak spots.

On break, Alex pointed the guy out to Philip, warned him that he might be trouble. A few months before, two guys picked up a raver kid who worked at one of the espresso shops down the street, lured him into an alley, and beat him within an inch of his life. The kid had spent two days in a medically induced coma, and his jaw was still wired shut. People thought these things didn't happen anymore, not in the days of *The Ellen DeGeneres Show* and the Human Rights Campaign and gay marriage in Massachusetts. But they did happen. Mostly to young guys who couldn't afford good lawyers and who were too ashamed to come forward because they had tried X that night or snorted a bump of something without asking what it was. This was something Alex had never learned in Cathedral Beach, or at Stanford, for that matter, where all things gay were couched in terms such as *heteronormativity* and *third gender* and discussed in hushed tones in empty dorm lounges by kids with multiple face piercings and trust funds.

Philip laughed at Alex when he tried to paint the guy in the baseball cap as some kind of threat. "He comes around all the time," Philip explained. "If he gets shit-faced enough, he might go home with some little twink. Right now it looks like that twink might be *you*." This last remark was said with just enough of a sharp edge.

Years earlier, in the months before Alex went off to begin his soon-aborted college career, when he was still living in his parents' oceanfront mansion and using his fake ID to get into bars such as The Catch Trap, he and Philip had a one-night stand. Like so many gay boys just out of the closet who end up in bed together, they had developed a friendship defined by equal parts frustrated desire and sibling rivalry. It was Philip who had come to the rescue when Alex's mother had discovered he was gay and strong-armed his weak-kneed father into cutting him off financially. It was Philip who had come to the rescue when Alex suddenly found himself without the means to continue at Stanford and nothing to live on, considering he had never worked a day in his life.

Just a few days after realizing he had no choice but to withdraw from Stanford—with a 3.8 GPA and the adoration of most of his professors—Alex moved into Philip's apartment in University Heights and got a job tending bar at The Catch Trap, where the only hard-and-fast rule for bartenders was that they hit the gym at least six days a week, with the added suggestion that an appearance in one of the many porn films that were shot in the area would lead to a substantial increase in customer interest. Alex took the first suggestion and ignored the latter, and now he had enough definition to tend bar shirtless, like the rest of his tip-hungry co-workers.

Philip said, "Just because you're too chicken to hit on him doesn't mean he's a gay basher." Wounded by this hard pellet of truth, Alex returned to his bar, which was buried at the back of the club, past the crowded courtyard.

Alex asked the guy if he wanted another drink, and the guy said, "You and your co-worker were talking about me." Alex waited for an indication that this was a question and not a statement of fact. None came, and Alex felt himself flush.

"How could you tell?"

"You have been staring at me since I sat down, and when you went to speak to him, he looked in my direction several times." His answer sounded robotic, without the slightest hint of sarcasm or amusement. He had no discernible accent, which meant he was from west of the Rockies, and his aversion to using contractions suggested he was either a Marine or playing the part of one quite well.

"We have a bet going about you," Alex lied.

The guy nodded and stared right into his eyes without any change of expression.

"Ten bucks says you're a Marine."

The guy licked his upper lip lightly with the tip of his tongue, the only indication that this statement had rattled him somewhat. "What's *your* money on?" the guy asked.

"Marine."

The guy nodded impassively, finished off his drink, and pushed the empty rock glass toward Alex. Alex poured him another one. "You have good posture," the guy said. "Your shoulders . . .you hold them well. Back. Not hunched over." The guy demonstrated, slumping forward, but still staring right into Alex's eyes with a blank expression.

Alex was tempted to tell the guy his heart had just melted into a pile of cheese, but he just smiled. As soon as he put a fresh cocktail in front of him, the Marine said, "There has never been an era except for ours that has condoned exclusive male homosexuality. Bisexuality, sure. Some of our greatest armies, some of our greatest soldiers had male companions—lovers. But they always maintained sexual relationships with women. It was always . . . *in balance.*"

Alex fought the urge to tell the Marine that if it was bisexuals he was looking for, he should try a high school drama club and not The Catch Trap. Sure, his lecture had been offensive, but something had entered his voice as he had delivered it: pain. The Marine's tone said to Alex, "I don't want to be here but I don't know where else to go." It was a pain Alex could identify with, even though everything else about the guy made Alex feel inadequate and desperate with desire. Alex wanted to be at Stanford, cashing in on all the golden promises that had been made to the children of Cathedral Beach, promises the world had broken because he was a fag. He wanted to be someplace where he didn't have to pump up his chest to make up for the fact that his career path had been shit on by his mother's homophobia.

"So you are a Marine," Alex said.

But before the guy could respond, a shrill voice trilled, "Oh, Lordy mercy! A *Muhreeeeene*!" One of Alex's least favorite customers had been standing just several feet away the entire time. But Alex had been so intently focused on the guy in the white baseball cap that he hadn't seen the man with the blond pompadour and ten-pound Rolex who went by the name Stephen Royce. Although Alex had many loyal customers, Stephen had become increasingly irate after Alex had refused several invitations to take a cruise on his yacht, which was rumored not to exist.

"Well, mercy me," Stephen crooned and put his arm around the Marine. "I always suspected there was something a little off about you, Alexander. I mean, I know full well that you're a castoff from the upper echelons of Cathedral Beach *high* society, but I must admit I had no idea you were a chaser." The Marine in the baseball cap winced at this term, a term for a gay man who sexually pursued Marines.

The Marine said, "I need for you to move your arm, sir."

Mouth agape, bushy eyebrows raised, Stephen Royce withdrew slowly, hands raised at the guy next to him as if heat were radiating off of him, which it practically was. "Well, excuse me. But given that I couldn't help overhearing this little interlude between the two of you, I thought I should step in and warn Alex here that despite what you see in the videos, it's the Marine who usually takes it up the ass."

The Marine said, "You are being inappropriate, sir." Alex heard the warning in the guy's voice. If Stephen Royce heard it, too, it inspired only anger in him.

"*Inappropriate?* Young man, you sitting at my bar is inappropriate."

"You are embarrassing this gentleman because he is not interested in you sexually. My sitting at this bar has nothing to do with that fact."

Stephen Royce flinched as if a glass of ice water had been hurled in his face. For a split second, Alex thought Royce might have been frightened off.

"You sure talk smart for a *baby killer.*"

The Marine delivered a solid punch to the bridge of Stephen Royce's nose without standing up all the way. Royce crumpled and hit the floor, red pulsing from both smeared nostrils. Alex was so busy marveling at the skill and efficiency of the guy's strike that he hadn't realized the implications, hadn't noticed the fear that had taken over the guy's face as soon as he realized what he had done. It wasn't that he regretted drawing blood. The official policy was don't ask, don't tell, but if you got the cops called on you in a gay bar, that was as good as telling.

"With me," Alex snapped, and grabbed the guy by one shoulder, dragging him out the side door and into the courtyard, then through a side door and into the alleyway. Alex kept shoving the guy forward toward the mouth of the alleyway, but suddenly the guy went down on both knees with the determination of someone falling into prayer and started vomiting. For a second Alex thought it was some aftereffect of violence, like the nosebleeds movie characters developed every time they used their powers of telekinesis. But the man kneeling in front of Alex didn't have supernatural powers; he was just giving Alex an eyewitness glimpse of the amount of alcohol it took for him to sit comfortably in a gay bar. Without gasping or apologizing, the guy finished vomiting, got to his feet, and stared at Alex as if he had simply paused to tie his shoelaces.

"You need to go," Alex said.

"He was being inappropriate."

"I know. But you don't want the cops called on you here. Not if you're actually a Marine."

Alex could he see the guy's muted version of protest in his eyes, in the way the lines appeared at the bridge of his nose. Then he nodded and trotted off toward the mouth of the alleyway.

×

By the time he returned to his bar, a stone-faced Philip and the lesbian manager were waiting for him and told him that Stephen Royce was being tended to in the office, screaming about some Marine who had tried to gay-bash him right there in the middle of the club. When Alex told them he had tried to chase the Marine so the police could be called, Philip looked to the floor to keep from laughing, and the manager's silence suggested that a mutual disdain for Stephen Royce and all his pretenses would keep this from going any farther.

After the relief of not having to tell bald-faced lies in front of Stephen Royce subsided, the disappointment set in, along with a kind of self-pity over the fact that he would probably never lay eyes on the baseball-cap-wearing Marine again. But half an hour later, as he was serving a drink, he pulled a napkin from the top of the stack, saw that there was something written on it, and paused. *My name is Mike. I would like to know yours. mtrecon@hotmail.com.* The childish sincerity and the courtliness of it had Alex grinning like an idiot, as the customers he was ignoring cleared their throats and tapped their fingers on the bar.

Mike Recon was waiting in the shadows on the other side of the street when Alex emerged from the bar. Philip saw him first, pointed in his direction, and then sauntered off down the sidewalk, staring at Alex over his shoulder with a bitter grin. Given who Recon had already shown himself to be, Alex thought getting a note and an e-mail address out of the guy had been a major triumph, so by the time they were standing face-to-face across the street from the club and away from all prying eyes, Alex was speechless and red-faced.

"Everything turn out all right?" Mike asked, sounding considerably more sober.

"You ran. I chased you. You got away."

"Maybe we should get out of here then," he said. When Alex met his stare, Mike flinched slightly and looked away, as if this forward a comment had taken all of his confidence. Alex pointed in the direction of his car, and they walked toward it.

Recon's sudden silence suggested determination—a determination to get his dick sucked in Alex's front seat. Since coming out, Alex had engaged in several one-night stands in backseats and seedy motel rooms, locations he probably wouldn't have been ashamed to have sex in if he were having it with women. But one-way sex wasn't his thing, even if the guy was a hot Marine. So when Mr. Recon slid his seat belt across his chest, stared straight forward, and placed his hands on his knees, Alex was relieved.

"Where should we go?" Alex asked.

"Someplace . . . not gay," Mike said. Alex felt the sting of rejection from this comment, given that he lived close by, smack in the middle of a gay neighborhood. Mike seemed to sense the tension in Alex's silence, because he met his eyes and said, "Someplace where we can just sit and talk. Like the beach, maybe."

"The beach," Alex said, and started the engine. He headed for Cathedral Beach. Stopping to consider which beach they should visit and which route they should take to get there would force him to consider things such as whether this guy's determination to get him alone might mean he wanted to leave him with his jaw wired shut. This was a risk Alex had long ago learned to accept. He always went for the straight-acting guys, the guys Philip referred to derisively as either "no-necks" or "cavemen."

They barely exchanged a word until they were driving down Adams Street, the main drag in the part of Cathedral Beach everyone referred to as the Village. They passed the darkened storefronts of designer furniture showrooms and the store that sold gourmet dog treats, where Alex had worked one summer. Alex realized how tired he was when he thought he glimpsed his mother rounding a street corner, her platinum blond hair cut in a perfect Jackie-O bob, holding her Louis Vuitton tightly to her hip, as if there were a small dog inside she was afraid of waking.

Now that he was cruising these streets, which had been desolate for almost twelve hours since the town basically closed down at about nine o'clock, Alex realized that some subconscious desire, something other than haste, had driven him to bring this handsome stranger here. After all, the guy was a Marine: what better kind of husband could a fag bring home to Cathedral Beach?

Silenced by these thoughts, Alex drove toward the the spot where Adams Street dipped and met up with the coastal drive that snaked behind a crescent-shaped lawn dotted with absurdly tall palm trees. There the Alhambra Hotel's lighted dome cast a pale glow down the seven-story pink adobe tower that supported it. They cruised past the lone high-rise condo that had gone up in the sixties, before outraged residents changed municipal codes and blocked anything over five stories from mucking up their view; then past a sandy beach formed by a concrete wall, where Alex's father had taken him swimming as a young boy, before pods of seals had taken over the beach, beginning what had grown into a decades-long battle between environmentalists from the University of California, San Diego and wealthy residents who insisted that the seals brought disease and sharks.

It was a windy night, and whitecaps tore into the rocky shore. He parked next to a set of wooden steps that led down to a narrow crescent of sand that stretched between jagged outcroppings. Mike looked around for nosy neighbors or trolling cops; then he decided it was safe and took a seat on a bench. "You live here?" he asked.

"I used to live here."

"Why did you leave?"

"I went away to school," he said. *My mother found out I was gay. She turned my father against me. Cut me off.* He kept these statements to himself as he stepped from the car and led Mike down the set of wooden steps.

Once they reached the sand, Alex realized how far in the tide was, but by the time the cold water washed across his ankles, Mike had seized him by the back of his neck and was dragging him into the band of darkness that hugged the base of the seawall, where the glow of the streetlights high above couldn't reach. Mike brought his gaping mouth to Alex's, made a comic sputtering sound that almost broke the mood, and doused Alex in rancid bourbon breath.

Alex shoved Mike's back against the seawall, sank to his knees, and swallowed Mike whole. For a while, there were just the sounds of the surf, the wind, and Mike's strangled groans as Alex built up enough momentum to do him serious injury. Convinced he had subdued the guy, Alex got to his feet, grabbed Mike by one shoulder, and tried to push him to his knees. When Mike's entire body went rigid underneath his grip, Alex only pushed harder. "*No,*" came Mike's firm, suddenly sober response.

"*What?*"

"I don't do that," Mike mumbled. "I'm not like that."

Alex snorted and didn't let up on Mike's right shoulder. Mike responded by batting Alex's arm away with one powerful forearm. A badly aimed blow, but strong enough to send Alex skittering backward across the sand, where he landed ass-first in the surf line, his upper half suddenly inside the glow of light from the streetlights overhead. "You're not like what? Like me? You're not one of me? Is that what you're saying?"

Mike didn't respond. Alex's anger was replaced by fear as he remembered that the guy who had just knocked him off his feet was trained to kill with his bare hands. Suddenly Alex wondered if this was what happened to that poor raver kid who had his jaw broken, if gay-bashings often had more acts to them than newspaper reports would have you believe. Mike took a step forward, his face in darkness. Alex shot to his feet and took off up the stairs. When Mike didn't call out to him, Alex assumed he was being chased, so he jumped into his car, locked the doors, started the car, and slammed his foot on the accelerator.

He was about to make a right turn off Coast Drive when he saw in the rearview mirror that Mike hadn't pursued him. Instead, he was standing atop the rock shelf that marked one end of the beach Alex had just fled. When the car's brake lights illuminated, Mike lowered his arms, turned to face the sea, sprinted for the far end of the rock shelf, and dove over the side and into the whitecaps below.

Alex pulled over, locked the car, and broke into a dead run, down the winding coastal road, past the entrance to the condo high-rise, jumping the white clapboard fence, and skittering out onto the now empty shelf of rock from which Mike had just taken a flying leap. He reached the end and was greeted by the sight of rolling whitecaps. He had just pulled his cell phone out to call the police when two strong, soaking-wet arms shot up under his armpits and clamped down on his shoulders with enough force to turn his ankles to jelly.

"What's your worst fear?"

"You are!" Alex said.

Alex fought images of a Hollywood-size shark rising from the water to catch him in its jaws. "Funny," Mike said. "Mine used to be drowning."

Mike threw his entire weight against Alex. They fell as one— Mike's body going straight and rigid, forcing Alex's to do the same—and hit the water like a splintered jackknife. The current pulled sharply on them, from one direction, then another, and the surrounding blackness was so total Alex might have mistaken it for death had it not been for the muffled roar of whitecaps over- head. They broke the surface just as they were drawn into the first swell of a fresh wave. Alex heard his own gasps, saw that the rock shelf they had jumped off was several yards off to the right. They were on a diagonal path toward the beach, and Mike was keeping them on it by kicking into the current.

When Alex tried to breathe, fire erupted in his chest. He started to spasm with deep coughs, releasing water he hadn't known had forced its way into his lungs. Mike had curved one arm around his chest now, lifeguard-style, as another wave drove them toward the beach. When they finally scraped sand, Alex felt total exhaustion overtake him as he tried to lift himself onto all fours. He almost fell face-first into the sand before Mike curved an arm around him again to keep him supported. His hacking coughs had the ragged edges of sobs, and as they grew more intense, he was distracted by the feel of Mike's hand kneading the back of his neck.

Alex sank forward and rolled onto his back, found himself staring up at Mike's shadowed face, unsure whether it was this brief frenzy of violence that had posed them like lovers or whether

Mike had deliberately positioned them that way. "Easy," Mike cooed, his voice as gentle as a mother's. "You were in perfect hands the entire time. I've been drownproofed. I'll take you to Las Pulgas sometime and show you a real jump. They've got a diving platform that's thirty feet up." He grabbed the back of Alex's neck and brought their noses together, clenched his teeth, and in a low growl said, "That's where you find the parts of you that are soft and make them *hard,* son. Because Recon Marines get hard by doing *hard* things."

"Why don't you just learn how to suck dick instead?"

The terseness and crudeness of this statement seemed to resonate with Mike as nothing else Alex had said to him quite had, and a rich laughter erupted from deep within his chest. Alex saw a light come into his eyes that had been all but extinguished earlier that night by bourbon and self-loathing.

Once he caught his breath, Mike said, "I'm sorry I made you fall."

"Into the ocean?"

"Before that. When I knocked you down."

"Oh. I see. . . . So you hurling me into the ocean afterward was, like, completely okay with you?"

"Yes."

"Why's that, Recon?"

"Because I went with you."

Then, somewhere overhead, a police siren hiccuped. Mike sat back on his haunches like a frightened dog; then he pulled Alex to his feet and ran them toward the shelter of a narrow cave that cut under the rock shelf. No doubt someone in the high-rise nearby had heard Alex's wail and called for help. Inside the cave, Mike pressed Alex against the wall with one arm. They could now see a police cruiser parked next to the white clapboard fence ten feet above the beach. The lights on the cruiser were flaring, but the siren had gone silent. The cop was probably just putting on a show for whoever had made the call. Silently, they watched the police officer's flashlight probe the spot where they had washed up, then travel out over the water. When the silence between them became oppressive, Mike looked back over his shoulder at Alex and said, "Sorry, dude."

Alex sank into a seated position, hands pressed to his mouth. Mike fell to his knees next to him, clearly terrified by this sudden transformation. The fact that Mr. Force Recon Marine couldn't tell that Alex was laughing only made Alex laugh harder. Because after meeting him piss drunk, decking a stranger, almost getting him fired, throwing up his guts, shoving him on his ass, and then almost drowning him, Mike had simply apologized to Alex as if he had done no more than step on his toe. Once Mike realized it was laughter shaking Alex's soaked body, he had to fight it himself, which he did by pulling Alex against his chest until the cop's flashlight disappeared and the cruiser pulled off silently into the misty night.

Once they were alone, Mike withdrew. Alex brushed past him, stepped out of the cave and onto the sand below. "Where are you going?" Mike asked.

"Home," he said. "I didn't take you there because you said you didn't want to go to a gay place. I live in a gay neighborhood." Even though it was too dark for him to see Mike's face, Alex turned to face him so his last words wouldn't be carried away on the wind. "You can come with me if you want. But you have to be *one of me.* That's the deal. I've played the other game, and nobody wins."

Alex started across the sand toward the steps. He waited until he had reached the sidewalk above before he looked back. When he did, he saw that Mike was behind him, carefully taking each step with a greater degree of consideration than he had done with anything else that night.

✕

John waited what he thought was an appropriate amount of time after Alex fell silent. Then he said, "So I guess I passed your test?"

"I'm sorry?"

"I didn't throw up or pass out, so I passed your test, right?"

"That's funny. I tell you a story about Mike and you think it's about you."

"Why bother telling me at all then?" John asked him. He told himself to shut his mouth. Between the sight of the asses on parade in the gay bar and the idea of Bowers getting blown by a dude, John could feel himself reaching a boiling point. All things considered, he thought he was being pretty goddamn accepting, but he was pretty sure the guy he felt shackled to wasn't about to give him a lick of credit, and it pissed him off.

"I do think it was about me," John said. "I think you were testing me. Seeing how much I could handle."

"Maybe," Alex said. "How much can you handle, John?"

"What you and Mike did on that beach isn't any of my business. And it doesn't have any bearing on what I'm doing here. Mike was murdered. We know who did it. We have to decide what to do about it." *You have to screw your goddamn head on straight and go to the cops,* he wanted to say. But instead he said, "That's our mission."

"I've got the feeling everything you do becomes a *mission,* John. Going to the drugstore. Opening a beer bottle. Yours is a world of *missions.*"

"Yeah, well, right now that's serving you pretty well."

"Right now I am in a truck heading I don't know where, because you feel indebted to Mike. Not to me. To Mike. Now, if your plans include impressing me with your fortitude and your fidelity to Marine Corps values, then I am eager to see what you have in store for me because we are not there yet, John. I'm sorry if this doesn't sit well with you, but you're still the man who almost cracked my skull open the other night. You're still the reason Mike's body is . . ." His voice caught, which struck John because he had sounded determined up until that moment. "If his parents get their hands on his body before I do, I will *never* get a chance to say good-bye. Do you understand me?"

"That's not going to happen."

"I hope not," Alex whispered.

"It's not going to happen, Alex."

He could feel Alex studying him, so he kept his eyes on the freeway. "He thought about telling you," Alex said.

"You told me," John said stiffly, because he didn't want to hear that again.

"But he was afraid to. Some Marines knew, John. Not you. He thought you wouldn't take it well." When Alex fell silent, John was confident he was being baited and kept his mouth shut. Alex continued, "To be honest, he thought something had happened to you. Something you didn't want to talk about." Another silence, and then, "He thought maybe you had been mol—"

When Alex jumped against his seat belt, John realized he had slammed the top of the steering wheel with one fist. "You want to know what I thought of your fucking story? I thought it was weird, all right? Not because it was about two guys slipping it to each other. You all can do whatever the fuck you want—I don't care. What was weird about it, what *got to me,* is that you told the story like it was something to be proud of, even though it was such a *struggle* for him. Now, I don't know what's politically correct or homophobic or whatever, but what I do know is that I don't have to down a bottle of the date-rape drug every time I go to bed with a woman!"

"And what do you think that means, John?"

"It means he was confused. It means he was different. Look, you may think I don't know anything about this kind of stuff, but I do, all right. I've got Marine buddies who have taken money to jerk off and screw around with guys they found on websites. They do it because they're hard up and guys like you are *really fucking eager* to pay for it. So when they can't find work they get what they need. No harm, no foul. I don't judge it. But that's *all* it is."

"You think Mike was after my money?"

"I think Mike was confused. I think he was different. I think he was *exceptional,* and I think that put him in a class by himself, okay? And I think it was lonely for him. And being with you—maybe it was *easier* than being with a woman. Maybe you asked less of him than a woman would. Maybe that's how grateful you were to have a hot Marine in your bed."

"Go fuck your sister, white trash," Alex said quietly. John flinched and forced himself to maintain his two-handed grip on the steering wheel. Apparently pleased by John's reaction, Alex said, "That's how it feels. Even when you take out the curse words and replace them with psychobabble."

"So it was a real marriage, then?"

"*You* are the one who is confused, John Houck. The reason Mike started using GHB is because he had a problem being naked in front of me after his right eye got blasted out of his skull and his legs got carved to pieces. And that has nothing to do with me and everything to do with you."

"Oh, yeah? Am I the reason he almost knocked you out cold when you tried to blow him that night? Did that have anything to do with me? He didn't even know me then."

"He knew men like you. The world is full of men like you. And I'm sick of it. And news flash, John, Mike was sick of it, too. That's why he was in Owensville with me, throwing your post-cards in a drawer."

"Bullshit. I'm not your mother."

"What the hell do you know about my mother?"

"Only what you just told me, which sounded like a lot of self-serving crap. A lot of stuff made out to make you sound like a big victim."

Alex barked with laughter and stared out the window as they passed over a lagoon that fed into the Pacific on the southern end of Carlsbad. The next town would be Oceanside, and then the long, dark expanse of Camp Pendleton. John realized he had sent Alex into a stall by bringing his mother into it, and he knew he should savor this small victory and leave it alone. But what kept the fires of anger burning was the contempt that had been in Alex's voice as he had accused John of being the one who was full of prejudice.

"Philip says you have a thing for Marines," John said. "It's like a . . . what's the word? A *fetish* with you."

"Philip thinks nine-eleven was an insurance scam," Alex said, sounding winded. "And you're *really* not my type, so don't worry."

"That's not what I meant."

"What did you mean?"

"Maybe Mike was just a *thing* to you. Like some kind of porno fantasy."

"And that would mean . . . what?"

"It would mean he wasn't—" John stopped dead in his tracks as he realized what he was about to say and what it truly would mean if he said it. His first thought was that he had walked into a trap Alex had set for him with his little tirade about men like John being the reason Mike couldn't be 100 percent cool with being a fruit.

"Say it, John," Alex said. When John didn't comply, Alex did the job for him. "That would mean he wasn't *like* me, right?" John didn't answer. "Well, John, even if you and I can't see eye-to-eye, you and Ray Duncan certainly can."

Alex flinched as if he could detect John's urge to clock him in the jaw, an urge that John fought by clenching the steering wheel with both hands. When John returned his attention to the freeway, he heard Alex let out a long, controlled breath. Another few minutes of this awful silence and Alex undid his seat belt and crawled over the armrest into the backseat. In the rearview mirror, John watched Alex curl into the best fetal position he could manage—maybe he was doing it to avoid more of a fight, or maybe he wanted John to feel like a chauffeur.

"Good night, John," Alex finally said in a soft voice that had no trace of his earlier words.

The best response John could manage was to give the guy a thumbs-up, just like the one Mike had given him as he was wheeled across the tarmac toward the C-17 transport plane that had carried him out of John's life forever.

8

Interstate 10 carried them east into Banning Pass, a dramatic gap between soaring mountains, where the flashing lights atop swarms of windmill generators looked like the running lights for a hundred crisscrossing runways. Weak sunlight almost the color of an eggshell began to swell on the eastern horizon as John crossed the border from arid coastal basin into desert.

Mount San Jacinto thrust itself into the sky on the southern side of the freeway. John had seen the mountain through several changes of seasons, remembered a wildfire one summer night that had turned its flanks into an orange honeycomb. Now he wondered if he'd ever be able to look at it again without seeing the photograph of Bowers and Alex riding one of the tramcars that took tourists up to its eight-thousand-foot summit. As soon as they passed San Jacinto, the necklace of communities that hugged the base of the Santa Rosa Mountains came into view, still twinkling in the lingering night. Their names—Palm Springs, Rancho Mirage, Indian Wells—evoked various paradises and mocked the world that lay north of Interstate 10, the high desert where John had spent the last of his teenage years.

Highway 62. Someone had told him it was the most dangerous highway in California, all those drunk Marines speeding back to Camp Wilson in Twentynine Palms at the end of their weekend leave, burning up the last of their gas money. Indeed, before Operation Iraqi Freedom, the only funerals John had attended, aside from the one for his parents, had been for fellow Marines killed in drunk-driving accidents. But 62 was also the avenue of his adolescence. It had always amused him that the directions for traveling from one half of his youth to the other were so simple: head west on I-10. Forty-eight hours later, take a left onto Highway 62 and stop when you hit Yucca Valley, the only godforsaken town in all the high desert that can boast a Kmart. Say good-bye to Spanish-moss-draped oak trees and to people who take their time saying things so they can be sure you get the message. Say hello to tiny heat-blasted trailers with monstrous Joshua trees in their front yards and to crazy tweakers who are convinced the powers that be will be undone by a revolution that begins smack dab in the middle of nowhere.

It was five-thirty in the morning by the time they reached Yucca Valley, late enough to wake his big sister during a time of need. In his absence, the town had acquired a Starbucks and a Walgreens and terraces of newly constructed homes on the hills north of 62, many of them modeled after New Mexico desert dwellings that looked like they would suit the Flintstones. He parked on a residential block just east of the highway. Alex woke as soon as John shook him. He told him to stay put, that he'd be back in a few minutes, but that he needed to wake up and stay alert until he got back. Alex nodded; then, as if he had just remembered the blowout a few hours earlier, he sat up with his head bowed, avoiding John's stare.

There was a pay phone in the parking lot of a strip mall off the highway. Patsy's phone number was still sitting in a drawer in a trailer he had no plans to return to in the immediate future, so he was forced to dial information to get the number.

Without warning, these simple actions blasted him back almost twenty years, to another pay phone, this one a few blocks from the Louisiana State University campus in Baton Rouge, where he had wiped out on his bicycle after riding it far outside the five-block radius around their home his mother had restricted him to. More frightened of his mother's anger than the warm flow of blood down the front of his face, he had used a quarter to call his sister, a senior in high school then, who, upon hearing the strangled sound of his voice, had rushed to him without any questions.

The top was down on her cherry red Miata when she pulled up. As she stepped onto the sidewalk, John pulled open the phone booth door enough for her to get a good look at him, and he braced himself for her anger. How surprised he had been when she had thrown her arms around him instead of clocking him across the back of the head. How tightly she had held his head against her shirt despite the blood on his face. How quickly and fully the smell of her had cut through the blood in his nose. Sunflowers by Elizabeth Arden. Years later, the sight of that same ovular yellow bottle with its thick white cap on the bathroom counter of a UCSD girl he was about to hook up with had so filled him with thoughts of his sister that he been forced to beg off at the last minute.

"Hello?"

John's mouth opened, but nothing came out. It didn't matter. As if she had been able to recognize the sound of his breathing, his sister whispered his first name in a voice that sounded shocked and fatigued.

"I need you to meet me," John said.

"John."

"Pick a place. Not in Yucca Valley but close."

"Where are you?"

"Just pick a place, Patsy."

The use of her first name seemed to startle her. "You're in trouble? You can't talk right now?"

"Yes," he said, even though he wanted to come up with something more obtuse, more coded than a plea for help.

"I'm looking after one of my girls' trailers out in Landers. She had to go to Fresno for a custody hearing. How does that sound? I'll head there right now, then call you."

"I'm not using cell phones right now."

"I know. You're using the pay phone right across the highway from where I live." A chill went through him, and he fought the urge to hang up and run. Then she said, "Sorry. This guy I dated a few months ago, he kind of stalked me for a bit. Used to call me from there all the time, tell me he could see me going to the bathroom. Stupid shit."

Against his will, John found his eyes drawn to the shiny new houses dotting the sandy hillside to the west. A far cry from the tract homes and trailers they had been forced to live in while she tried in vain to find a suitable husband. He'd heard through the grapevine that she had come into some money, mainly because she had eventually married her boss, a man John had never met, and inherited his bar. "What happened to your husband?" he asked.

"He's been dead two years, John." There was no irritation in her voice, just soft parental condescension, as if John were an infant and she had just asked him not to put Play-Doh in his mouth.

"Should I bring anything?" she said quickly, seemingly unnerved by his silence.

"Just meet me," he said. "Please."

She gave him directions, and about fifteen minutes later he and Alex were traveling north on 247, known more affectionately as Old Woman Springs Road. After they passed through his sister's high-end neighborhood and crested the hill it sat on, the scorched earth beneath them began to rise and fall like petrified ocean waves, and there was a limitless expanse of cactus-studded sand stretching out toward the few barren desert mountains on the far horizons in almost all directions.

Landers wasn't a town so much as a massive spread of trailers without any real center that had been dubbed "the land of endless vistas." At some points a space of almost five city blocks lay between each inhabited plot of sand.

"Your sister lives out here?" Alex asked.

"No. Out here I can see everyone who's coming. There's nowhere to hide."

"What does your sister need to hide from?"

"Ray Duncan needs to hide."

Alex studied him, his blue eyes sleep-glazed, as if he wasn't sure of John's sincerity. Maybe the guy took it as an apology for their earlier fight. For all John knew, maybe it was.

John returned his attention to the road; up ahead he saw the trailer Patsy had described. It sat behind a chain-link fence. The trailer had been painted baby blue, and there was a children's play-set in the front yard, in the shadow of an enormous, multibranched Joshua tree. Ribbons of various colors had been tied along the top of the front fence. There was nothing that spoke more to him of the desert than a run-down trailer whose owner had gone to every pathetic attempt to dress it up that she could afford. In Louisiana, nature itself would bring canopies of greenery to the most impoverished of homes. In the desert, the unforgiving light allowed hardship few disguises.

"Is that her?" Alex asked. But John ignored the sight of the woman sitting on the trailer's front steps as he pulled around the side of the trailer so he could park the truck where it was hidden from the road. As they walked around toward his sister, John realized he was keeping his eyes on the ground in front of him, even as he heard Patsy's hiking boots scrape against the concrete steps as she shot to her feet.

At the last possible second, he lifted his eyes to her. By then Alex had stepped forward and offered his hand, and Patsy Houck took it, the gesture tinkling the swarm of silver bracelets on her right wrist. She studied Alex with a furrowed brow and parted, speechless lips. His sister looked more beautiful than he had ever seen her. Her hair was a thick brown mane, with her token white streak dyed in the front. She'd had a boob job, but he was struck by the brightness in her eyes, the clear vision of a woman who had been released from most of her worries.

All this he took in while she gave Alex the once-over, and indicated with a rude silence, which was not her nature, that she wasn't quite sure what her brother was doing riding around the high desert with a gay guy who wore chest-hugging brand-name polo shirts.

"Can he wait inside?" John asked.

Patsy nodded. "There's coffee," she said, and her mouth stayed open, as if she had more to say about what pleasures awaited them inside a strange woman's trailer, but then her eyes caught John's, and the sound of the front door shutting behind Alex seemed to lock them in a cell together.

"Whatever happened to Tina Gray?" she asked him in a bright voice, as if they had been standing there chatting for hours. "You guys dated for what—almost a year, right? She lived out here with her mom, right? Did they move away?"

John nodded. Tina Gray had taken his virginity in the back-seat of her mother's El Dorado, forever dashing John's childish suspicion that women never really enjoyed sex, they just put up with it so men would leave them alone. Tina Gray had convinced him that there was no more beautiful a sight in the world than the creases that appeared in a woman's thighs when she rocked her legs back to allow you in.

John said, "She ran off with some guy who worked at Denny's. Told me she didn't want to be with some jarhead."

"You weren't even in the Marines yet."

"I know. I'd only said something about it once to try to impress her."

"Bitch," Patsy whispered, and John almost turned away from her and from this forced gesture of sibling camaraderie. "All I remember about her is that she was short, chubby, and blond, like all your girlfriends. I'm going to go out on a limb and say you're probably still going for the baby-faced beauties, right?" He thought of Mandy, who fit this description to a tee, and the idea that his big sister could still read him after ten years brought blood to his cheeks. "Did you leave the Marines?"

John nodded, studied the road in both directions. The sun had crested the horizon, shortening the shadows of the Joshua trees all around them. The blacktop road was empty. The wind rattled a dozen small things across the vast emptiness surrounding the trailer.

"Why?"

"Because it was time."

She nodded, eyes to the ground, sucking on her lower lip

briefly, her way of saying she knew she was being lied to and she hated it but she didn't want to drive him away. "I sent you an e-mail a couple of months ago. Did you get it?"

She didn't add that it was an e-mail containing the location of their brother's grave. He nodded, and for a few minutes neither one of them spoke. He had visited the grave many times, usually after fortifying himself with a couple of shots of Southern Comfort from a bottle hidden under the front seat of his truck.

"I left a sergeant," he said. "Three years in Recon. You know, Force Recon—"

"I know what it is," she said softly. "That's a big deal, John." She was doing her best to sound pleased, but he could detect the condescension in her voice; she knew he was trying to impress her, as always, and, as always, she wasn't quite sure how to react to it. Even though she had never come right out and said it, the Marine Corps had been her last choice for him, and he knew it.

"John . . . who's Alex?"

"He's being framed for murder. And the man who did it got away because of me."

He saw her shock turn to disbelief, and before she could open her mouth to question him, he began telling her the story, except for the part about Bowers being more than an old friend and comrade, except for the part about how he had been given Danny Oster's home address the day before.

While he spoke, Patsy sank to a seat on the top step, her clasped hands resting against her lips, her eyes focused on him with increasing desperation as the details of the story he told her seemed to push her further away from the real reunion she had craved for so long. John ran out of things to say, and Patsy finally allowed herself to stare past him. Then, without so much as a word, she got to her feet and started walking toward the spot where her Jeep Grand Cherokee was parked in the Joshua tree's perforated shade. The car looked new and recently washed, except for the thin coat of sand along the running boards from the ride out there. Patsy opened the passenger-side door and removed something from the glove compartment; then she started for John with an envelope in her hands. For a second he thought of the note Mandy had spied his sister trying to shove under the door of his trailer and figured she was going to force her own kind of reunion after all.

But when she handed him the envelope, he saw the words typed across the front: SERGEANT JOHN HOUCK, USMC. He opened it, pulled out a single sheet of paper, and unfolded it as Patsy moved beside him. It was a hand-drawn map, and it took John a minute to realize that it was the road they had just come out of. To the west of Old Woman Springs Road, a few miles to the south, an X marked a spot.

"When did you get this?"

"My night manager called me around closing time last night, said someone left the envelope on the bar. I asked him to bring it over on his way home. That's why I wasn't that surprised when you called this morning. I figured someone knew you were coming my way."

"Did your manager see who left it?"

She shook her head. It didn't take John much effort to trace Duncan's motions. After leaving the trailer park, he had headed for Patsy's bar. Patsy had held on to her last name, so it hadn't been that hard to trace the connection. Maybe Duncan had been waiting for him, expecting him to run to her, and when he hadn't, he dropped the letter. The spot marked with an X was just a short drive north from Patsy's bar.

"Stay with him," John said. Patsy started shouting questions at him, but he was already walking toward his truck, and in his mind he was already gunning it down the blacktop.

He was going seventy-five down Old Woman Springs Road, weaving in and out among camper-shell-crowned pickup trucks on their way to work in Morongo Basin, when he saw the green Jeep Grand Cherokee following from about five car lengths away. When he reached the spot marked on the map, his sister was gaining on him, and within less than a minute, the Jeep joined him on an unpaved road that had been ground down by tire tracks, which kept the unobstructed sand-shifting winds from covering it over entirely. They passed a lone trailer, then a second one that looked abandoned, then there was nothing but open sand leading to a wide valley between two mountains, chocolate islands in a sea of chalk dust.

Something blinded him briefly: harsh sunlight reflected off a nearby surface. When he parked the truck, his sister did the same behind him and hopped to the ground.

"I wanted you to stay with him!" he called to her.

"Yeah, and I want a nice, healthy husband and a private plane. What the hell was in that envelope?"

Instead of answering her, he headed toward the spot the reflection had come from, heard her footsteps behind him and then several crunches of sand that indicated they had been joined by a third party. When he turned he saw his sister frozen in her tracks a few paces behind him, her open palms in front of her, as if she were trying to hold the sand in place. A three-foot-long sidewinder curled its way through the sand between them, its rough scales giving it traction. John held his ground as well, waiting for it to depart and waiting for Patsy to run back to her Jeep because she hated snakes more then anyone he had ever met. But she did no such thing. Once their unwelcome visitor had departed, she lifted her eyes to John's; then her eyes focused on something behind him, and she pointed to it.

A shovel had been driven into the sand several yards away, and a tiny shaving mirror had been duct-taped to the top of the handle. When John pulled the shovel free, an envelope slid across the sand; it had been slightly buried under the tip of the blade. He opened it and removed a single sheet of paper with a single line of text in the center: CUT HIM LOOSE AND WALK AWAY, OR . . . John started digging. A few minutes later he hit something solid, got down on his hands and knees, and unearthed a metal cash box that could be purchased at any office supply store. A second envelope was taped to the lid.

He opened it and pulled out a note that said . . . IT ALL GOES TO PIECES.

From behind him, his sister said his first name as if she thought she could imbue its single syllable with all the warning in the world. But before he could entertain the idea that there even was such a thing as fear, John opened the box.

Inside was a severed hand covered in dried blood. On the index finger was a silver ring with a red ruby in the center, the same University of Arizona graduation ring Mike Bowers had worn on a chain around his neck during their deployment. Behind him his sister started cursing into her palms.

John rarely prayed, but he did believe moments of silence could work some effect on the soul. For just a short time they allowed him to imagine he was hollow and that the evils of the world could pass through him like a mist, leaving only a light stain on his insides. But the severed hand in front of him had held him safely against the ground as a storm of shrapnel and white flame had swept over him; there was no breathing that out.

When he turned around, he saw that Patsy was hunched over, as if she were sick to her stomach, her wide-eyed stare fixated on the blackened fingers visible in the open cash box. Her hands were still covering her mouth and she didn't seem to see her younger brother at all.

"Give me your phone," John heard himself say.

She stared at him for a few seconds. Then, when she saw his outstretched hand, she seemed to remember his request and handed over her cell phone. Her cell carrier's information service put him right through to the Owensville Sheriff's Department at no charge, and when a female deputy answered, John said, "I need to speak to Ray Duncan."

"*Captain* Duncan is not in right now," the deputy responded. "Is there something I can help you with, sir?"

"Yeah. Give him a message for me. Tell him when he gets to the middle he's going to hit steel."

×

When they got back, Alex was inside, nursing a cup of coffee at a tiny kitchen table exactly like the one in John's trailer, his rigid posture suggesting he was afraid of breaking one of the many ceramic animals that lined the shelves above his head.

John set the cash box down on the table in front of Alex and opened the lid with both hands. As soon as he saw what was inside, Alex reared up as if the table had caught on fire, one hand shooting to his mouth, the other holding his gut as if it had been pierced. He made a sound that John didn't have words for, then shook his head violently as tears sprouted from his eyes. *A necessary evil*, John told himself. *You couldn't have made this easier for him. He had to see this the same way you saw it.*

"This is how Duncan is going to play this. So think hard about how you're going to play it. Real hard. Because this came with a note: 'Cut him loose and walk away, or it all goes to pieces.' Do you understand what that means, Alex?"

Still frozen halfway between sitting and standing, his eyes screwed shut, his hands clasped against lips in tortured prayer,

Alex had no response except to shake his head as if he were turning down an invitation to jump into a wood chipper headfirst. John heard his sister say his name softly from across the room, and he held up one hand to silence her.

"Now, I know you don't think there's any authority that can help you in this, but you need to think real hard about that, Alex. Real hard. Because this man has Mike's body, and if we don't do something about it, he's going to send it to us in pieces. So you take some time and you *think*."

When she saw he was headed for the front door, Patsy stepped out of it ahead of him and held it open behind her. He had one foot across the threshold when Alex said, "What about *your* decision?"

"I've made it!" John said. "I'm not cutting you loose. Mike Bowers saved my life, and you're the only thing he left behind. That's not up for debate."

He drew the door shut behind him before Alex could use any words to distract himself from what sat right in front of him.

×

After John finished telling her the story of how Bowers had saved his life and lost an eye for it, Patsy cracked the driver-side window of her Jeep Grand Cherokee and lit a Virginia Slim. "And if he doesn't go to the authorities? What then?"

"I teach him how to defend himself."

"Against who? Ray Duncan?"

"Against whoever he runs into on the road to being a complete fucking idiot."

"So you teach him how to fight? Then what? You wash your hands of him?"

"I'll get out of California, probably. I've always wanted to see

Montana." He thought of the CHP study guide sitting in the kitchen drawer of a trailer he didn't feel safe returning to.

After a few seconds of silence, he realized she was glaring at him as if he had cut wind. "You're shitting me, right?" Patsy asked.

"It's not going to come to that," he said, with a glance back toward the trailer. "Not after what I just showed him."

"*The Hunt for Red October,*" she said quietly. "The Russian guy. Sean Connery's friend. The whole movie he's talking about how he wants to see Montana. Then he gets shot at the end and before he dies he says, 'I would have liked to have seen Montana.' Just like you did right now."

"I don't remember the film that well, Patsy."

"Well, sometimes when we're scared and stupid, old shit just comes up. Old memories we didn't know we had." She pursed her lips and stared back at the seemingly lifeless trailer a few yards away. "Montana," she whispered. "What the fuck, John?"

"California hasn't been so kind to me, Patsy."

"Iraq was nicer?" she asked. The anger in her tone told him she had taken the comment as an indictment of her parenting skills. "Maybe you should look at how you've treated California."

"I'm trying to do something *right now,* Pats. Something good."

"And you're already planning the vacation you're going to go on afterward."

"I was going to start cadet training in a few weeks. For the CHP."

"You're not exactly paving the way for a career in law enforcement here."

"Yeah, well, I knew I wasn't going to be able to wear a uniform again until I set things right with Bowers."

"Good. So go back in there, get what's in that cash box, and take it to the police."

"That won't work."

"Why the hell not, John?"

"Because it's not what he would have wanted! Bowers was about the man standing next to him. It's what made him a great Marine. It's the reason he saved my life and never asked for any credit for it. He wasn't a lawyer. He wasn't about justice. He wasn't about *setting the record straight*. He left those jobs to God, the president, and the men they chose to do their work for them. What he did was take care of the man standing next to him, and whether I like it or not—and believe me, I don't, Patsy—that man is Alex Martin. So that's what I have to do."

"You're still a Marine, John. You're still repeating words you never bothered to learn the meaning of."

"What would you know about being a Marine?"

"Don't you try to pull rank on me, little brother. I was cleaning up after devil dogs when you were still jerking off down the hall to my Victoria's Secret catalogs. I've been in this valley a decade, and it's full of the messes Marines make after their M-4s get taken away. Most of those messes have names like Debi and Kristina, and they come into my bar with their arms in slings thinking I'm actually going to believe them when they tell me they fell down the front steps."

"I've never lifted a hand to a woman in my life. You know that."

"Do I? It's been ten years, John. Honestly, what do I really know about you?"

"You know what I'm telling you right now. Just because you don't want to hear it doesn't mean it's not the truth."

She dropped the butt of her exhausted cigarette through the crack in the window and rolled it all the way up. The AC blew strands of her chocolate-colored hair back over her left shoulder, making her look like something out of a music video. John said, "You do the job that gets put in front of you. Not the one you want. Not the one you picked ahead of time. The one that gets put in front of you by war or by God or whatever. That's what it means to be a Marine."

Patsy fought an eye roll by rubbing her temples with the middle three fingers on each hand. Her loud exhalation turned into a groan. Then she said, "So, what do you want from me then? Money?"

"We're going need a place to stay for a little while, no matter what he decides."

"A hideout," she whispered. "Jesus. I thought I might have to bail you out of prison someday, but this I wasn't prepared for."

"Why'd you think you'd have to bail me out someday?"

Her smirk vanished, and with what looked like effort, she met his eyes. "I was pretty sure that as soon as you weren't a Marine anymore, you would try to kill Danny Oster."

The remark blindsided him, reminded him of how close he had come to driving to Redlands, even with someone else's nine-year-old child in the front seat of his truck. Patsy furrowed her brow and stared down at her clasped hands as if she had just imparted terrible news. Maybe the name Danny Oster was too much even for her to bear.

Then he saw a figure out in the sandy distance, walking toward them across the expanse behind the trailer, vaguely familiar but too far away for him to make out. Patsy saw it, too. "Who is that?" John stepped out of the Jeep and pulled the Sig from the holster at his waist. Patsy followed him, and then stopped cold when she saw he had drawn his weapon.

After a minute, John recognized Alex's blond hair. He had taken off the light jacket he'd been wearing the night before and untucked his dark green polo shirt.

"I didn't even see him leave," John said.

He holstered his weapon and passed through the back gate in

the chain-link fence. He and Alex were a few yards apart when Alex stopped walking. His shirt was soaked through with sweat, and his hands were caked with sand.

"You buried it," John said.

"It seemed like the right thing to do," Alex said.

"It is if you don't want to take it to the authorities."

Alex was silent.

"Or if you don't want *me* to take it to the authorities."

"I love the way you say that word, John—*authorities*. Like it gives you a warm feeling all over. Is that how it feels to be protected by the system?"

"You tell me, Mr. Cathedral Beach."

"I don't live in Cathedral Beach anymore. And you never did. So we don't have that working in our favor now, do we?" John had no response to this. "So tell me—what's next? Since you're not going to cut me loose."

Before he could answer, John looked back over his shoulder at his sister. She was holding the fence with one hand and studying Alex with a pinched expression, like he was a girlfriend of hers who had demanded her real opinion of a dress that didn't fit her. She hadn't mentioned the possibility of turning them in herself, and he was willing to bank that she was grateful enough to have him back in her life that she would go a good ways with them.

"Here's the deal," John said. "I'm going to teach you how to defend yourself no matter what choice you make. That means I'm going to teach you how to fight. But if you choose to use what I teach you on Ray Duncan, you're on your own. Got it?"

"How else would I use it?"

"You could end up running from this for the rest of your life, and God knows who you would meet along the way."

"Fine, then. Yes, John. Please. Teach me how to kill."

"I'll teach you how to win a fight with your bare hands. But first I'll have to find out what's standing between you and your ability to kill another human being."

"And then what?" Alex asked.

"I'll get rid of it," he answered. He let this hang for a minute. Then he said, "Whether or not you kill anyone is up to you. But let it be said just for the record here"—he looked back at Patsy, who was staring at him with glazed eyes—"I extended two offers of protection to you, and this is the one *you* chose."

"Fair enough," Alex said quietly.

"Do you accept?"

At first Alex smirked at the formality of it, but when he saw that John was dead serious, he raised his head slightly, studied John intently for a few seconds, and without a trace of hesitation in his voice said, "I accept."

Behind him John heard Patsy give a weak voice to what he was feeling inside—she cursed under her breath and started toward the trailer. Alex watched her departure with a skeptical expression.

"Looks like you should talk to her," Alex said.

"I've got my sister covered. Thanks."

"Really? It's been—what? Ten years?"

Once again, John was reminded of the fact that Alex had been given all sorts of facts about him, while his knowledge of Alex grew inch by painful inch with each passing hour. John told Alex to take a shower and then he started back toward the Jeep, where Patsy had slipped behind the wheel and started the engine.

She rolled down the window as he approached, but remained silent as Alex walked past them and went back inside the trailer. Instead of chewing him a new asshole, his sister said, "I might have a place. It's out of state, but we can leave tonight."

"You're coming with us?"

"This is a friend, and it's a big favor. It's with me or not at all."

He doubted the truth of this statement, but he wasn't in a position to argue.

"Who?"

"Let's just get there, okay?"

Her reticence relieved him. He truly didn't want to know. His sister had been annoyingly accepting of wackos throughout their time in the desert, and there had been no shortage of Indian shamans, recovering drug addicts, and all-around loonies in her past. She must have thought she didn't have the right to judge people too harshly, considering the universe had taken so many advantages away from them, such as parents and affordable health care.

"I'm going to withdraw some cash," she said. "I figure we'll need it."

"I can't ask you to come in on this, Patsy."

"Good," she said. "'Cause you didn't."

She took the Jeep out of park, his signal to step away as she backed out of the lot and onto the two-lane blacktop that led back to Old Woman Springs Road.

Only after her Jeep had faded from view did he realize that she had patted his hand gently before he had stepped away from her vehicle, the first time they had touched in ten years.

9

Forty-five minutes after they crossed the border into Arizona, John turned down the Carrie Underwood song on the radio and said, "How much longer?"

Patsy said, "We'll probably get there just before sunrise. I figure you'd prefer it that way."

The digital clock said it was almost midnight, and they had been on the road for almost two hours already, which meant she wasn't taking them much farther than Arizona, possibly New Mexico if she put the pedal to the metal. She had convinced John that they should go in one car—hers—and had suggested that they leave his truck in the one place Duncan knew they had already been: the location off Old Woman Springs Road where

Duncan had buried the cash box. If they had been declared fugitives, there was no mention of it in the news, and the fact that Duncan hadn't turned to the media suggested he had a darker plan in store.

Alex was sleeping peacefully in one of the bucket seats in back, his head resting against his balled-up jacket, his lips parted. Something about Alex's slack jaw and the way the passing headlights streaked his face reminded John of a lance corporal who had died right in front of him, just seconds before being loaded into a Black Hawk, so he tried to avoid looking at him in the rearview mirror.

Why shouldn't he be sleeping like a baby? John thought. *Now that I'm covering his ass.*

"You know," Patsy said quietly, and John realized she had not turned the radio back up after he had turned it down, "he might just be out to prove something to you." She was watching Alex in the rearview mirror to make sure he wasn't listening.

"He said I wasn't his type," John said.

"I didn't say he wanted to get in your pants," she whispered. John was startled by how easily she was able to use this phrase when two men were involved. "Maybe he just wants to prove he's not a sissy."

"He almost shot an officer of the law in my trailer," John said as quietly as he could without whispering. "And it was clear he didn't have the slightest damn clue how to even hold a gun. He's impulsive and irrational, and if I don't do something about it he's going to get himself killed."

He didn't want to consider the possibility that there might be more truth in what Patsy was saying than he was willing to believe. But what did it matter? Doing right by Mike meant giving Alex the skills to survive whatever he chose to confront. That was where it ended. That was where he *needed* it to end.

"John?"

"Yes, Patsy."

"When I made that comment about Danny Oster. About you—"

"Trying to kill him?"

"Yeah." She gave him a quick glance and then returned her attention to the road. "You didn't say anything."

"What was I supposed to say?"

"Can we not play it like that? I know it's been ten years, but today hasn't really been the reunion I was hoping for, and you got to admit I'm meeting you a lot more than halfway here."

"A couple of days ago an old buddy of mine . . . not just a buddy; a guy whose life I saved . . . he brought me a file on Oster he got from a PI buddy of his. See, I had told him the story one night after I got wasted—"

"The story?"

"Of what happened to Dean."

"I know, John. What is it that *happened* to Dean again?" Her gaze was dead ahead, but her hands had tensed on the wheel and her voice was tight, sure signs she was gearing up for one of her subtle but effective strikes. And he couldn't help but wonder if she was forcing them to visit the past again because she didn't want to know what John had considered doing with the file Charlie had brought him.

"I don't want to do this," John said quietly. "I really don't want to do this."

But Patsy seemed undeterred. "Because, see, John, the story Dean told me that day is that you misinterpreted what you saw. That what you saw were two guys roughhousing on a bed and you lost it."

John checked the rearview mirror, saw that Alex was still sound asleep, his body rocking sluggishly with the Jeep's motion.

"Is that why Oster's pants were around his ankles? You think I made that up? He lied because he was ashamed, Patsy. Because part of him thought it was his fault."

"Is that what he told you?"

"No," John said. But when he didn't finish the thought, Patsy shifted in her seat, sucked in a long breath through her nose that signaled her irritation, signaled the fact that she was holding back in a way she never would have when they were younger. In terms of cutting through any bullshit that was shoved her way, Patsy had been a better mother than their own mother, a career nurse who had only paid serious attention to her kids when they were bleeding or in acute physical pain.

"What did he tell you, John?"

"Please, Patsy."

"I'm the one who buried him. I have a right to know."

He was suddenly dizzy, as if he were about to take a jump off the high board, what it felt like to get ready to unload something that had tormented him for so long. "He said he lied to you so you wouldn't hate me. So you wouldn't think I failed."

"Why would I think you failed?"

"Because I was supposed to be watching him that day and I was down the street at Tina Gray's. Because I should have known that Oster was a freak who was spending way too much of his time with a seventeen-year-old boy. Because he was my responsibility."

"Says who?"

"Me. I say it. Because it's the truth, Patsy."

Her stunned silence seemed to hang over them both like a kind of humidity. Finally, in a voice that had a threat of tears in it, she said, "Tell me this isn't the reason I haven't heard a word from you in ten years. Please, John. Tell me this isn't the reason I've spent the past five years watching every newscast, waiting for some mention of your name."

"He was my responsibility. It was just the way things were in our house. And it's the way they should have been because, God knows, you were doing everything else."

"He lied to both of us, John. He lied because he didn't want either of us to know what happened in that bedroom."

"I know what happened," John hissed. "I was there! I *saw* it!" Patsy lifted one hand at the anger in his voice, and at first he thought she was trying to shut him up, but then, when she glanced behind her, he saw she was warning him not to wake Alex.

A long silence passed between them until Patsy found her voice again. "If you want to take this on, go ahead. I can't stop you. But you listen to me, John, and you try to remember this along with everything else you can't seem to forget. I never made Dean your responsibility. Not because I didn't think you were up to it, but because I loved you. And I would never ask someone I love to throw their arms around a hurricane."

He yearned to believe her, but part of him thought she was just so eager to have him back in her life that she would say anything to try to cut him free of their broken past.

"We better cut it out before we wake the baby," Patsy finally said.

"I think I'm going to join him."

She was silent as he undid his seat belt and squeezed into the back. He crawled up onto the bench seat at the very back of the Jeep, but, of course, sleep didn't come. There was nothing to see outside of the windows except the glowing ember at the tip of his sister's cigarette where she rested her arm out the open window. For a while she flipped stations on the radio. Then, at about two o'clock, they entered some stretch of Arizona where the only broadcast they could pick up was something that sounded like late-night Navajo hour, lots of throaty male voices coughing out primal chants. They sounded too much like the involuntary guttural noises he had heard the wounded make in combat: tremulous sounds that came from the chest, the stutter of words failing to force themselves through closing throats. He wasn't about to ask her to turn off the radio, and Patsy seemed determined to listen to it, maybe because it was keeping her awake, so John somehow made it bearable by telling himself that the sounds of dying men were exactly what the Navajo singers were trying to emulate. This meant they shared a dark knowledge with John. This meant he had comrades out there in the dark.

When Patsy gave up and killed the radio, John heard a rattling sound behind him, turned to look into the tiny cargo area, and saw the rattle was being made by the Spartan sword, still sticking up out of the cardboard box containing the last pieces of Mike Bowers's life, which he had removed from his Tacoma before parking it in the desert. John turned, bent over the back of the seat, and pried open the flaps of the box. It was too dark to see inside, so he reached behind him and turned on one of the dome lights, which sent a faint glow across half of the bench seat without rousing Alex.

He froze when he saw that the dark mass gathered at the bottom of the box was Mike's dress blues, several gold buttons staring up at him like coins in the bottom of a grime-covered fountain. Their condition, as well as their position, beneath tattered hardcover novels and framed diplomas, was too appropriate a symbol of what had become of Mike's life for John to linger on them for too long.

Is this what Mike would have wanted you to do? he asked himself.

How could he possibly answer his own question? How could he know what Mike would have wanted when Mike had kept his real life a secret? John couldn't ask a question of the smiling man in the photos hanging on the wall inside his secret home. He had never met that man because he had never been allowed to meet that man.

Whose fault was that? Was it Mike's fault? Or was it the fault of the guy sleeping soundly a few feet away from him?

✕

John woke up right after Patsy left Highway 89 and began to follow a gravel road down a scrub-covered slope into a broad valley studded with bushy trees that had hardy white trunks. Massive sandstone rock formations straddled the horizon, but soon those were lost to the trees that suddenly crowded the unpaved road they traveled. They passed through a cattle fence that had been left open for them and a humble wooden sign that had something written on it John couldn't make out. Something about something being "the answer," but John couldn't tell if the first word was *Atonement* or *Acceptance.*

The fact that the name of whatever place this was wasn't posted at the front gate made John both relieved and nervous at the same time. Duncan might have a harder time finding them, but just what the hell had his sister gotten them into? "Atonement is the answer"? She'd gone through a lot of phases after they moved to the desert, but organized religion hadn't been one of them. Maybe that had changed after he left home.

There was enough sunlight to sparkle off the waters of a creek moving slowly several yards off to the right, and if John hadn't been paying close attention, he would have missed the large ranch house that sat just off the road in the middle of a wide clearing fringed with Douglas fir trees. Patsy continued, slowing down as the trees thickened around them. Some of them looked newly planted and were struggling to survive in the parched earth. John had been to Arizona a few times, and the redness of the place always got to him; it made the desert landscape of his adolescence seem anemic by comparison.

Patsy pulled to a stop near a smaller version of the house they had just passed. Without any words of introduction for their new home, she stepped out of the truck and started down a dusty trail that cut through the trees toward a small house with thick cinderblock walls, a low, flat roof, and a line of clerestory windows running along its side walls. John was relieved to hear the steady *thrum* of central air conditioning. They stepped through the front door and found themselves inside what appeared to be a small summer-camp cabin.

Patsy advised them that she would be back in a minute. There were four bunks in all, two against each wall. At the back of the house were a small kitchenette and a bathroom. For a moment John was reminded of his barracks during boot camp; then he saw the frames hanging above each bed, went to one, and made out the words of a prayer printed in calligraphic script: *God, grant me the serenity to accept the things I cannot change, the courage to change the things I can . . .*

"Looks like your sister thinks the best way to teach me how to kill would be for both of us to stop drinking," Alex said. He was sitting on one of the beds with a heavy blue book on his lap. It looked like he had fished it from the drawer in the nightstand. He held it up so John could read the words *Alcoholics Anonymous*. When John didn't laugh at this joke, Alex rose silently from the bed and headed for the bathroom. John turned to the half-open door to the house, knowing full well just who it was from Patsy's past that would design such a place.

He walked outside, into the strengthening glare of the sun. Just up the bank of the creek was a small circle of trees with a stone bench in the center. There was a man sitting on it, a baseball cap shoved down over his head, a cigarette sending up a curl of smoke from his right hand. He didn't move as John entered what looked like a meditation garden. Behind the bench was a statue of Jesus on a stone pedestal. Right next to John, a matching pedestal supported a statue of Buddha. There was no denying it was a beautiful spot. Just above the tree line, on the horizon, you could see the sharp-edged sandstone formations that people around here called *mountains*. They were changing color in the light of the rising sun.

Eddie Shane took a sip from his coffee, pulled a rumpled soft pack of Marlboro Reds from his shirt pocket, and extended it to John. John held up a palm. In the years since he had broken Patsy's nose, Eddie's watery blue eyes had slipped deeper into his face and the lines around his mouth had multiplied, as if the skin around his jaw were tightening to the degree that it might tear at any given moment.

"There's coffee up in the house," Eddie said, as if they had already spent the past few weeks in each other's company. "I can run up and get you a cup. I imagine you don't want any of the other men to see you. That's why we put you down here. Privacy and all."

"We can't sleep in the same place," John said. "That's not going to work."

Eddie's fixed expression suggested that he had moved past the place in his life where he could be surprised by anything other than death. "You and your friend, you mean? She didn't tell me his name. She hasn't told me much at all, so you don't have to either if you don't want to." When John didn't thank him for his offer of coffee, Eddie nodded slightly at his own cup as if he were prepared to face the fact that solicitous remarks weren't going to get him back in John's good graces.

John felt foolish for having let the comment slip from him, but the truth was he hadn't known what else to say, such was the shock of seeing Eddie, whose departure Patsy had celebrated as much as John had. But clearly he had cloaked himself once again in what he had once referred to as the "the language of recovery," a phrase that had seemed absurd the first time John heard it come out of the mouth of a big-rig driver from just outside Dallas, Texas. The truth was, it wasn't smart for him and Alex to be sleeping under the same roof, not if John was going to achieve any status as an instructor, but he could have asked Patsy to buy them a tent to pitch out in the woods.

In the silence that followed, Eddie lifted his gaze to John's, and the two men just stared at each other. Eddie wore the resigned look of a lifelong inmate whose execution day had finally arrived. In a flat, emotionless voice he said, "I did wrong by you and I did wrong by your sister. I hit your sister because she told me what I was and it wasn't who I wanted to be. I hit her because I couldn't accept the truth and I left you without saying good-bye. If there's anything I can do to make up for it, please let me know."

"You rehearsed that one, didn't you?"

"Yours wasn't the only home I left in the middle of the night, John Houck."

"How many of them did you go back to with that little speech?"

"All of them. Including yours. But you were gone by then. Iraq, I hear."

John nodded, braced himself for some smart-ass remark about the ongoing war on terror, but Eddie apparently thought better than to deliver one. But his slow nod gave the impression that he was equating his own recent struggles with the ones John had been through over there, and that made John's blood boil.

After the silence between them grew uncomfortable, John said, "So, what is this place? Some kind of AA church?"

"AA doesn't have churches. This is my own deal. A recovery

home for men like myself. Usually I've got a full house, but right now attendance is low. I've got four up in the main house, so you guys have got down here all to yourself . . . which your sister said was how you would want it. I've also got land. Your sister said you would want that, too. There's a couple acres of it over there that I haven't touched yet. Maybe I'll sell it off someday. I don't know. About twenty miles up the road, land prices jump sky high."

John nodded, wondering how a big-rig driver, and a drunk, could come by this much land this close to one of the nicest parts of Arizona. Eddie must have sensed he had a question he didn't feel comfortable asking because he cleared his throat and said, "When you go through the kind of things you went through, when you see that kind of stuff, I mean—"

"War," John said clearly and forcefully so that Eddie would have a chance to be very confident of the statement he was about to make.

"Yeah, war. I guess it can make things in the past seem like they're further away than they actually are." He studied John, who did his best to give no reaction. "I'm just saying—you and me and your sister. It wasn't that long ago."

John knew what he was trying to say, but he decided to let Eddie twist a little bit more by playing dumb. "Guess it's a good thing you apologized, then."

"Apologies are for pussies," he said quietly, but his choice of language betrayed his anger. "I asked if there was anything I could do to make up for it. But it looks like I'm already doing it, given that I haven't asked you who you're with or just why you need to hide out here with a bunch of recovering drunks and speed freaks like myself."

John tried to freeze the man off with a glare, but it did nothing to deter him. Maybe his most recent benders had not forced him to suffer the way a wounded Marine might, but it was clear they had showed him far greater horrors than the pissed-off brother of a woman he had punched.

Eddie had shuffled off in the direction of the ranch house just up the creek by the time John realized that he hadn't thanked the man. It didn't matter, he guessed, given that Eddie hadn't waited around for a thank-you.

×

When he got back to the outer cabin, John found Patsy and Alex standing together in the tiny kitchenette, unloading several bags of groceries that Eddie had apparently purchased for them prior to their arrival. Once again, the sight of them behaving with the relaxed air of tourists on a weekend getaway made his fists clench, and he stood in the doorway like an angry father waiting to be noticed.

"These are just some basics," Patsy said. "Make me up a list later and I'll make a run." In the car the night before, he had already made up a list of the essentials he would need. It would land him on some kind of watch list if it fell into the wrong hands.

"Where are you staying?" John asked.

Patsy studied the list he had just handed her. Alex busied himself loading bottled water into the fridge, as if he were about to be caught in the middle of a marital squabble. "Up at the house," Patsy said casually, but she had stopped unloading bags and was giving John a level stare, both hands open against the counter in front of her.

"Add a tent because we can't both sleep in here," John said.

Alex pulled his head from the fridge, gave John a shocked stare. Patsy glared at him as if he had just shoved Alex off his feet. He should have known they would interpret it as a homophobic comment and found some way to head it off at the pass.

"I'm going to be doing my best to simulate a training environment here, and during no part of my training as a Marine did I ever sleep under the same roof as my instructors." The surprise went out of Alex's expression, and he returned to the task of loading the fridge. Patsy didn't look like she would be so easily deterred.

"We're here because you want to help Alex. How's that going to be possible if you're too freaked out to sleep under the same roof with a gay guy?"

"Can I talk to you outside?"

"I'm not sure," she answered.

But she followed him out the door and toward the edge of the creek. Once they were face-to-face, she brushed strands of hair back from her forehead, folded her arms over her chest and cocked one eyebrow, as if she were about to get a lecture from a five-year-old.

"Eddie Fucking Shane?" he asked when the silence became unbearable.

"You all had a nice chat?" John didn't respond. She continued, "I'm sorry. You have a problem here?"

"I have a problem with the fact that he broke your nose. Yeah."

"I did, too. That's why I didn't marry him."

"Are you sleeping with him?"

"Aren't you a little *busy* to be this concerned with my private life?"

"Aren't you a little too old to be dicking me around like this?"

She dropped her arms from her chest, sucked in a deep breath, and stared at the creek next to them for a few minutes. "Eddie asked me if he should write you a letter when he came to see me. To apologize. I told him you probably didn't want to hear from him. He said if that was the case, then he shouldn't contact you because the way they do things in AA, they're not supposed to unburden themselves at someone's else expense."

"That's nice of him. How could he afford this place?"

"He couldn't. I gave him most of the money. Efrem left me enough to live off for the next ten years, and between that and what the bar rakes in, I had it on hand."

"Eddie's apologies sound pretty profitable if you ask me."

"I *didn't* ask you. And given the help I've been doling out recently, I'd take those AA meetings up the creek over what you're about to do out here any day." She pulled the list out of her pocket and grimaced at it. "Jesus Christ, John. Since when do *I* know how to pick out ammunition clips?"

"You're going to stay with him? Up in the main house?"

"Yes, John. You want to know why? Because he's the only man I've ever met who will go down on me for three hours."

His cheeks on fire, John brushed past her and started for the cabin. "Oh, for Christ's sake, John. We sleep together every now and then, out here in Arizona. Where I don't even live." When she saw that this had stopped him, she continued. "I give second chances, John. I don't do third or fourth chances, but Eddie's only on number two. And guess what? So are you."

"If he hurts you again, I'll kill him."

"Or you could just stick around."

Before he could only fumble for a response to this, Patsy started for the main house, John's grocery list held out in one hand beside her as if it gave off a sour odor.

✕

Inside the cabin, in one of the nightstand drawers, John found a pad and paper, which he removed quickly, before Alex could emerge from the shower. John carried the pad, paper, and a pen into the woods, and followed the creek in the direction Eddie had pointed earlier that day when he had said there was additional land.

The trees thickened a little along the creek's bank as he walked up the gradual slope. He came to a large clearing that looked like it had once held a storage shed, or possibly another house, that had burned to the ground. The large boulders lying in various locations throughout the clearing suggested they had been placed there by human hands, adornments to whatever structure had once occupied the dusty expanse between short, dry pine trees.

He sat against one of the boulders and proceeded to draw an outline of a male figure. He didn't bother to add any facial features. The number-one rule of hand-to-hand combat was that your opponent did not have a face. He had a head with two soft spots on either side called temples that could only effectively be struck with pinpoint accuracy. He had two highly vulnerable areas in the middle of his head that had only the softest layer of tissue for protection; these were called eyes, and targeting them was the perfect way to bring him to his knees. John had been trained to the degree that he could ward off any attacker's blow with a quick series of defensive movements that could end in the attacker's death, but he had no intention of teaching all of these to Alex.

Many of these moves were about striking a sensitive part of the assailant's anatomy so that their instinctive physical reaction would override their conscious thoughts. But for Alex, John would have to streamline this, teach him only the best places to strike, leaving out the blows everyone learned from the movies. Uppercuts to the jaw were out. They had to be delivered too forcefully, and the risk of injury to himself was too great. Punching a guy in the nose looked great on TV, but a skilled assailant could train himself to endure the watering eyes and bleeding that might follow.

On the figure he had just drawn, he drew a line out from the area where the figure's eyes should be. Then he drew two lines down the center of the figure's throat, both about an inch from where his trachea would be. These were the vagus nerves. Strike them hard enough and you could stop a guy's heartbeat, one of the primary causes of accidental death during martial arts competitions. Then it was time for the arteries, which he marked with crosshatched lines. There were the jugular and carotid arteries in the neck, and the subclavian artery above the collarbone. All of these were susceptible only to knife strikes, and considering they hadn't even attempted unarmed fighting yet, John thought it might be too ambitious to include them. But when you sit down to draw a map of how to kill a man with one strike, you can't do things halfway. He got to his feet, tore the diagram from the notepad, and folded the diagram in half.

Back inside the cabin John found Alex passed out on one of the beds, a copy of the big blue AA bible he had brandished earlier open on the covers next to his chest.

On the diagram he had just put together, John wrote the words STUDY THIS above the figure's empty head and left the paper on the nightstand.

10

John and Alex ran down the bank of the creek, past the clearing and into the woods, along the path John had staked for them in the hours before dawn, when Alex was still fast asleep. They followed a trail of red flags over fallen logs and through low-hanging branches, a cruel parody of the race both had run on the night they first met; only this time John was in the lead, and Alex was hot on his trail, running with a red-faced determination that suggested he believed this was only the first of many physical challenges he would be forced to endure that day.

Once they completed five miles, John stopped and, without allowing Alex a chance to catch his breath, started for the clearing. The night before, he had asked Patsy to purchase him something he could wear around his neck, and she had come back with a long necklace of puka shells that made him look like a surfer. But he was able to tape a photograph of Mike Bowers to it, which meant it would serve its purpose nonetheless. In the cardboard box of Mike's belongings that still sat in the cargo bay of Patsy's Jeep, John had found a leather photo book that contained three-by-five versions of the photographs he had first seen hanging on the wall inside Mike and Alex's home. It was a shot of Mike leaning on the balcony rail of what looked like a motel room. He looked handsome and serene and without a care in the world.

"Your opponent doesn't have a face," John told Alex, who had furrowed his brow and wiped sweat from his eyes to get a better look at the photo of his dead boyfriend. "Every time we practice, this is where you look." He tapped the photo, saw Alex fight the urge to lift his eyes from it. "Never into my eyes unless I tell you otherwise. Got it?"

"Does that mean you're my opponent?" Alex asked.

John ignored him, as he had vowed to ignore every smart-ass comment Alex might make during the course of his training. He was confident the kind of verbal discipline that had been used on him in boot camp was out the window—Alex would probably just try to bitch-slap him. Instead, John began to explain to him how to assume what was referred to as the basic warrior stance: feet shoulder-width apart, a slight bend in the knees, elbows bent at a forty-five-degree angle, arms held high enough to defend the face without blocking vision. Alex speedily executed each instructed movement, making it clear he was eager to rush through this prelude to more exciting things. So, John told him to stand straight and then gave him all the physical instructions again, this time in a different order than Alex was expecting, which threw Alex for a loop, made him curse under his breath.

"Relax," John said quietly. "We have all day."

"All day on *this*? You're kidding, right?"

John gave him a thin smile and repeated the directions, in a different order yet again. And the day wore on, the sun arcing high overhead and Alex biting down on his frustration. John didn't bother to tell him that someone with no fight experience had to ingrain the basic stance on his muscles, had to train to assume the stance from any given position under an assault from any direction. John didn't bother to tell him that this was how it was done—through drill, the repetition of physical movements until they become reflexive.

But there was another facet to this process, one that made John feel as if he was getting away with something: even though he wasn't breaking Alex, he was training him to be obedient—hypnotizing him through the repetition of simple and seemingly meaningless commands.

After two hours of this, John added another layer to the exercise: Alex had to assume the basic warrior stance from three different positions: flat on his back, down on all fours, or sitting cross-legged. John would announce the position, then clap his hands, and Alex would have a split second to assume the stance. If he got it wrong, they had to start from the same position again before moving on to another one. A few times, Alex landed flat on his ass, and John turned his back, which instantly silenced Alex's curses. Then they would resume: the steady cadence of John's instructions and the shuffle of Alex's feet as he leaped into position forming a hypnotic rhythm.

John knew from his own training that he and Alex were being slowly and inextricably bound together in a subtle way. It was not that he was gaining control of Alex's mind, it was that both men, in concert, were gaining control over Alex's muscle memory. Would this process give John the power to demand that Alex go to the authorities? Probably not, but it would make the other movements Alex needed to learn easier to teach.

As Alex's resistance faded, as he became more comfortable with assuming the basic stance from all three starting positions, John was finally able to note how willing Alex was. Small movements such as these, repeated for hours on end, were enough to drive most new recruits to the brink, but Alex's face had gone lax, his eyes had glazed in a way that suggested he was envisioning the movements before he executed them. For a while John assumed Alex's willingness was simply evidence that he was eager to show John he was up to it. But then another possibility occurred to John, and it stole some of the fire from his voice: maybe Alex was just showing him how willing he was to kill.

Patsy brought their lunches on a plastic tray. She walked right into the middle of the clearing without giving them a word of warning and set the tray down next to one of the boulders. Her eyes lingered on Alex, and seeing no cuts or bruises, she left them to themselves. They ate separately and silently, and when John set his plate aside and walked back into the middle of the clearing, Alex followed.

The remainder of the afternoon was spent on moving without leaving the basic stance. Alex was ordered to follow John's every move, eyes focused on the picture of Mike that hung around his neck, without ever leaving the basic stance. Half of the clearing was in shade now, so John had the two of them start in the sunlight and made shade the goal; the minute Alex left the stance or faltered by even a step, they walked back into the hot sun.

Again and again they crossed the clearing like dancers, until the sun started its final plummet toward the western horizon and shade began to spread across the entire clearing. John clapped his hands loudly to signal that they were done, then took off into the woods, onto the same circuit they had run that morning. Alex followed without protest.

After five miles, they both turned toward the creek. John fell to his knees and doused his face. Alex pulled his sweat-soaked shirt from his body, dipped the shirt in the creek, then squeezed it out over his head. When he saw John looking at him, Alex gave him an easy smile. At first John thought it was the smile of a student who knew he had aced a test, but then he felt the familiarity of it. Even though he felt that on some level this was what he had been shooting for, the simple smile frightened him, and he found himself looking down at the creek water. He could feel the pained expression on his face.

"Was I not supposed to look you in the eye yet?" Alex asked.

The photo of Bowers was still hanging from John's neck, like a badge of honor, or, at the very least, a memorial of some sort. What had seemed like a simple psychological training technique earlier that day now had a weight to it his neck couldn't support. Quickly John pulled the string of puka shells from around his neck and extended it toward Alex in one hand. Alex just stared at this offering with a look John could only describe as wounded, all evidence of the smile having left his face.

John tried to force a casual tone and said, "Why don't you hold on to it when we're not training?"

Alex gently pulled the badge from John's grip, collecting the length of the necklace in both hands. Now that he had handed over the badge, John was able to take in the scene he had unwittingly fallen into: he and Alex, half naked, at the edge of a creek, water running down the softly defined muscles of Alex's alabaster torso. He wanted to make a break for it, but he saw this as a childish urge; at best, a pathetically inadequate response to a deeper fear within him, a response that wouldn't do anything to alleviate the fear he felt. And it was fear—fear, plain and simple—that men like Alex spoke a language that sounded like English but looked like Latin when written on the page, a language that John could fool himself into thinking he was fluent in, right up until he might ask for a drink of water and get a kiss on the mouth instead.

For a while, Alex stared down at his hands, as if what he held inside his fists was evidence of some great disappointment. Then he got up and walked off toward the cabin without so much as a good-bye.

×

Someone was shouting in the woods. John awoke with a start, grabbed the gun resting underneath the cot Patsy had bought for him. He unzipped the flap of the tent and stepped out into the darkness, now silent save for the insistent flow of the nearby creek. Another volley of shouts—pained, agonized even. Male. But nothing about the man's voice sounded remotely familiar.

Gun raised, he followed the direction the shouts had come from, through the low, spidery branches, and stopped when he saw Alex several yards ahead, sitting cross-legged in the dense foliage a few yards from the bank of the creek.

On the back porch of the main house, a tall, gangly figure in a baseball cap and a T-shirt that hung from his emaciated frame paced the back porch as if he were looking for something. He paused every few seconds to peer through the back door into the main house. "*Fuckin' quit this!*" he shouted. "*Just fuckin' quit this, all right?*" He jumped up and down like a spoiled child. Then he picked up a wicker chair and hurled it across the porch, knocking over a table, shattering what sounded like an ashtray.

In a low voice, Alex said, "I think someone had a few cocktails." Now that his presence had been recognized, John lowered the Sig, pointed it at the ground with one hand. Just then Eddie burst from the back door, holding a double-barreled shotgun, speaking in a low but determined voice, too quietly for John to hear him. John stepped past Alex, out of the cover of branches, and onto the open dirt.

Eddie saw him, stopped talking, took a minute to register the gun in John's hand, then continued. Every few words John could make out phrases such as "conditions set forth" and "rules you agreed to" and "three strikes." He held his ground, not sure if he had made his presence known to support Eddie or threaten him, or just make it clear that he was willing and able to do either one if the situation called for it.

From behind him, Alex said, "Don't you have enough on your plate, John?"

"I didn't ask you."

Eddie must have found the right combination of words, because the gangly lunatic erupted with pathetic sobs, and gestured wildly as if he were about to make some grand point that was suddenly stolen from him by the intensity of his remorse. Eddie held his ground, then shifted the shotgun to one hand, pressed the other between his failed pupil's shoulder blades, and led him around the side of the house.

Once they were gone, Alex said, "He wasn't going to go to Iraq. The invasion. Mike wasn't going to go. I talked him out of it."

This information was too huge, bigger in some ways, than the revelation that Mike had lived with another man. For some reason, John couldn't accept it while standing, exposed, on the bank of the creek, so he stepped back into the foliage, moving past Alex, who must have thought he was trying to make a quick escape because he raised his voice and said, "I threatened to leave him if he went. I forced him to make a choice, and for a while, it looked like he was going to choose me. But he was just afraid to, and he was lying. One night he came over to my apartment, and he was all tense and shut down. I knew something was up, so I looked in his rucksack while he was in the shower and I found a flight itinerary. They were flying him to Germany the next day with some other men from his unit, and that's when I knew—I knew they were just repositioning him.

"I confronted him about it, so he told me. He said he had come to tell me that night because he didn't want me to suffer through knowing about it. I threw him out of my apartment and told him I never wanted to see him again. He begged me not to let him go and I threw him out. I threw him out because I knew there would be no honor guard at my door and I knew if he died over there, I would have to find out from CNN and that if I went to his funeral nobody there would know who I was.

"But then I spent the whole night staring out the window and I realized I couldn't let him go. I had memorized his flight number and I knew he had two connections; the last one was in Atlanta. I didn't get to Lindbergh Field in time, so I booked myself a flight to Atlanta that would get me there half an hour before he left, but it was delayed, and by the time I got to his gate, they were already boarding. I saw him and I started running and I called his name, and suddenly the two guys next to him—guys from his unit—they turned and stared at him and I saw the happiness on Mike's face turn into fear in a second, and I just froze where I stood because I knew if I went any farther, Mike would have to find some way to explain me to those men.

"He was always giving me a thumbs-up if I did something right, so it was the only thing I could think of. . . . I could only hope that he knew what it meant. That he would know I would wait for him until he came back."

John saw Mike being wheeled across the tarmac at Balad, bandaged and injured almost beyond repair, and remembered Mike giving him a thumbs-up in the moment before the C-17's enormous belly swallowed him.

Alex said, "Funny how you finally make a decision and everything gets so simple that it feels like you've never made a decision before in your entire life. That's how my life was after that moment. Simple. True."

Alex paused and stared at the flowing water in front of them, as if he thought John needed a moment to digest this juxtaposition of Mike's Marine life and his personal life. What John needed was an answer to the question of why Mike hadn't been able to invite him up to the house if their lives had been oh, so very *true*.

"He gave me a thumbs-up right back," Alex said. "I guess it was like our wedding day. But that's all it was. Two thumbs-up in a crowded airport terminal. That's all it could be. You two got to have a better good-bye even after you almost got him killed."

Before John's anger could find his voice, Eddie called his name from across the creek. Now Eddie was standing by himself.

"Everything all right over there?" Eddie asked.

"I could ask you the same question."

Eddie seemed to consider his response. "That wasn't his first slip. I'm not about only giving one chance."

"Fine. I don't need to know."

"Yes, you do. Otherwise you would have gone back to bed." Eddie started for the back door before John could respond.

When he turned around, he saw that Alex hadn't moved an inch, and he figured he was waiting for a response. John said, "How much are you going to get to blame on me? You think I'm supposed to stand here and be your whipping boy for everyone who ever called you a name? You knew exactly what you were signing on for the minute you found out Mike was a Marine and you went after it full-throttle. But then when *you* got afraid, you tried to have it both ways. That's why you had to have your *wedding* in that airport terminal. Because you gave him a choice he couldn't make."

"The Marines wouldn't allow him to be my boyfriend and be a Marine. You know that."

"That was not the choice you forced him to make. You asked him not to fight. You told him he would lose you if he did. If you really knew who he was, if you really knew the type of Marine he was, then you knew what you were doing to him was blackmail. And that doesn't have anything to do with you, him, or anyone else in the world being gay."

John had started to move past Alex through the low branches and said, "Besides, why would I care about a wedding I never would have been invited to?"

"Would you have come?"

"Maybe."

"I don't believe you. And Mike wouldn't have believed you, either."

"See, I doubt that, Alex." He spun, didn't silence himself even though he knew his anger was about to get the best of him. "I think *you* were the reason I was never invited up to that house, because *you* were the one who didn't want me there."

Alex's silence told John that he had scored a point, so he headed back to his tent before the game could begin again.

×

The next morning, after their five-mile run, John led Alex to a spot he had found that morning where the creek widened by several feet as it made a sharp turn around a high ledge of water-polished sandstone. The depth of the creek at this spot was a good five feet, just enough to be able to make out the six bright red bricks John had bound together with duct tape and dropped to the creek's bottom. Alex spotted them right away, held them in his stare as John gave him the instructions: retrieve the bricks from the bottom of the creek and drop them at John's feet in sixty seconds' time.

Alex gave John a long, wary look, as if immersing himself in water on John's command was equivalent to going all the way on the first date. Then John pulled his stopwatch from his pocket, gave him the go signal, and Alex tore into the creek as John took several paces back toward the tree line. As Alex dove under the surface, John made out the sharp smell of tobacco from some-where nearby, then looked up the bank to see his sister standing partially hidden in the trees, like some FBI agent who liked to taunt the Mafioso she was keeping under surveillance.

Eighty seconds later, a soaking-wet Alex dropped the bricks at John's feet, gave him a wide-eyed and expectant look. "Eighty seconds," John told him. Then he picked up the bricks in one hand, walked to the bank, and tossed them into the center of the creek. "Sixty this time."

"Am I supposed to be learning how to swim here?" Alex asked between gasps.

"This is strength training."

"Cruel and unusual strength training."

"Strength training involves real pain or it isn't worth shit."

"Why's that, John?"

"Because if I'm going to teach you how to crack your oppo-nent's skull with your foot, you need to be willing to break your heel."

For a second it looked like Alex might burst out laughing, and just the tease of amusement that flashed in his eyes made John want to strike him, because it implied that Alex was the one indulging John and not the other way around. Alex took a step back at the sight of whatever expression John had allowed onto his face, lifted both his hands to signal that he was ready.

This time Alex retrieved the bricks in seventy seconds' time. When John informed him of this, he said, "How about this? If I make it under sixty seconds, I get to ask you a question."

"One-word answers only," John said. Then he hit the stop-watch and gave him a go signal. For six more rounds, John's prediction proved to be true: Alex couldn't make it under sixty seconds. Then on go-around number seven, Alex completed the challenge in fifty-eight seconds. For a few more seconds he stood in front of John, dripping like a wet dog, hands open as he waited to hear the verdict.

"Ask."

"Who's Dean?"

"One-word answers."

Maybe the frustration of having flubbed his own game got to him, because it took Alex another few tries before he was able to get under sixty seconds again. Then, with heaving breaths, he dropped the bricks at John's feet and said, "Is Dean your brother?"

"Was," John answered.

Four more tries and Alex finished in fifty-five seconds. "Shoot," John said.

"Is Dean the reason you hate me?"

"I don't hate you."

"One-word answers."

"No!"

Against his will, his eyes cut up the creek to where Patsy was still watching them from a distance. He was sure she was too far away to hear their words, but she was sitting on the bank of the creek, knees to her chest, arms folded around her knees, eyes locked on John as if she were trying to read their exchange from his facial expressions. Was she the reason their brother's name was on Alex's lips, or had Alex only pretended to be asleep when they talked about him in the car?

John said, "We're done here. Any more of this and you'll be on your back for the rest of the day. I need you on your feet." He started off toward the clearing and heard Alex's footsteps as he fell into step behind him.

Eddie had told John that he didn't currently have a full house. That meant he had empty beds. In accordance with the note John had left for his sister that morning, the mattresses from those beds had been stripped and deposited in a pile in the middle of the clearing. John spread them out side to side. Then, without warning, he seized Alex's right arm in two places, bent at the knees, and threw Alex's entire weight over one shoulder and onto the mattresses. Just as John expected, Alex flailed his limbs when he hit, and he rolled over onto one side, grabbing handfuls of mattress in an attempt to right himself.

"You fall like that in a real fight and you'll break your arm and take yourself out of the game," John said. "You won't be on a mattress, and you won't have a clear idea of what's lying on the ground around you. Learning how to fall is learning how to get back in, and learning how to get back in is learning how to—"

"Win?" Alex asked with a sneer.

"No. Kill. Get up."

Alex followed this instruction, but he did so with his eyes on their feet, and his upper lip curled back over his top teeth. To the ignorant observer, it might have looked like Alex was just struggling to draw breath, but John could read the expression for what it really was: anger and disgust. Was he losing the trust he had earned the day before?

Alex lifted his eyes to John's chest, stared at it for a few seconds. "Where's the picture?" he finally asked. John felt himself flush with embarrassment, told himself that he hadn't brought the necklace with Mike's photo on it because they didn't need it, not today, not when Alex was learning how to fall. But he knew Alex wouldn't believe this for a second, which made him wonder if it was actually the truth. Alex gave him a slight, wry smile, as if he could hear these thoughts in John's head and took a kind of masochistic pleasure in them.

John turned on his heel and marched back through the woods toward the cabin. Once he reached the threshold he realized he had not asked Alex where the necklace was. But he didn't have to look hard for it—it was coiled in a nightstand drawer. He waited until he entered the clearing to put it back on, waited for Alex to smile warmly at him, to read this small gesture as something more monumental than it seemed to be on the surface. But Alex didn't seem impressed in the slightest.

He ordered Alex to assume the basic warrior stance he had learned the day before. Alex complied, eyes staring dead ahead as John backed up several spaces, bent an arm in front of him, and rammed Alex from the side, sending him flying over his other leg. Alex hit the deck, teeth gritted, eyes screwed shut, and before he could catch a breath, John began manipulating Alex's limbs as if he were a mannequin, molding them into the defensive prone position: falling leg bent, arms still bent in the defensive stance position, chin tucked to chest.

"On your feet," John said. Alex answered by hesitating for several seconds, then rising to a standing position. John told himself not to indulge him, that the blow hadn't been that hard. "You want hard? We'll lose the mattresses." He told himself he wasn't angry, told himself he was beyond anger. Then he backed up several paces and slammed Alex from behind, bent arm hitting the guy's lower back like the bumper of a car. Alex flew forward but managed to roll onto his side before he hit, breaking the fall with his lower back, keeping his arms bent and his chin tucked.

"Good," John said quietly. But the way Alex stared at him, eyes wide and unblinking, nostrils flaring, made John feel like an abusive husband complimenting his wife on how well she had taken to the stairs he had just thrown her down. He extended one hand to Alex to help him up. Alex stared at it for a few seconds, then got to his feet on his own, eyes locked on the photo of Bowers hanging from John's neck as if he were drawing strength from it. John tried not to linger on this insult, a powerful one in the tiny universe they had created in the center of the clearing. He told himself he had to reassert his authority. He told himself that neither of them could move forward if he didn't get some respect back.

He backed away as Alex assumed the stance. Then he ran at him, seized the back of his neck and his left wrist, pulling his arm out from his body to immobilize him as he bent him at the waist, forcing him to stare down at his own two feet. Then John swung his rear leg high, preparing to sweep it down so his boot heel struck Alex's ankle. His plan had been to yank him off balance before the strike, to scare him into thinking his Achilles tendon was about to be struck.

It half-worked—but Alex realized what was about to happen and sank his teeth into John's thigh. It came as such a shock to John that it overrode his conscious thought. He released Alex's wrist, but there was no stopping his own rear leg, which he had already swung high and was coming back down to the spot where Alex's leg had been. But Alex shot to a straight-up standing position and threw John off to the side. John felt his legs go out from under him, and then the sky filled his vision and he felt like he was in a brief free fall. Then he heard the crack of his shoulder impacting the dry earth and he knew Alex had managed to throw him off the edge of the mattresses.

His world spinning, he was on his feet. He could sense the pain coming and knew the only way to ward it off for another precious few minutes: rage. He spun, saw Alex standing there, wild-eyed, staring at him. So John threw a classic punch, saw it connect with Alex's nose, saw Alex's head snap back, strings of red spewing from his nostrils. He hit the mattresses on his ass, and John realized he was bearing down on him even as the edges of his blurred vision came back into focus, then seemed to stretch like plastic wrap being pulled at the edges.

"You stupid son of a bitch! I'm trying to help you!" He heard the curses tumbling from his mouth, tried to tell himself they were coming from some other place, someplace right next to the spot where he had heard bone snap when he hit the earth. "What does a man have to fucking do for you, anyway? What does a man have to do for you that's ever fucking good enough? Huh? Can't you see what I'm—can't you see what I'm—"

His sister's frantic cries distracted him, and the minute the words stopped flying from his mouth, he could feel the pain: nails driven into his right shoulder and acid filling the veins of his right arm. What was he even saying? *Can't you see what I'm trying to do?* He saw the look of horror on Alex's face, realized it had nothing to do with what John had said, with what either of them had done.

Patsy started running toward them; then she took a good look at John and stopped in her tracks, her mouth falling open. John decided to follow everyone's lead and looked down at his right arm, saw the shoulder was inches lower than it should have been, saw the bloody tip of white bone jutting out from the side of his forearm, like the stub of a small branch that had been torn free from the bark of his arm.

Then the full force of the pain hit him as if someone had pulled so hard on his right shoulder he had caused a rip down the middle of his torso.

He threw up, hit the earth on both knees, then keeled forward into blackness.

11

Everything seemed like a dream until they reset his shoulder. He remembered being carried out of the clearing, seeing the blue sky get laced with pine branches, then being set down inside some cool, dark room and listening to Eddie and his sister argue in hushed whispers about whether they should take him to the hospital. He didn't hear Alex's voice, but this wasn't the comfort he wanted it to be because all he could see was the twin strings of blood shooting from Alex's nose, and the vision, as it replayed again and again in his mind, filled him with something that felt like dread.

Then there was an unfamiliar voice close to him, telling him in a trembling whisper to relax and be still. Then a piece of wood was slipped between his teeth and he tried to force himself out of his body and into some far corner of this unfamiliar room. He heard the snap of his shoulder clicking back into place, felt his torso rise up off the bed involuntarily from the agony of it, and then he passed out in the middle of his own strangled cry.

When he came to, he was sure it was days later, but then he saw his sister sitting on a wooden chair in the corner of the room, and she was wearing the same outfit she had worn earlier that morning as she watched Alex lug bricks from the creek and lay them at John's feet—beige-colored jeans and a lime-green T-shirt with the name of some dive bar written across it. It looked as if they were in the main house—a small room with three beds just like the ones in the outer cabin and adobe walls. More framed prayers and sayings on the walls. John went to sit up, then saw that his right arm had been set in a cast that was still drying.

"Eddie took his guys into town for an AA meeting," she said. "You passed out before the stitches, but you should probably buy flowers for the guy who reset your shoulder. Poor thing. You called him names he'd never heard before, and he was a skid row drunk, so that's saying something. And that scream you let out—well, it was pretty funny, watching what it did to a bunch of guys just a few days off speed. I mean, they were jumpy to begin with, but—"

"Where's Alex?"

Her sarcastic smile vanished. "Maybe that's the last thing you should be asking."

"He can't leave." His voice sounded raspy and distant. He knew he shouldn't feel this weak from a broken bone; it wasn't the first time in his life he had worn a cast. He dreaded the thought that his exhaustion came from somewhere else. He had lost control over Alex, and there was greater pain in that proposition than there currently was in the right side of his body.

Patsy said, "He didn't leave unless he walked." John fell silent, allowed his body to go lax, even though he was afraid of the exhaustion that threatened to overtake him. "Tell me why I shouldn't shut this whole thing down," Patsy said.

"Because you don't have that kind of power."

"I have some, John. I have the power to call the authorities and tell them what happened to Mike Bowers, and I also have the power to tell them what you two are up to."

"What are we up to?"

"Trying to kill each other for one."

"That is *not* what I was trying to do out there!"

"Oh, really? He said you were trying to teach him how to *fall*. And somewhere along the way you threw some kind of high kick, and then his nose got broken. So explain to me how this *training environment* of yours works, John. Enlighten me!"

She was bending over the bed, and he realized how immobilized he was—by pain, by fatigue, and by the cast that had been applied a few hours before. Part of him thought she just wanted payback for the way he had torn into her about Eddie two days ago, but he was too tired to deny the obvious. She had seen what had taken place out there; she had seen John's anger and how easily it had exploded to the surface. And it had scared her as badly as it scared him.

"What did he say to you?" she finally asked. Her voice was quieter now. Clearly she thought John's silence meant she was on the verge of getting some admission out of him, and suddenly she was humble and gentle. "He must have said something to set you off. I could hear him asking a bunch of questions down by the creek . . ." She trailed off and he broke eye contact, stared at the ceiling.

"He asked about Dean," he finally said. "He wanted to know who he was. He wanted to know if Dean was the reason I hated him."

As if their brother's ghost had just walked into the room and taken up a post next to John's bed, Patsy turned her back to him and moved to the chair she had been sitting in earlier. "What did you say?" she finally asked.

"I told him I didn't hate him."

"Is that the truth?"

"I'm trying not to. That's all I know." John's answer surprised both of them. Patsy stared at him for a long while, as if something in his tone had given her some hope and she needed to study him to make sure it had been sincere.

"Try harder," she finally said, but there was no real anger in her voice, and he realized this was her way of saying that she wasn't going to call the authorities, whoever that might end up being. That she wasn't going to "shut this thing down." Not yet.

"I never said Dean's name in front of him," John said. "Did you?"

"I told him we had a brother who died recently. That's all." She allowed these words to hang in the air between them, pathetically inadequate as they were to describe Dean's life, his history, and his effect on their family.

"Get him for me," John said. "Please."

Patsy left the room without another word, leaving John to watch the last light of day retreat across the ceiling and then vanish into that strange, seemingly lightless glow that fills the evenings in the desert, as if the very earth and everything struggling to live in it maintains a kind of radiance from having been pummeled by unrelenting sunlight all day. There was a small clock on the nightstand, but John kept himself from counting the minutes. It was dark by the time he heard footsteps outside the room. He didn't dare reach for the nearby lamp lest he start a wildfire inside his right shoulder. But when the door opened on its hinges, he saw only one shadow, his sister's. She turned on the lamp for him and avoided looking into his eyes as she said, "He won't come. He says when you're ready, you can go see him."

He closed his eyes to absorb the pain of this slight and once again saw the blood coming from Alex's nostrils, the horrified expression on Alex's face as he hit the earth. After all he had paid witness to in Iraq, how could a bloody nose have this effect on him? Maybe killing was easy when it was your true intention. What made life unbearable was the pain you caused when you were trying to do the right thing.

"John?"

His vision misted, and he blinked furiously. He had avoided tears, but Patsy had seen the first threat of them. Maybe his pain gave off some kind of vibration detectable to a blood relative. She stood over the bed, staring at him expectantly. But when he went rigid again, she withdrew and told him he needed to rest.

✕

In the middle of the night, he awoke to the sight of his sister standing over him in a baggy nightshirt, her hair sleep-rumpled. She extended a glass of water toward him, opened her other palm to reveal two blue pills. He took them from her with his good hand and swallowed them before she could tell him that they were for the pain.

He drifted off within minutes, awoke to the sound of slow, shuffling footsteps and the faint light of early morning. Patsy was in the chair across from the bed, fully dressed and freshly show-ered, but paying him no mind as she turned over a large envelope in her hands. In his drugged haze, he assumed it was a good-bye letter, that she was leaving him to deal with Alex on his own. The thought of it forced him to shut his eyes and do his best to wish himself back to sleep.

What felt like just a few minutes later, he awoke again to the sight of Patsy standing over the bed, checking his pulse on his good wrist. "What are you doing?" he heard himself ask her.

"Taking your pulse."

"Why?"

"Because I don't know what else to do."

Fair enough, he thought, and then he drifted off, starting awake now and then, once as his sister was tying a splint to his cast.

There was no good-bye letter waiting for him when he woke again, this time with a finality that told him the blue pills were leaving his system. But the silence in the house told him that once again Eddie had taken his men off-base. He swung his legs to the floor and managed to get to his feet. He straightened, and for half a second it seemed like there wasn't going to be any pain. Then it struck with such force he landed ass-first on the bed, as if he had been shoved into a seated position by a giant hand.

He was still trying to control his breathing when he heard the gunshot. This time he ignored the pain as he shot to his feet, went to the window, and looked out at the slanting orange sunlight of dusk. He heard footsteps racing down the hall toward him and turned. Sweat broke out all over him at once, and he recognized it as a sloppy misfire of his trained response. When his sister flew into the room, he gasped audibly, released the hundred visions of possible assailants that had strobed his mind's eye in an instant.

"Did you bring a gun?" Patsy asked him.

"Where's Alex?"

"I don't know. *Did you bring a gun?*"

"It's in my tent, and the shot came from there."

"Eddie took the guys into town."

"Get to a room with a phone and lock yourself in it. Give me your cell."

"John, you dislocated your shoulder and broke your arm in two places. What the hell are you—"

"I'll use the goddamn cast if I have to!"

She took her cell phone out and stuffed it in the pocket of his jeans. He left the room, suddenly finding himself in an unfamiliar hallway, given that he didn't remember being carried inside the house. He was halfway across the back porch when he realized he was barefoot. Then came a second gunshot, definitely from the direction of the clearing. And the gunshot sounded familiar. If it wasn't his Sig, it was one exactly like it. He splashed across the waters of the creek and into the dense foliage on the other side, made his way through the lower, shielding branches.

He was coming up on the clearing through good cover when he made out the lone figure standing in the middle of it: Alex. His nose had been sloppily bandaged, and he was walking away from one of the large boulders. From his position, John had a sideways view of Alex as he lifted John's Sig in a two-handed grip. There was a classic mistake in his grip; he rested the butt on top of his free hand, but instead of balling his hand into a fist for better support, the hand was lax, fingers open, like he'd probably seen Jack Bauer do it on *24*. He fired at the row of aluminum cans he had placed on top of the boulder—his shot was just a few inches too high.

John withdrew into the branches, pulled the cell phone from his jeans pocket with his left hand, and scrolled through the phone book until he found a listing for Eddie's home number. He punched *Send;* Patsy answered in a hoarse whisper, as if she thought the house itself was surrounded by cannibals. "It's Alex. He's practicing a little shooting."

Her breath went out of her. "When did you teach him how to shoot?"

"I didn't. Looks like he's trying to teach himself."

And he's not doing such a bad job of it, he thought. After a few more deep breaths she said, "Can you tell him to stop? If he's still shooting when Eddie gets back, we just might lose our lease here. Eddie's still pissed we didn't take you to the hospital."

He could hear the real questions she was asking him: *Can you talk to him at all? Can you ask him to forgive you?* To these questions as well John answered, "I'll see what I can do."

He moved back in the direction of the creek so he would come up on Alex from behind. He kept his steps slow and careful as he approached, and he saw Alex go rigid at the sound of them. But Alex didn't acknowledge John's presence in any real way; he just continued to focus on the row of aluminum cans twenty yards in the distance.

"You're not so bad at that," John said quietly.

Alex responded by firing another shot, too high again. Right behind him now, John reached out, brushed Alex's left shoulder with his hand to give him a warning, then pushed down gently on his left bicep. "Lower," he said softly. "And you do it with each breath. Breathe in, finger on the trigger, breathe out, and fire. The gun rises slightly above the target as you inhale, then back down to hit it as you exhale."

After a few seconds, John felt Alex inhale, saw the gun barrel rise slightly, then descend. The bullet tore the middle can from the row. A perfect shot. John laughed despite himself, was about to pat Alex on the back when Alex spun.

He raised the barrel right in front of John's eyes, aimed at the spot just above the bridge of John's nose. John's first instinct was to lash out with his right arm, which bucked against its cast, then against the broken bone inside it. The pain crippled him, so when Alex ordered him down onto his knees, he didn't have a problem going along with the order.

He closed his eyes; then something brushed his face, and

that's when he realized that some sort of hood had been slipped over his head and the pressure against the back of his neck was being made by the barrel of his own gun, still hot enough to singe the hairs there. "You had your chance to train me. Now it's my turn. Stand up."

Branches clawed at him as Alex drove them into the woods.

"You're going to pretend you're somebody else, John Houck." The controlled sound of his rage filled John's stomach with a cold bath.

"How am I going to do that?" he asked. Alex held John's left hand against the small of his back and moved the gun barrel to a spot between John's shoulder blades as he steered him out of the clearing. He could hear the creek flowing off to his right, which meant they were headed in the direction of the property John hadn't explored.

"You're going to shut up and listen to every damn word I say," Alex answered him. "Because you're going to *be* this person. You're going to walk in his shoes no matter how ugly it gets. Of course, imagination goes only so far. I've got some props to help you along the way."

John would have preferred to hear madness in his voice, but instead Alex's voice was cool and controlled, like someone in shell shock. "I'm sorry I broke your nose," John said.

"I'm not, John. You want to know why? Because you showed me just who the fuck you are."

"And who's that?"

"A white-trash closet-case piece of shit, John," Alex snarled. "You wouldn't have accepted Mike, because you wanted to fuck his pretty ass, and that just wasn't okay with you. Because you were too busy trying to be a real man. A real man who fell down on the job and put his entire team in danger. A real man who walked out on his sister ten years ago—"

John tore his hand free of Alex's grip and took off, making a hard left so it would be harder for Alex to aim at him. He didn't run because the accusations were true; he ran because he knew full well that if Alex had managed to convince himself of these lies, then he might well be capable of any kind of violence he could dream up. Just as he reached up for the hood with his left hand, his right side impacted with a tree trunk, and his entire world caught fire. Maybe if he hadn't been blinded, he wouldn't have seen the stars that strobed his vision in such brilliant Technicolor. They were the only things to distract from the exquisite agony of the impact. He had no sense of up or down, just a vague sense that his knees had come to rest on broken twigs. He retched, thought he was going to vomit, then coughed up a phlegm ball, which smeared his lips.

For what felt like an eternity, he rocked back and forth, as if it would help the pain to subside. Then, when he had managed to steady his breathing, he felt the gun barrel brush against the back of his head, and in a clear and controlled voice Alex said, "Did you ever stop to ask yourself why I never suspected you, John? Did you ever wonder why I didn't think you killed him? After all, you were the only one who ever got to be alone with him after he was dead. Maybe chasing me out into the woods the way you did was some big cover."

"You know that's not true."

"How? How do I know that, John?"

"Because when I caught up with you, I would have killed you."

"No, John. I don't know anything about you anymore. Up until yesterday I thought you were just a sad sack of shit trying to do right by me. But you showed what you really wanted."

"What's that?"

Alex's voice blasted right into his ear. "You wanted to punish me, didn't you, John? You wanted to show me what it takes to be a real man like you. Problem is, John, you're *not* a real man. Maybe I'm not, either. But the least I can do is show you what it takes to be like me. And don't try to fool me into thinking you're tough enough for whatever I throw at you. I know you left the Marines before you went through SERE."

SERE stood for "Survival, Evasion, Resistance and Escape," an immersive, demoralizing training program Recon Marines went through to teach them how to survive in enemy captivity. In a simulated environment, trainees were given a false piece of intelligence they were required to keep secret; then they were taken hostage and subjected to days of psychological torture designed to toughen them to the degree that they could stand up to anything short of having their fingers cut off. John had never been able to get a single SERE graduate to tell him the extent of what they had been put through, not even Mike. Sure, he'd heard the same stories everyone had heard. Trainees being forced to piss in their waterproof boots and wear them for days on end. White captives being forced to wear Klansman hoods and drag their fellow black captives around on leashes. But these stories had the smell of urban legends, and the avowed secrecy of almost everyone who went through the program hinted at even darker experiences. Had Mike shared some of these with Alex? Was that why Alex was bringing it up, because he was about to use some of them?

Alex said, "You were supposed to, though. But you pussed out and left the Marine Corps because you almost got your captain killed."

"You need to cut this out," John heard himself say, and the tremor of genuine fear in his voice turned his stomach. "You need to cut this shit out right now."

Instead, Alex drove the gun barrel up under John's chin, and the sound that came out of John was mostly a roar, but there was a word in it: his sister's first name. As if on cue, John felt the hood get ripped up over his mouth, and suddenly he was chewing some kind of fabric. From the shape it took once Alex shoved it inside his mouth, John assumed it was a sock.

Alex lifted him to his feet by the back of his neck and said, "Listen to every word I say to you. *See* what I tell you to see."

Alex shoved him forward. The temperature dropped suddenly, and even though he was hooded, he thought he could feel a deep darkness on his skin.

12

They were standing on a dirt floor, and there were loose rocks underfoot. John was willing to bet it was some kind of cave. A small one, though, because when Alex started to speak again, his voice didn't echo.

"Eighteen, John. You remember eighteen?" To avoid choking on his gag, he nodded in response. "You were eighteen when you joined the Marine Corps, right? Ran away from home because you wanted to be some big hero?"

Again he nodded. Alex's instructions had been to visualize every word he said to him, so John did. Saw himself standing outside the Marine Corps recruiting depot in San Diego, felt the shaking in his legs as he and his buddy Clyde Travis paused for the first time in several hours to absorb the full impact of what they were about to do. They had hitched a ride down from Yucca Valley with a tattooed, cigarette-swallowing former gunnery sergeant who had been more than happy to ferry two willing new recruits to their new home. Only when they reached the threshold to their new life did John wonder if they were making a mistake. He said so to Clyde, who had called him a pussy, which was funny now, considering that Clyde had washed out in the second week of boot camp and ended up managing an AutoZone.

"Imagine you've had a secret your entire life, but you know that if you drive to this little bar all the way across town, you'll find someone you can tell it to. You'll be able to get it off your chest once and for all, and chances are they won't judge you or call you names . . ." Alex trailed off, as if the power of the memory he was referring to in the most general of terms had overtaken him.

"You're eighteen," he said, then swallowed before he continued. "You're eighteen and you've just gone away to school. You're finally free from your parents, who would probably slam the door in your face and keep it shut for the rest of your life if they knew this little *secret* you had."

Alex turned him around, pressed down on his good shoulder, and John felt his ass come to rest on a wooden chair. Alex retreated slightly; then John felt strands of rope being wrapped around his stomach, the same rope he had asked Patsy to buy for one of their upcoming endurance challenges.

All of his plans to train Alex seemed absurd and haphazard now, and he had to fight the urge to laugh at his own stupidity, his arrogance. Although, if either quality could get him out of this fucker of a situation, he would have welcomed them both back with open arms. It was clear to him now that all he had managed to do to Alex so far was blow the top off the well of grief and anger inside him.

"You're gay, John. Even though you've never laid a hand on another man in your life, you know damn well you're a full-on cock-sucking fairy. Are you working with me here? Are you seeing this?" When John didn't answer Alex asked, "Are you *feeling* this?"

He felt the final tugs as Alex tied the knots that secured John to the chair and nodded as deeply as he could. "I'm telling a story, John. That's all. I'm telling you a story so you can understand. Isn't that what you want, John? To *understand* your good buddy Mike? To understand the things men like him go through?"

Liar, he thought. This was a story about Alex, eighteen and visiting his first gay bar, and he was pretty sure it was a story that ended in violence, which John had stupidly brought to the surface the minute he broke Alex's nose.

"You're eighteen, John. You've barely been at college a few weeks, barely have any real friends, so it's easy for you to slip out every night and drive clear across town to this little gay bar in the middle of nowhere. See, you've checked out the bigger clubs, but they're too much. Your fake ID worked but there's too much of everything there—too much sex, too much music, too many drugs. You need a quiet place where you can find someone who will listen, someone who will make you feel less like a *mistake* in a universe intended for assholes and Marines."

Footsteps. The sound of something metal clinking on a table. John fought images of knives and pliers, realized he had heard nothing more dangerous than the pop of a bottle cap. An open beer bottle was passed under his nose, and it amazed him how a smell that had previously made his mouth water could be turned into a stench by cold darkness and a coil of rope.

"So, you park across the street and you watch the men who go inside and you're kind of amazed because not all of them look like the pathetic faggots you've seen in movies or on TV. They're not dressed up like women and they're not wearing tube tops and feather boas and all kinds of sissy shit." In recounting the story, Alex's voice had taken on a clipped masculine tone, as if he were speaking in the voice of his former self, the young man he had been before the story he was telling came to an end.

"And you wait, and you wait, and you wait for the courage to go inside that bar, but it doesn't come. Not the first night. Even though you sit there downing a bunch of beers you bought with your fake ID. So you go back to your dorm, lie to your roommate about where you've been, and lay up all night planning what you're going to do when you go back. It takes you two weeks. Two weeks of sitting in your car drinking beer before you finally step out and cross that street, flash your fake ID to the guy with the mustache who's working the front door. Then you're inside and you see some pool tables and a long bar. No sex club. No guys in assless chaps. Nothing like you've been told. Nothing like you've been taught to fear.

"And the men inside. They look like *men,* and some of them are smiling at you. Sure, the rest are looking at you in a way you're not used to having other men look at you. But a couple of guys, they come over and say hi, but they can see how drunk you are and mostly they're just welcoming you to the place, because they were you once and they know how many beers it took you to come inside, and this isn't like those big dance clubs. This is one of those bars where people try to take care of their own."

From the sound of his voice, John could tell that Alex was retreating, walking back over to the table where he had opened the beer bottle. He could see where this was headed and he dreaded what props Alex had selected to help him imagine the ending of this tale. He tried to speak, but nothing came out. He swallowed and found his mouth was dry.

"A few of them offer to give you a ride home because they can see how drunk you are, but you refuse because you're not ready for them to know your last name or where you go to school. You try to walk as straight a line as you can out the door. And then you see him. He's waiting for you right next to your truck. Handsome. Tall. Blond hair, blue eyes, and a smile that lights up the street. Later, when you look back, you'll remember that he was standing in the shadows, just outside the halo of the streetlight, and you'll realize the cowboy hat wasn't just a prop—it was supposed to hide his face. But for now he's the most beautiful thing you have ever seen, and when he asks you if you want to take a ride in his truck, you know there isn't really a choice for you. That you've turned down too many opportunities, ignored too many promising looks—there's no way you can dismiss this man, and you're just drunk enough to think he might be the last one you'll ever need to meet.

"And then he curves his arm around your back and starts walking you away from your car, and just the feel of his arm around your back—well, it's like your destiny has finally reached out to you and told you which way to go."

John felt something whip through the air in front of his face, followed by a crash that lashed the hood with broken glass and enough beer to soak clean through it until he tasted Budweiser on his lips. Alex had clearly smashed the beer bottle against some hard surface, probably a pot or a pan he was holding right next to John's head.

"The pain's too great at first for you to feel it, and for a second, you think the bottle just came down from the sky and hit you in the head. And then—"

John was rocked backward, then pitched forward, crying out in pain as his arm was jostled and the chair was dragged along the dirt floor with John canted forward at a forty-five-degree angle. "Then, suddenly, the guy's dragging you into an alley and you see other guys waiting for you. And you *know* instantly what it means. You know you're being punished by God, by your parents, by everyone you have ever met, everyone who ever knew your secret. Because all you wanted was to feel less alone. All you wanted was to have them smile at who you actually were."

The chair stopped but it was still pitched forward, and John had no choice but to throw his good arm out and brace it against the dirt.

Something exploded just over John's head. Alex was striking a hard surface several feet above the chair, probably the wall of the cave. Again and again Alex struck the stone wall until John felt chips of rock lacing his exposed neck. The worst of the sound was centered in the pipe and not the rock, a resounding clang each time it made contact with the wall.

"Is this you, John?' Alex cried. "Could you have done this?"

The banging stopped, leaving John's ears ringing. Then beer splashed down John's back as Alex emptied one bottle over the back of his head, then another. It poured under the hood and into his mouth, soaking through the sock stuffed in his mouth and into the back of his throat.

"Only it's not beer, John. See, the pipe isn't enough for them. The beating—well, that was just meant to bring you to your knees. Now, they need to show you how they really feel about you."

John coughed despite himself, and the beer-soaked sock came halfway out of his mouth. Alex finished emptying the last beer bottle over the back of John's hood; then John heard the sound of the empty bottle hitting the cave floor and rolling. He coughed again, and the sock came out enough for him to spit it out all the way.

"No!" he managed between coughs. "I never would have done that to you or to any man."

Alex lowered the chair down onto all four legs and turned it.

When he ripped John's hood off, John blinked, allowing beer to get in his eyes. When Alex started using the empty hood to wipe his face clean, John grimaced and turned away, then relented. Once his vision had returned, he saw they were indeed inside a small cave and there was an electric lantern sitting right next to the opening, turning Alex into a backlit silhouette.

"I never would have done that to you," he said.

"Not me," Alex said. "Mike. They did it to *Mike.*"

He tried to take in this new information at the same time he tried to catch his breath, but he couldn't swallow it: the thought of Captain Mike Bowers being beaten and pissed on in an alleyway at age eighteen. How could the Mike he had known have emerged from that experience to be a man of impeccable skill and laserlike focus? Sure, John could see someone surviving that kind of beating and going on to become a Marine but the kind of deranged, suicidal Marine who plows his Humvee right into enemy fire while shouting a dirty version of his favorite country song at the top of his lungs. He couldn't see that person becoming Lightning Mike Bowers.

"You don't believe me?" Alex finally said.

"What does it matter?" John whispered. "What does it matter what I say to you or do for you? You think I live to hate you, and nothing's going to change your mind, so fuck it."

"Oh, please, John. Don't act like you're out to prove something to *me.* Don't act like you're trying to accept me, to accept who I am. That's a load of bullshit. The reason you think you're so damn heroic is that you hate my guts and you're doing all this anyway."

"Maybe so. But who says that has anything to do with the fact that you're gay?"

Alex barked with laughter for a few seconds; then he stopped himself just as his laughs started to sound crazed and desperate.

"The question is, can I accept *you,* John? Can I accept the fact that you need to pretend to be a hero because something bad happened to your little brother? Something that might have made you turn your back on the man who saved your life, if he'd lived long enough for you to find out who he really was?" John didn't have the energy to deny this, probably because he knew it to be the truth, so he allowed Alex to continue. "What did you call yourself last night? My whipping boy? Maybe. But what am I to you, John?"

When John didn't answer, Alex closed the distance between them, bent down until their faces were almost level. "I think the only reason you signed on for this is because as long as you have me to hate, you don't have to really accept the fact that Mike *chose* me to live with him, to love him, and to fuck him. It's Mike you're angry at, isn't it?"

"What does it matter? Next to yours, my anger looks like a light fucking rain."

Alex smiled, but it was more like a grimace. Then, quickly, as if it were meant to be a sneak attack, he said, "What happened to your brother, John?"

"The reason you can't understand why I would agree to help you is because you are too cynical and too . . . *indulged* to even begin to understand the principles, the values, that I lived by. That Mike lived by. We were—"

"What happened to your brother, John?"

"I don't do things because of how they'll make me *feel.* Because of how they'll—"

"*What happened to your brother?*" Alex roared, face cherry red, veins pulsing in his temple. Maybe it was a device, because something about the seeming insanity of Alex's sudden anger made John relax, as if nothing he might say could make things any worse.

"He was raped," John said quietly. "By a man who lived in our street. A friend of his. Danny Oster. Oster went to Mexico for a while after I almost beat him to death. But now he's back and he's changed his name to Charles Keaton and he's living in beautiful Redlands, California, where I guess he's about to find some other confused, emotional kid just like my brother and try to get him alone, when his parents, or his brother, or whoever's supposed to be watching him is somewhere else."

Alex withdrew, his brow furrowed and his breaths slowing. "How do you know he raped your brother?"

"I saw it. With my own two eyes. I walked into the bedroom, and he had Dean flat on his back and he was ramming himself into him and Dean was making sounds like he had been speared in the gut!"

Alex averted his eyes from John's, as if these details were too much for him to absorb. "On his back," Alex finally whispered, and then John realized Alex was asking for clarification on this detail, so he nodded.

"I had a choice," John said. "The day I decided to track you guys down I had all the information I needed to do some real harm to that man. But that morning I got a phone call from this guy—a few months before I had gone to him to get a present for Mike, a Spartan sword, just like out of *Gates of Fire*. When he called to tell me it had arrived, I knew, deep in my gut, that I could get that sword and do whatever it took to find out where Mike was. Or I could sit in my trailer all day, staring at Danny Oster's new address and wondering what I could do that would hurt him the most until I got sick of wondering and decided to take some action.

"The reason it wasn't an easy choice is because if I sat down with Mike, I knew I would have to tell him the truth about what happened that day in Ramadi. I would have to tell him that the reason he had to save my life is because I had just gotten an e-mail from Patsy telling me that Dean had killed himself, and I didn't tell Mike about it. I didn't come clean about my mental state when we're going into a hostile area and Mike lost an eye because of it. He needed to hear that. I owed him that. The sword was nothing. What I wanted to give him was the truth."

"Instead you got me," Alex said.

"Yes. And I haven't turned my back on you for one moment."

At first John didn't know how to read the wide-eyed expression on Alex's face, because it seemed like the first time Alex had looked at him in such a manner. He looked concerned and afraid at the same time, and even though John was staring him right in the eye, Alex's expression didn't change.

When he crossed the cave again, John felt a surge of triumph, but he tried to keep it hidden as Alex untied the ropes that bound John to the chair. Even when he was free, John didn't get to his feet.

Before he stepped out of the entrance to the cave, Alex looked back at him over one shoulder and said, "I'm sorry about your brother."

This simple statement, delivered without any of the anger or sarcasm John was used to hearing out of Alex, kept John glued to the chair. The tension in his chest threatened to give rise to a small seizure, and when he started to blink back tears, he told himself they were just a result of having beer poured in his face.

13

When he was within sight of the main house, Patsy shot up out of the chair on the back porch where she had clearly been waiting for him. Behind her, the house was lit up like a fishbowl, and he could see the men inside crowding the kitchen, where one of them had just finished cooking something and was passing out servings to his excited patrons. It was too dark for Patsy to see the condition he was in, but when she smelled the beer on him, she cursed under her breath. "Shouldn't be drinking on the stuff I gave you last night," she muttered. Then she curved an arm around him, felt his soaked shirt against her skin, and fell silent.

She steered him through the back door of the house, then through another door and into what was clearly the master bedroom, where her suitcase sat at the foot of the bed and there was real furniture and something besides prayers hanging on the walls. She sat him on top of the toilet, took time pulling his shirt off him and around his cast. She dabbed at the cast with her fingers to make sure it wasn't beer-soaked.

"Y'all fought?" she asked softly.

She saw a response in his eyes, and it seemed to take the wind out of her. She pursed her lips, indicating that she was biting her tongue, hard. Then she turned her back to him and turned on the bath and for a while they sat there in silence, she watching the water fill up and he hearing the sound of the lead pipe striking the wall of the cave over and over again.

She turned off the faucet. Then she set a short stack of bath towels between the toilet and the tub, told him he could use them to rest his cast on, and left him alone with his next mission: a hot bath.

He was halfway between nightmares and being awake when Patsy shouted his name a while later. When he didn't respond right away, she threw open the bathroom door, without regard for his nudity or the fact that she had roused him from a doze. His cast had been sliding off the stack of towels, was about to go under when he sat up as straight as he could. He asked her what was wrong, and she opened a towel for him to step into. "Is it Alex?"

Without answering, she wrapped the towel around him, kept her eyes on the floor as she steered him into the bedroom. Mike's face filled the television screen above a banner that read GAY MARINE SLAYING. In voice-over, the Headline News anchor was detailing the stellar service record of former Marine Corps captain Mike Bowers. Then John found himself staring at Ray Duncan, in full uniform, including a wide-brimmed khaki hat, standing before a phalanx of microphones. His backdrop was the brown brick sheriff's station and the rolling hills that cradled his town.

Eyes locked on the sheet of paper he held in one hand, Duncan said, "This Sunday, the body of Michael Bowers, twenty-nine, was discovered in a wooded area ten miles east of the Owensville town line. The body was badly mutilated. Exact time of death has not been established." *Badly mutilated.* John dreaded the thought of what other injuries Duncan had added to the body to cover up the fact that he had buried one of Mike's hands in the desert.

The reporter took over for Duncan, and suddenly John was staring at himself. His last official Marine Corps photograph swelled to fill the screen. He wore his dress blues and cover, and the flash had flattened out his face. Then, right after him came Alex, a candid party shot. His cheeks had the blush of a few drinks, and he had a Glo-stick around his neck. The reporter spelled out that both men were believed to be on the run. Both men were wanted for questioning.

"They're not saying you're on the run together," Patsy said quietly.

"They don't need to. Duncan's saying exactly what he wants to."

"Which is?'

"Both men are wanted for questioning. That means they think we're both alive and well—and together. In each other's arms." He turned to see if she was getting his meaning. "Duncan's trying to make this thing out like it's some big gay love triangle."

"You tried to *report* this murder," Patsy said. "He accused you of having PTSD. He showed you the door."

"Exactly. It's not me he's trying to frame. He's just trying to get me out of the picture. Then he can claim Alex had an accomplice who moved the body while I was chasing him into the woods. In the meantime, he thinks I'll cut the guy loose if the entire country starts to think we're slipping it to each other."

On television, news crews pursued an impeccably dressed

woman up the front walk of a sprawling pink mansion surrounded by a high stone wall. Her platinum blond bob looked like it would hold its form in a monsoon, and her cream-colored pantsuit had a flared collar. Her enormous sunglasses made it impossible to tell whether she was ignoring the reporters with stone-faced dignity or outright contempt. Charlotte Martin, Alex's mother, had her son's long, full-lipped mouth and delicate chin. She had only one statement for the media, and apparently she had released it in writing earlier that day: "I am saddened by the circumstances in which my only son has found himself. But given that he left my life several years ago, I cannot be held responsible for what he has invited into it since."

"Jesus," Patsy whispered as the words hovered on the screen for a few seconds. "Woman can't even say Alex's name."

But John was too taken by the phrases *left my life* and *my only son.* Odd choices for a woman looking to distance herself from the situation, and further proof that Alex hadn't told John the entire story of his departure from Cathedral Beach.

The report ended, and Patsy used the remote to kill the volume. Neither of them spoke for a few minutes. "The cash I gave Eddie for this place," she finally said. "It was under the table. I'm just saying—this place can't be traced to me. If you need to stay here, we probably can."

She had taken a seat at the foot of the bed. When she lifted her eyes to his, he thought she was going to defend herself. Instead she said, "Should we tell Alex?"

Dressed in a pair of Eddie's too-short blue jeans and a T-shirt for something called an AA roundup, John led Patsy down the creek toward the outer house, where the clerestory windows revealed a glow coming from several bedside lamps inside. When he saw that the front door was shut, he expected it to be locked, but it wasn't, and when he swung it open, he saw that Alex's bag was missing, and the bed he had been sleeping in was perfectly made, as if he had never been there at all.

Patsy brushed past him through the front door, gave the entire house a once-over, and seemed to come to the same conclusion as John. "Shit," she whispered, and then she seemed struck by a thought and ran past him. He turned and watched her jog in the direction of where she had parked her SUV when they had first arrived.

He felt blindsided and shamed by the panic that filled him. Given the events of the evening and the day prior, he didn't think there was room for another emotion inside him, but this was pure panic, plain and simple. Being branded a fugitive was something he had anticipated days earlier, and it had come as almost no shock to him, but this empty room—there was terror in it, the terror that he had failed utterly and allowed Alex to slip through his fingers and into a blind fall.

Patsy burst through the front door a few seconds after John found the note lying on the kitchen counter. "He took the Jeep," she said through gasping breaths. John showed her the note, which said, *I hope you will hear from me soon, Alex.* Patsy backed away from the note as if she thought it were about to self-destruct, and her hands went to her mouth. "Oh, no, John. He had a cell phone. What if someone called and told him—"

"I had the ammunition clips you bought me out in the tent earlier, but he took them when he started shooting. Check the cabinets for them."

"Where are you going?"

Instead of answering, he stopped in the doorway and said, "And there's something else. It's a diagram. Got a man's torso and head and shoulders on it. See if it's in any of the drawers or if he took it with him."

"Why?"

"Because it's a diagram on how to kill a man, that's why."

In almost no time at all John covered the distance between the house and the cave where Alex had held him captive. The electric lantern was still there, and when he turned it on he saw the empty chair, missing its seat, and the coil of rope that had been used to tie him to it. No Ka-bar knife. No Sig. Not even the lead pipe had been left behind.

Cursing under his breath, he ran back to the house, found Patsy waiting for him out front, her arms crossed over her chest as if there were a chill in the air only she could feel. "I didn't find it," she said. "Where did you go?"

He threw open the front door as if he were about to confront a band of insurgents, as if something about the room might have shifted and given up some evidence of Alex's intention in the few minutes he had been gone. His sister had to say his name several times in a row before he could feel his feet again.

"'*I hope* you will hear from me soon,'" John said. "Like there's a chance that's not going to happen."

"What does that mean, John?"

"I think you're right. Somebody called his cell and told him about the story, and now he knows where Mike's body is and he's planning on doing something about it. And he needs Mike's knife and my gun to do it. I think he's going to try to kill Ray Duncan."

Patsy sank to a seated position on the foot of the bed; then a thought struck her. "How the hell did he get the keys?"

"Where were they?"

"In my purse," she said. Then her face seemed to cloud over, and suddenly she was running out the front door and toward the house. John followed her, calling out to her, and she called back that everything was fine in an absurd attempt at placating him, even though she was running so fast John could barely keep up with her. She bypassed the back porch. Some of the men were watching television in the living room. John followed her around to the front entrance of the house, stopped calling out to her because he didn't want to draw the attention of any of the men. Was she afraid that Alex had stolen her entire purse?

To his shock, she tried to close the front door behind her in John's face, but then she was drawn to the sight of her purse turned on its side on a table inside the white-walled foyer. The sight of it lying there didn't seem to give her any relief. Breathless, her brow furrowed, she hurriedly went about stuffing the contents of her purse back inside it. That's when John saw the envelope, the same envelope she had been turning over in her hands early that morning as he drifted in and out of a drugged haze, the same one he had assumed was a good-bye note.

He tried getting her attention by saying her name. When she ignored him yet again, he snapped, dug into her purse with his left hand, pulled the envelope free, and was shocked to see her holding on to it, panic in her eyes. Then she released it, brought her hand to her mouth as if she expected John to sock her in the jaw. He turned the envelope over and saw his first name written on it in blocky handwriting that at first seemed only vaguely familiar. Then he recognized it, and the breath went out of him. It was his brother's handwriting.

For a while they just stood there, Patsy breathing into her hands, the sounds of some cop show thudding against the walls. At one point John looked up to see Eddie standing in the doorway, but when he saw their postures and the look on John's face he retreated without comment. When John turned for the door, Patsy said his name in a trembling whisper that had the threat of tears in it. He stepped outside anyway, walked a few paces away from the house, waited until he heard the sound of Patsy's footsteps crunching the gravel behind him.

"How long have you had this?" he finally asked.

"Since he died. I found your trailer, tried leaving it, but the damn envelope was too big to fit under the front door, and I figured—" Her voice caught, and John remembered that Mandy had told him that Patsy had tried to leave a note for him. "I figured it wasn't the kind of thing you left under somebody's door. It was with him, John. It was with him when he died."

A suicide note, he thought.

"You should have given this to me, Patsy."

"You were distracted. You had other things on your—"

"You should have given this to me, Patsy."

When she didn't respond, he turned, saw her bowed head and heaving chest as signs of surrender. "I know, John," she whispered. "But I wanted a shot at you first. I wanted to see if I could get you back."

He had no answer for this, and when he started walking away from her, she didn't follow. He walked all the way back to the outer house, where the front door was still open and the bedside lamps inside gave off a deceptively welcoming glow.

John pulled the door shut behind him and locked it, sat down on the foot of the bed Alex had used, and opened the envelope.

The envelope was large because it contained an entire sheet of watercolor paper that had been folded in half. At first John thought it might be a store-bought, oversized greeting card. Then he saw that Dean had glued an old tattered photograph of John and Dean to the front flap, taken a few days after they had moved to the desert. They stood in front of a one-story tract home with salmon-colored stucco walls just south of Highway 62 in Yucca Valley. The two young men posed on the dried patch of dirt that passed for a front lawn were doing their best to look happy to be in each other's presence, if not the high desert. The bill of John's baseball cap with the New Orleans Saints logo on it shadowed his glower, but Dean's red curls were exposed and his smile was a metal-studded rictus thanks to braces, which flashed against the deep red of his first California sunburn.

John could remember the picture being taken, could remember how Patsy had tried to force them into this tiny moment of celebration. With trembling fingers he opened the card and took a few seconds to squint at the tiny block letters that passed for handwriting, too tiny and too controlled, and he wondered if his brother had spent his last days under the influence of something speedier than heroin. He began to read.

John,

I know you're probably pissed at me for doing what I did. I wish I could say I'm sorry, but I'm not. And it's not because you left me in Yucca with that stupid bitch—I won't even bother to say her name! It is because I think as hard as you tried to be good to me, you couldn't understand what it was like inside my head. All these voices, all the time, telling me I'm a piece of shit. And I hate to say this, John, I really really do, but a lot of them sounded just like yours. I know what you wanted, John. You wanted me not to cry so much. You wanted me not to be so sad all the time about Mom and Dad, and what I need to tell you is that I stopped, I stopped being sad about them, and I stopped being mad at you for leaving. (I know you left because I lied—I'll get to that.) But see, what happened was when I stopped being mad and sad, shit really got bad. It really got bad.

Okay. Sorry. I had to stop because my friend is coming over with the stuff soon and he just thinks I'm going to sell it. He doesn't know anything. Whatever. You don't need to know all that and it probably makes you mad, so I'll stop. What I was saying was . . . I know you wanted me not to be sad all the time and you wanted me to be stronger so the other boys at the school wouldn't pick on me, but see, I think looking back that you were upset because you could tell what I was, you could already tell the way I was going to be. I know you probably don't see it that way. I know you probably think you were doing the best you could do, but I could tell, John. I could tell that you were never going to accept me, so I lied to you, but that's *why* I lied, John. I hope you can see that today. Now that I'm gone. I hope you can see that. It's not like I blame you for it, but I figured I should tell you so that you can understand.

That day you walked in on me and Danny, he wasn't raping me. We had been doing it for a while and I really liked it, and we were even going to move away together when I was eighteen. He wanted to go to West Hollywood because he said guys like us could get along there but I knew that wouldn't be far enough away from you. But I was so afraid. I thought if you knew the truth you would kill both of us, but if you thought he had raped me, I would get to live. Problem was, I didn't expect you to go to that bitch. (I won't say her name. She is *dead* to me!) So I had to lie before she started asking questions, even though I knew you would never forgive me. Can you understand that, John? I was trying to keep myself alive. I was afraid of you. I loved you—not in that way!!! But I was afraid of you. I wasn't surprised when you ran away. I knew how badly you wanted to be a Marine. I know you did good and stuff. I got into some bad shit, John, but I tried to turn my life around and I went to see that bitch we call our sister and she wouldn't give me any money. She just gave me your e-mail and said that you were at war and everything and I should write you, and so I told her who the fuck does she think she is ordering me around. . . . You don't need to read this. The point is, she knew already. She knew I had lied about Danny, and she said if I wanted to turn my life around I could find him and apologize and I should tell you what really happened. So I guess that bitch got to order me around after all. Ha ha ha.

John, I'm sorry for what I'm about to do but I know that if you knew what it was like to be me that you would understand. I'm sorry that God was never kind to our family. And I know you're probably sorry for the way you treated me and I wish I could have given you a chance to tell me in person, but it's time for me to go now.

Dean

"Your li'l bro"

After he finished reading the note, John rose from the bed and left it lying on the comforter next to the spot where he had been sitting. He got a beer from the fridge, his first in days now that his job as drill instructor had come to an end, and spent a few minutes trying to use the bottle opener with his left hand. When his sister knocked on the front door, he opened it for her and brushed past her without meeting her expectant gaze. She moved past him into the house, probably toward the note, and he walked through the darkness toward the creek, waiting for the predictable emotions to come.

Instead he felt anger, pure and simple, and he realized that for so long he had nursed his rage toward Danny Oster, and next to that whirlwind, his brother had been nothing more than a birdhouse rocking in the winds of other men's perversions. The idea that an anger that had driven him so completely had been based on a lie—that was just too overwhelming to swallow all at once, like staring down at a corpse and demanding that you immediately accept the fact that you yourself will become one someday.

He started for the meditation garden and realized from the numbness in his legs that he was in a kind of shock. He sat down in front of a Buddha statue and tried to lose track of time until he heard twigs crunching underfoot.

Patsy stood next to the bench off to his side, probably so he wouldn't have to look at her if he didn't want to. "Are you sorry for the way you treated him?" she asked, a tremor of anger in her voice.

"Should I be?"

"You never lifted a hand to him in his life. He wasn't afraid you'd kill him. He was afraid you'd reject him. That's a different goddamn ball game, and he knew it." He realized her anger was on his behalf, or at least she believed it was, and this silenced him even further. "What he left out of that little note is that he had been dealing heroin for three years. He also left out that he and that buddy of his owed his supplier almost fifteen grand and that his buddy had skipped the country rather than pay his portion of the debt. So rather than face up to anything he had done, he decided to get good and numb and check out. But not before blaming *you* first."

"He came to see you," John whispered.

"Yes. He did. And he had track marks up and down his arms and he didn't say a damn thing about owing anyone any money. He wanted three thousand dollars, and I told him the only way he was going to get it was if he let me check him into rehab and if he started trying to put his life back together. And he could start by telling *you* that he had lied about Danny Oster."

"He admitted it to you? That he had lied?"

"Yes. He told me you would have killed him if he hadn't. The same . . . *crap* he wrote in that letter. And when he saw I wasn't going to budge, he called me a stupid cunt and left."

"Why didn't you tell me this the other night in the car?"

"Why, John? So I could be *right*? I don't want to be right anymore. I want to be able to sit down and have a meal with my brother and talk about what's going on *today*."

He wasn't ready to accept her belief that he hadn't played a hand in Dean's suicide. For the first time in his life, he felt diseased, as if a sickness of his had caused his brother to lie to him, and that same sickness had caused Mike Bowers to lie to him about who he was.

"You wouldn't have killed him, John. He knew that."

"Death isn't always the worst thing that can happen, Patsy."

"No. You're right. It isn't. For the one who gets to die, it's pretty easy."

He knew exactly what she had meant, had groped from the same logic himself in his long nights of mourning a brother who was still sixteen in his mind, but it always seemed to wiggle out of his hands like a wet fish. He got to his feet suddenly, which startled her, and that's when he realized that she had slowly been trying to close the distance between them.

In the darkness, it was impossible to see her face, but he looked right at its shape as he said, "A fate worse than death is life in prison, and that's what Alex is going to get if he kills Duncan, or tries and fails. Mike wouldn't have wanted that. It's the only thing I can be sure of. So I have to stop him."

"How the hell are you going to do that?"

"I need to get to his friend Philip in San Diego. If he didn't go there, Philip might know where he's gone. I need wheels, Patsy."

A long silence settled between them. Then Patsy said, "I'll drive."

She told him to wait for her while she talked to Eddie, collected some things, and got ready. Then she was gone before either of them could say another word about Dean's suicide note or the names he had called her from the grave. He was walking back toward the cabin when something glinted at him from the darkness to his left. He went to the spot, at the edge of the dirt road they had driven in on, and found the shattered casing of a cell phone. Alex's cell phone. He recognized the Samsung logo above the cracked plastic display.

Alex had gone to the effort to back over it more than once.

×

After thirty minutes Patsy called the phone in the outer house and told John to meet her next to the garage. When he got there, he saw that the door was already up, the overhead light was on, and his sister was stepping inside the driver-side door of a battered Toyota Tacoma pickup with a dented camper shell on the back. It sat parked next to a dusty green Ford Explorer that Eddie probably took on more respectable trips than a hunt for a would-be killer.

When he got in the Tacoma's passenger seat, he saw that Patsy had shoved her hair up under a Phoenix Suns cap. But when she turned to pull her seat belt over her, he saw that the back of her neck was covered in brown bristle, and without asking her permission, he reached up and pulled the cap from her head. Startled, she turned and stared at him wide-eyed as he took in the fact that she had chopped off her lustrous brown mane. She looked like a punk rocker, or a woman who needed to disguise herself.

And for what felt like too long, too long considering Alex was probably burning rubber toward his date with death, John fingered the chopped ends of her hair. "They're going to figure out I skipped town," she finally said. "They'll see I made an ATM withdrawal before we left. Pretty soon my face will be all over the news, too."

"He shouldn't have called you all those names," John said.

She shook her head and looked down at the steering wheel as if he had paid her a petty compliment she didn't feel she deserved. Gently, she pulled his hand from her new do and set the hand on his knee, but she didn't let go out of it. "Just tell me I wasn't dead to you and everything should be all right," she said, trying to sound flip and almost pulling it off.

"You weren't."

He knew full well that the things his brother had said about him were far worse than the names he had called their sister. Names were one thing, blame was another, and he had laid that one right at John's feet. Maybe John needed his sister to cry over it for him, or maybe he needed the anger between them to dissipate and there was no other way to do it.

People talked about therapy and change and the power of Christ, but maybe you just had to wake up one day and say you weren't going to do it anymore, you just weren't going to act like someone who felt that way, and you had to begin by saying words that felt strange on your tongue, even if they resonated inside your heart.

"Maybe when this is done, you and I can have a meal." After a few seconds of trying to control her breathing and failing, she closed her fingers around his and nodded, tears spilling down her cheeks, jaw quivering.

She let go of his hand after a while, wiped tears away with the back of one hand. "Sounds good to me," she said, and then she started the engine as if they were on their way to a Sunday BBQ.

But when her eyes passed over his, he saw the fear in them and was reminded that he was not the only one risking everything.

14

Loop 303 took them around the western edge of Phoenix. After just three days in woodsy isolation, the city's massive, twinkling expanse seemed like an alien landscape, one he was unfit to inhabit. He barely knew the city, but Mike's ghost loomed so large in his life now that the entire expanse of it seemed like a graveyard dedicated to him. Somewhere out there were streets Mike had played on as a kid, the university classroom where he had first learned of the Spartans' brave stand at Thermopylae, the alley where he had been beaten and left for dead. Look at any city through the right memories and it could become a graveyard as haunted as a former battlefield.

They had given up listening to the radio because one of them would keep switching to the nearest available news station, which usually led with a report on the two fugitives connected to the gruesome murder of a gay Marine.

They were about an hour from Yuma and two hours from dawn when Patsy pulled off onto a side road that seemed to go nowhere. Inside the camper shell, Patsy made a makeshift cot of grease-stained blankets and whatever else she could find, and John eased himself inside. He watched dawn rise over the Anza Borrego desert through the camper shell's grease-stained windows, knew they were two hours from San Diego and their only possible lead on Alex's whereabouts. Before they had left the house, Patsy had used whitepages.com to find a single listing for a Philip Bloch in San Diego. She had MapQuested the address, which was in University Heights, the same neighborhood where The Catch Trap was, where John had almost abandoned Alex when he had insisted on getting that box of Mike's belongings out of his car.

At a gas station, Patsy bought him a prepaid cell phone—practically untraceable unless law enforcement already knew of the purchase and you were stupid enough to use it for criminal activities for more than forty-eight hours after purchasing it. Considering Patsy had made it out of the gas station shop unscathed, John felt safe dialing Philip's number on it as they pulled out of the gas station's parking lot.

Philip answered after one ring, sounding groggy from sleep. It was nine-thirty. John prayed he had simply worked late or had been up all night worrying about Alex. "Are you being watched?"

"I don't think so."

"Check outside right now. Any Crown Vics or other vehicles hanging around that you don't recognize?"

"No. I checked already. This morning, when they let me go."

"When who let you go?"

"San Diego PD. Hanrock County Sheriff's. It was like a big

party downtown. They had me in an interrogation room all night. I think I made them happy, but they told me not to leave town."

The bottom of John's stomach dropped out, but he knew he couldn't get into it on the phone. "Can you meet me somewhere?"

Silence. Hesitation.

"Is he with you?" Philip asked.

"No. He isn't."

"Tell me what that means."

"I will. If you meet with me."

"Should I bring a gun?"

"I'm not. I lost mine. Someone took it." He prayed this was enough to convey his meaning because he had no interest in getting more specific over the phone. He told Philip he would call him back with a place; then he hung up on him before Philip could come up with a response.

A few minutes later, they were driving past the address for Philip Bloch that Patsy had found online. Philip lived in the second-floor unit of a stucco duplex with mud-colored walls and ornate iron bars over all the windows. A long driveway led to the garage in back, but after a brief scan of the street John was able to confirm Philip's statement that there was nothing that looked like an unmarked car waiting for them outside.

Next John instructed Patsy to head over to Pacific Beach, to a run-down motel where he and some old buddies once rented a room for a weekend when they were fresh out of boot camp. They had spent the weekend chugging Coors while they discussed the prospect of going surfing, which none of them actually knew how to do. Patsy didn't protest when he asked her to go inside and use cash to get a room. She came back with the room number, and John handed her a sheet of paper and told her to take dictation.

Ten minutes later, when Patsy returned from the room she had paid for, John called Philip back. He answered after the first ring, and John gave him the name and address of the hotel and the room number. He hung up just as Philip went to ask another question. Once this series of steps was completed, he started to breathe easier.

At exactly the moment he said he would, thirty minutes from their last phone call, Philip pulled into the motel's parking lot. He was driving a white Ford Escape with all sorts of gay bumper stickers on the rear bumper. Patsy watched him as he went for the room, and John watched out the back of the camper shell to see if Philip had been followed. Traffic on the avenue continued to flow, nothing slowing or stopping or turning to follow Philip into the motel parking lot. A minivan with kids in the backseat turned into the Carl's Jr. across the street, but that was it.

"He just went in," Patsy said as John continued his survey.

Now that he was inside the room, hopefully Philip had picked up the note that Patsy had left for him on one of the bed pillows. Hopefully he was reading John's instructions to get on the 5 and head south for Border Field State Beach, a relatively desolate expanse of coastal chaparral and angry coastline right next to the Mexican border. He was to look for any car that might be tailing him by switching lanes every so often. A following car that was willing to switch to the right lane with him but not back to the left was probably a tail; tails instinctively hated changing lanes into their blind spot and would fall back before doing so. If he saw a tail, he was to call the number for the cell phone John had given him. If not, he was to call when he reached the entrance to the park. And last, he was to wad up the note in one hand and carry it with him to his car to indicate compliance.

Fifteen minutes after he entered the motel room, that's exactly what Philip did. He even raised the wadded-up note in one hand, as if he were waving good-bye to someone he didn't care to look at. Then he got behind the wheel of his car and headed for the 5. They followed.

"Tell me we're not trying to win the sympathy of the border patrol here," Patsy finally said.

"If we stay far enough north of the border, we should be good," John said. And the truth was he needed open space to make sure Philip wasn't being tailed, and he couldn't think of another beach nearby that wouldn't be crawling with surfers on this bright, sunny day. Only the bravest dared enter the treacherous waters off Border Field, a watery graveyard to hundred of immigrants foolish enough to try that doomed crossing. But maybe the choice had been prophetic, because if he failed in what he wanted to do, he might have to cross that border to avoid the consequences.

×

Philip called when he reached the entrance to the park, then made a disgusted sound in his throat when he saw the Tacoma pull up right behind him and realized he had been followed the entire time. John leaped out of the back of the camper shell, phone pressed to his ear, and ordered Philip to unlock his passenger-side door. As soon as he shut the passenger-side door of the Escape, Patsy backed up enough so she could pull a U-turn, then headed out of the park, past the chaparral expanses on either side of Dairy Mart Road, and in the direction of the waiting spot they had picked out in the run-down residential blocks just south of the 5.

Without being distracted by the sight of his new chauffeur, John ordered Philip to drive deeper into the park. Philip kept his mouth shut and followed orders, and soon the whitecap-strewn deep blue of the Pacific appeared ahead. John had been right; all that awaited them was an empty expanse of windblown sand and angry whitecaps. They were a good distance from the border fence that jutted into the ocean, looking pathetically frail given its auspicious purpose.

He told Philip to stop. The guy's eyes were bloodshot, and he looked like he had shed a few pounds since John had last seen him. But he was freshly showered, his hair a wet pile on his head, and was giving off the scent of lotion that smelled like the stench someone might get from dousing roses in pineapple juice.

"What happened to your arm?" Philip asked.

"Let's get out. I've got a better view that way."

"Don't you want to stay hidden?" Philip said.

"I do, but I need to see if anyone's coming."

"And if someone is?"

"Then you're going to drive this thing straight for the border fence while I head in the other direction."

Philip glared at him. "And why would I do that?"

"Because the alternative is Alex spends the rest of his life in jail for murder."

Philip stepped out of the car. John followed suit, walking slowly around the nose of the SUV until his back was to the roaring ocean, and Philip was backed up against the grille, arms folded over his chest, refusing to look in John's eyes, like a defiant child.

"Where is he?" Philip finally asked.

"I was hoping you could help me with that. I need to know if he has any other friends he would run to—"

"Why did he *run*?" Philip snapped. "If you were protecting him, why did he run from you?"

"Because I think somebody called him and told him what had been done to Mike's body and it sent him into a state of rage. And now he's out there with my gun, which apparently he already knows how to fire. Do you know who taught him to fire a gun, Philip?"

"Well, I sure as hell didn't call him. As for teaching him to shoot, my guess would be the other Marine in his life. They were two fag boys living in the middle of Hicksville. I imagine it was a skill he needed."

"You use that word a lot more often than I do," John said.

"Which one? *Fag*? You barely know me, so it's not like you've had time to count." They were circling the source of anger between them and getting nowhere fast, so John decided to plow right in.

"The police kept you all night? You must have given them quite a story."

"I didn't tell them a damn thing you told me. I just told them that you came to the club looking for Alex. I told them that you and Alex had had some sort of fight and you didn't make it clear what it was about. I told them that you two left together. I was just confirming what they already knew. They questioned everyone at the club."

"How did they get to the club in the first place?"

"The same way you did. They knew Alex used to work there."

"Is that all you told them?"

Philip exhaled loudly, tongued his upper lip briefly, and crossed his arms more tightly against his chest. "I told them Alex always had a thing for Marines—butch, straight-acting Marines like yourself. I thought it was better to let them believe you guys were fucking than to tell them what you told me. Then they started asking me questions about Alex's history. Other men he had dated. Where he might be. The same questions you're about to ask me, it sounds like."

John couldn't avoid the contempt Philip had for him; it was as naked as Alex's anger toward him during that first phone call, before Alex had believed Mike to be dead. True, he had never made much of an effort to prove himself to Philip, and that would probably be impossible now, given that Alex had fled his protection and given that the resentment radiating off Philip's very being seemed ingrained. But it struck John as pathetic, full of defeat, or, at least, the perception of it, as if Philip believed John had already beaten him to a pulp and the only recourse he had was to pop off some nasty remarks about it. Could Philip not see that John was the one with the broken arm, the one who stank of auto grease?

"They asked you about other people in Alex's life?" John asked.

"Yes. I told them there hadn't been any other men in Alex's life for the past three years because he gave his entire life to Mike. Even when Mike was in Iraq, there was no one else. No one. And I told them that Alex was not capable of murder. On any level!"

"And me? Did they ask about me?"

"Of course they did, and I said I didn't know you at all." It sounded like an insult. John turned away, scanned the beach and the distant fence, the expanse of wind-whipped chaparral leading off in the direction from which they had come.

"Alex isn't capable of killing anyone," Philip said, as if John's silence had begged the question. John stayed silent, didn't mention the reenactment the day before, replete with smashed beer bottles and a lead pipe. "The only reason he went with you was to prove his manhood. That's all. Shit, after all the time they spent together, Alex got as caught up in that macho Marine Corps bullshit as Mike was."

"How did I get such a big role in his life?"

"For Christ's sake, you were practically the other man. He lost his shit when Mike asked if he could invite you up to the house."

"What? He thought Mike and I would run off together?"

"No. He thought you had power. The power to make Mike pretend he was straight again, even if it meant kicking Alex to the curb. It's not like it would have been the first time he'd been thrown out. His parents did the same thing when they found out he was a fag. They stopped paying his tuition, cut him out of their life insurance policy." They had also left him a luxurious cabin in the mountains for him and his boyfriend to play around in, but mentioning this wasn't about to get Philip on his side. "So, in walks this big, hot Marine, and Alex just gives him his entire life. He gave up on everything else."

"He said he made a decision," John said.

"What the hell does that mean?"

"Most people call it a *commitment,*" John fired back. "Now, I'm sorry he didn't make it to you, but maybe if you care about him enough to get over it, you'll start telling me where the fuck he could have gone!"

This outburst stilled Philip. At first John thought the guy had been mortified by his anger. Then in a gentle voice Philip said, "A commitment, huh? Pretty soon you'll be calling it a marriage. You've come a long way in a short time, John Houck."

"Maybe not such a long way. You saw what they're saying about me on the news."

"They're not saying it."

"They're implying it."

"True," Philip said. Then, after studying John for a few tense seconds, he said, "I don't know where he could have gone, John. That's the truth. I've told you all I know. Christ, I've told you all I *want* to know."

✕

Philip dropped him off at the entrance to the park and he walked the few blocks to where Patsy was waiting for him on a wide street, lined with one-story tract homes, that had an expansive view of the roaring freeway. After he finished telling her his new plan, she let her hands slip from the steering wheel and into her lap and gazed out the windshield as if she had just been given a terminal diagnosis.

"She's probably got reporters all over her house," she said.

"I doubt she invited them inside. And that will just make her place easier to find."

"You're a bigger part of the story than she is. How do you plan on getting through them?"

"I'll get her to meet with me."

"I have money, John." She let this hang in the air between them, and then looked away from him nervously. "We can turn ourselves in, hire us a good lawyer—"

"And where does that leave Alex?"

"Wherever the hell he chooses to be. That's where it leaves him."

"Tell me you didn't come with me just so you could convince me to give up."

"All right, let's say you get to his mother. She'll turn you in—"

"Not if I tell her I know where her son is, and I'll only tell her if she doesn't call the police on me."

"Right. A son she doesn't care about—"

"Then why is she using phrases like 'my only son' and 'he left my life'? Alex wanted me to think she was a bitch because there's a story there and he didn't want me to know the other side of it."

"So there's a story there. Fine. How's that going to help you find him?"

"Because Philip stood out on that beach and told me that Alex has no friends, no people in his life other than Philip. I think that means something happened in Cathedral Beach, and it was bigger than Alex coming out of the closet. I think it involved people in Alex's life that Philip never knew about."

"And you think one of them is hiding him?"

"Maybe," he said. "But the other option is we try to shadow Duncan until Alex shows up with my gun. So why don't you take your pick?"

After a few seconds, she started the engine. "We should wait until dark. I'll find someplace we can stay parked until then. It's supposed to rain tonight, too, but I guess it's not the time to shop for a cute umbrella."

John said, "Get me a good raincoat and we'll call it even."

×

Two news vans sat parked across the street from a salmon-colored mansion with a peaked, red-tiled roof visible above the fifteen-foot stone walls that bordered the front of the property. Palm trees the size of small high-rises sprang up on the other side of the walls. John thought they looked like a piss-poor attempt to distract from the fact that the house was built like a fortress, like they were intended to suggest there was a tropical paradise on the other side. But apparently it looked great on film because two different reporters addressed their camera crews with the pink palace as their backdrop. They wore brightly colored raincoats and stood under the cover of jerry-rigged tarps.

John's heart skipped a beat as he realized they were reporting on him. But then he was able to stabilize it with deep breaths. Patsy didn't seem to be having any such luck. From where he lay, stuffed into his large raincoat, his cast already plastic-wrapped, he could see her through the open back window. Her baseball cap was shoved down over her head but she was glancing every which way, as if trying to determine which direction each raindrop was coming from.

Patsy pulled off onto a side street lined with a hodgepodge of Cape Cod–style cottages, Spanish mission revivals, and Victorians. Vine-laced white picket fences ran next door to wrought-iron gates, as if every kind of rich person's architecture in the world had come to Cathedral Beach to retire.

The number he had for Charlotte came from information, and

he was confident she wasn't going to answer it herself. It was a pretentiously accented male voice on the answering machine, probably a butler or assistant, unless Charlotte had gotten remarried without Alex or anyone in the news media finding out about it. Butler it was, John realized, when the message finished with, "Mrs. Martin asks that in light of recent events, the news media respect her privacy. Public comments will be made only at the appropriate times and the media will be well advised beforehand. Thank you and good day."

After the beep John said, "Your son hasn't killed anyone but he will if I don't stop him. Only you can help me do that." He gave her the number for the phone and hung up.

Patsy had nothing to contribute from the front seat. For a long while—almost twenty minutes—they listened to the rain hammering against the truck. Finally Patsy said, "Maybe you should try again."

He did, and once again the machine picked up. John said, "Alex said you threw him out because he was gay. I don't buy it. I think he did something, something that hurt you. That's why you still call him 'your *only* son.' That's why you told the media 'he *left* your life.'"

Fifteen minutes later, the phone rang. Patsy jumped, then spun in her seat. John answered without saying a word. The person on the other end of the line said, "Who is this?" The woman's voice was soft but insistent, like a kindergarten teacher's.

"My name is John Houck." Silence from the other end. Patsy's grimace told him she thought this was a bad move.

Charlotte Martin said, "Is my son with you?"

"No. He's not."

"Then how may I help you, Mr. Houck?"

"I need you to meet with me."

"I've been led to believe that you're a dangerous man," she said quietly, and with what sounded like only mild offense, as if someone has asked her to dance to a fast song.

"Your son is being framed for murder, and if I don't stop him, he's going to kill the man who's trying to frame him."

"And who would that man be?"

"You can pick the place."

"As I have said already, I've been led to believe that you are a dang—"

"What's dangerous is that your son is out there with my Sig Sauer, which he knows how to fire, and a Ka-bar knife, and no one knows where the hell he's gone. Now, you can look at this in one of two ways. You might have information that could help me find him before he does something profoundly stupid. Or if it's really true that he *left* your life, maybe this is an opportunity to get him back."

"This is *very* strange," she whispered. "Very, *very* strange." He felt like saying that her tone sounded strange. He couldn't tell if it was sarcasm or genuine anger. Maybe being kept prisoner in her own home had kicked a dent in her composure. He hoped so, and went in for the kill. "There are two news vans across the street. The map says there's a nature trail behind your house, but I can bet you there's some reporters camped out there, too. If you need me to find you a way past them, I can."

"Do you know where the Alhambra Hotel is?" she asked him. They had passed it on the way to her house, a seven-story pink adobe building with a lighted gold dome. He told her he did, and she said, "There's a big lawn just downhill from it, right on the water. There's a bench there. Sit there until someone comes for you."

"Not someone. *You*."

She had hung up on him.

15

The crescent-shaped lawn below the Alhambra Hotel was empty. Just as Charlotte had told him, there were several benches lining a curving path. Beyond a white clapboard fence, rocky outcroppings jutted out into the sea. The beach where Alex and Mike had taken their first dive into the ocean together had to be nearby, but he couldn't see it through the fog. At one corner of the lawn was a darkened clubhouse with a bridge club schedule on a hand-painted sign out front. John took shelter against one corner of the structure, assessing the consequences of following Charlotte Martin's order.

Because he was confident it was a test, he sat down on the bench for about a minute. Then he got up, walked back to the clubhouse, and scanned the darkened coastal drive on the other side of the broad lawn for approaching cars. Just above the street, the bottom of the Alhambra's property line was marked by a white clapboard wall topped with lattice panels. Above that, the flat rooftops of what looked like villas were clustered around an open space John figured was the hotel's swimming pool. When he was confident he had another opening, he went back to the bench, sat down on it, and stared stupidly out at the roiling ocean until he felt eyes on the back of his neck.

They were a foot apart when the approaching stranger tilted his umbrella back, revealing cueball eyes and a bushy brown mustache. "Your name is Mr. Smith," he said, and it took John a second to realize it wasn't a question. "My name is Franklin, and Mrs. Martin has asked me to tell you that as night manager of the Alhambra Hotel I have explored all the various definitions one can find for the word *discretion*. So if you could please—"

And then he recognized John, and the mirth left his expression. His lips parted, but nothing came out as he realized he was standing a foot away from a fugitive connected to a gruesome murder currently all over the news and all over his town. But Franklin said no more, and John fought the urge to ask the man if he had just come up with another definition of the word *discretion*.

"With me, please," he said. John followed the umbrella across the lawn, then across the street and through a service entrance. Then they were moving through a narrow, rain-soaked alley, past a row of Dumpsters and then through an open door to what looked like the hotel's brightly lit kitchen. "You might want to keep your head down," Franklin said politely, even though John still had his hood on. Another doorway brought them to an interior staircase with a dark green carpet that had white blossoms printed all over it.

John smelled stale perfume mixed with cigarette smoke, then

the smells of cooked meat coming from room-service trays that had been left outside the doors to rooms. Being rich meant you could discard odors the way normal people discard old socks.

On the seventh floor, Franklin held up a hand and stepped out into the hallway. Once he was confident the coast was clear, he waved John through, and John felt as if he were on his way to a sexual rendezvous with a married woman.

The walls and doors were mahogany with brass fixtures, and the Oriental carpet that ran the length of the halls was run through with dark blues and reds. Unlike the other floors he had glimpsed on the way up, this one seemed to have been preserved in the period of the hotel's construction, and the doors were spaced far enough apart to let him know that they were suites. At the end of the hallway they came to a second staircase, with a dark wood railing and a red velvet rope blocking the bottom step. Franklin unhooked the rope, noticed John's hesitation, and said, "The Soledad Room is closed this evening."

He nodded, followed Franklin up the stairs. At the top step, they entered an expansive square room that seemed to take up the entire eighth floor. The walls were half plate-glass windows. Off to his left, he could see the cove and its bluff lined with mansions, their security lights fogged with shifting halos by the lingering mist. Two rows of tables, cleared of everything except their white tablecloths, ran down the center of the room. Booths lined the walls, their backs low so as not to block anyone's view.

Charlotte Martin was sitting in a booth in the far corner, a view of the whitecap-strewn ocean visible behind her. Someone, probably Franklin, had lit several tea candles on the table in front of her. The only other illumination came from the massive lighted gold dome that covered the hotel's roof; it bathed the borders of the room in a dull glow.

As he approached her table, Charlotte Martin rose to her feet slowly and extended her hand. Her hair was slightly mussed, as if she had just stepped out of her private plane. Her black turtleneck sweater gave her curves without giving them away. He figured she had had several face-lifts, but he couldn't tell where any of them began or ended.

John took a seat, expected her to break the ice, but instead she looked out the window to her left. John followed her vision to where the street in front of her mansion was lit up by the bright lights of news cameras. The reporters camped out in front of her home were all about to go live for their eleven o'clock newscasts. From this height, he could see the mansion's long, rectangular swimming pool, could see the floor-to-ceiling windows, covered by blackout curtains, that looked out onto it. How had she gotten out?

"What does *soledad* mean?" John asked.

"Loneliness," she said quickly, as if she were pleasantly surprised that he had asked the question. "Which is, I guess, what an intellectual might refer to as *irony,* given that this could be such a romantic room under different circumstances. Of course, there's a nearby mountain with the same name, so it kind of kills the joke, don't you think? Can I get you a drink?"

"I'd rather it just be the two of us."

"There's a bar right over there. I'd be more than happy to make you one myself."

"No, thank you."

"I see. You want to stay alert, is that it? You're afraid I might try to gay-bash you with my right shoe?" Instead of answering, he took the time to register that she had bought into the implication on the news that he and Alex were a couple. He decided to let her believe this because of what it might reveal about her. When he didn't respond, she returned her attention to the view of her house below. "They're nice enough, I guess. Earlier I went to visit my mother-in-law in the hospital and they didn't try to *shock* me the way they did the first time. See, I'm learning that's what they do. They just shout the most insane question they can think of to get your attention. This morning one of them asked me if I thought my son practiced unsafe sex." She laughed into her drink before downing a quick swallow of it.

"Your mother-in-law is sick?" he asked.

"Alex didn't tell you?"

John was about to answer when he realized Alex had indeed told him that his grandmother was dying, just a few nights earlier as they sped past highway signs for this very place. "Are you in love with my son?" she asked him. When she saw how startled he was by this question, she set down her drink and crossed her arms in front of her. "I think it's a fair question, given the lengths you're going for him."

His first instinct was to say he hadn't known Alex long enough to be in love with him. This was the safe way out, the politician's answer. But he needed Charlotte to stay polite for as long as possible, and it seemed to him she was more likely to do that if she thought she needed to prove to her son's lover she wasn't a homo hater. "Yes," he heard himself answer. Once the word left his mouth, he felt a stab in his gut, as if just muttering this response would make it true. But then he saw that the reality around him had not shifted in the course of a single word—the tea candles still flickered, the mist still crawled over the shore below, and the smooth swell Charlotte Martin's breasts made against her sweater threatened to draw his attention as much as her words.

"Well, then, you should know that he's a very determined young man. And from the look of things, he's not very interested in doing things your way."

"He's mad as hell and has been for a long time. I'm not sure if that's the same thing as being determined."

"And you blame me for that?" He decided to let her twist on this one, wanted to see if she was a woman prone to defending herself. She cleared her throat and sat forward. "I see. So it's all my fault. Perhaps he would have preferred to have been born in my hometown. I'm sure he would have just adored Colton, where I would have been a career waitress, and a sensitive young man like him would been beaten to a pulp every day on the way to school."

"So you married well."

"People take expressions like that for granted, Mr. Houck. Married well. As if all I did was buy the right hat. There are so many years, choices, sacrifices, and disappointments that go along with *marrying well*. More than thirty years ago I was cleaning up after a drunk who told me that girls with legs as good as mine didn't need to attend college. Tomorrow morning I will be hosting the Sisters of Light charity luncheon in the lower ballroom of this hotel, regardless of whether the news media decide to make an appearance. Over the past five years I've raised almost twenty million dollars for that organization. One of my board members told me just the other day that at the rate I'm going, leukemia might become an ancient memory in our lifetime." She studied him for a few seconds. "I take it you're not impressed."

"It sounds like good work," he said quietly.

She didn't seem convinced by his tone. "So tell me, what is this *story* my son told you?"

"It's short. You found out he was gay, and then you cut him off and threw him out."

Her glare was so steady he had to fight the urge to shift in his seat. She uncrossed her arms and leaned back into the booth. She took a sip of her drink, then set the glass down gently, as if she were afraid it might break from the tension of her grip.

"My son had an affair with a married man. This man was not only one of my husband's business partners, he also had two children and lived several blocks away from us. When his wife found out about the affair, she tried to kill herself. She wasn't successful. When she came to, she hired a good lawyer and took her husband for almost everything he was worth, thus killing a thirty-million-dollar beach resort project *my* husband had been working on for five years.

"When I confronted Alex about all of this, he looked me dead in the eye and told me that he thought I would prefer that he sleep with a married man from Cathedral Beach rather than some fag he picked up in a bar. Those were his exact words, by the way, lest you should accuse me of *homophobia*."

Along with confusion, John felt shame and embarrassment for Alex, because there was no denying that the story fit with so much of what he had already learned about him. What had Philip said? Would we be here if Alex could love someone like him? Before Mike, it had been a married man old enough to be Alex's father.

"As for my son being cut off? It's true we decided to withdraw our financial support of his education. We thought it only fair that if he was going to go around screwing up his father's business deals by thinking with his groin, then he should be on his own for a while. Learn the real value of a dollar." She stopped suddenly as if she didn't like the taste of her own words. "Has he? Learned the value of a dollar, I mean."

"He's been too busy learning the value of a gun."

"And who's been teaching him that lesson, Mr. Houck?" John kept his mouth shut and gave her a weak smile that hurt his cheeks. "I see—so you have other vested interests here. If my son actually does decide to pull the trigger on—I'm sorry, just *who* is it that's framing him for murder again?" She furrowed her brow deliberately, held her hands out as if she were waiting to hear the price of a lousy haircut.

"If you want to talk names, why don't you give me the name of your husband's former business partner?"

"You don't honestly believe this man is harboring my son, do you? He left Cathedral Beach years ago. I wouldn't be surprised if he's dead drunk in a gutter somewhere."

"You didn't know about the affair until his wife found about it, so I'm not putting any stock in what you know."

She flinched at the bite in his voice. "I'm sorry, Mr. Houck. Did I hurt your feelings? I just assumed, since you're a man who's been trained to kill with his bare hands, that you would find all these sordid matters of the heart to be superficial and petty. Amusing even."

"Alex said you were a bitch. I was hoping he was wrong."

"My son enjoys telling lies to get what he wants. And it sounds like his victim routine worked on you quite well." She gestured to him with an open hand, took a drink with the other. Even though she didn't know the truth of his relationship with her son, John felt the bite in her words.

"You flew into a rage at your son because he screwed up your access to millions of dollars you didn't need. And you faking a lot of self-righteous moral indignation strikes me as funny, 'cause you're the one who's got a system worked out for meeting strange men at nice hotels late at night—a system so good it can get you past three news crews who would kill for a sound bite."

Her strained laughter didn't quite make it past her throat. She took a deep breath and said, "And *you*, Mr. Houck, are *in love*." She drew out the last word as if she were mocking the concept of love itself. "That's the only way I can see a man like you buying into this kind of victim-driven nonsense."

"Give me the name of—"

"Arthur Walken," she snapped. "Developer, cheat, and lover of young boys. Last I heard he had relocated to Chicago." Her words were rushed, breathless. He couldn't tell if divulging Arthur Walken's name angered her, or if she were still smarting from the implication that she had affairs of her own, an implication she had not responded to. "Can you really see a thin-skinned young man like my son hiding out in the Midwest? I can't. He's not cut out for snow. You know, regardless of how I feel about the choices my son has made in his life, I have nothing against homosexuals. Nothing, truly. But I'm not a fan of the *oppressed,* the *victimized.* When an entire group of people come together and try to make some kind of identity out of what they don't have, they usually end up convincing themselves they can do whatever they damn well please."

Suddenly John was no longer in the Soledad Room. He was back in his trailer, listening to these very same words come out of Ray Duncan's mouth. He had heard the sentiment before, dozens of times, about blacks, Mexicans, even the Army, but Charlotte's phrasing had been almost identical to Ray's. Had he mentioned Duncan's name yet? No. He hadn't wanted to come off as a complete loony from the get-go by trying to convince her that a real cop was tied up in all this.

"Is that all you wanted?" she asked.

"Just about."

"Well, if you do find him, there's something else he should know, something you might be able to tell him that would convince him to stop all this nonsense." John responded to her dramatic pause by raising one eyebrow. "He's about to inherit fifteen million dollars." She let this sink in as she took a sip of her drink. "His grandmother is ill, as I told you, and Alex is named as the secondary beneficiary on her life insurance policy. Alex's father was the primary of course, but given that he died first, all that money goes to Alex. And maybe to you as well—if things work out, of course." She gave him a mock toast. "Congratulations, Mr. Houck. It looks like you've married quite well."

"Does Alex know this?"

"Of course not. He's too ashamed to come back here, too ashamed to visit his grandmother on her deathbed."

"But you aren't. You visited her just today, didn't you?"

"I did."

"That must mean there's something in it for you, too."

"My mother died when I was thirteen. Suzanna Martin is the only mother I've ever had."

"And let me guess: you're the third beneficiary."

"I am. But I'll never see any of—" She stopped speaking instantly, as if she had been struck with a small stroke, but everything about her composure remained intact until she cocked her head to one side, as if John had told a riddle.

"Your son is implicated in first-degree murder right around the time he is supposed to inherit fifteen million dollars. Are you not putting this together? How many of those goddamn drinks have you had, lady?"

Charlotte snorted and shook one hand at him, the prim schoolteacher once again. "Mr. Houck, if you're going to imply that I'm playing some kind of—"

"How much time have you spent in Owensville?"

"My husband used to keep a place there. Plenty of time, I'd say."

"Ask me again."

"Excuse me?"

"Ask me again who I think is trying to frame your son for murder."

She didn't comply, but she stopped stroking the side of her glass with her index and ring fingers.

"Ray Duncan," John said.

She gently closed her eyes and sucked in a short breath through her nose. Stripped of the title of captain, the name was still familiar to her. A laugh caught in her throat.

"Ray?" she asked incredulously. But her use of the man's first name and her strained attempt at humor only further convinced John that he had landed on the right track.

Slowly she placed both hands on the tablecloth in front of her and rose to her feet. She collected her raincoat off the seat next to her, then her umbrella from where it was leaning against the edge of the table. John didn't move as she walked past his chair, down the empty aisle between empty tables, taking her time fastening the buttons on her raincoat, her head bowed as if the act required every bit of her concentration.

John continued. "He's missing a piece of his thumb, isn't he? I don't know. Maybe it's just a blister or maybe it's something more permanent. He hasn't been able to use his right thumb for a while. That's all I'm saying. It gives him a distinctive handprint, especially when he's got blood on his hands. Was it some kind of accident? Maybe he tried to get your pants off too quickly?"

She stopped walking, her back to him, continued fastening the buttons on her coat. John got out of his chair and started closing the distance between them. He expected her to start moving again when she heard his footsteps, but she had gone stock still, so still he wondered if when she turned to face him again she would have another person's face.

"What did my son do to deserve you?" she asked.

The hard edge had left her voice; he saw an opportunity to break her, if he didn't move too fast. He said, "Your son gave up everything for something he believed in. At first I thought he and Mike were hiding out up there on that mountain, and maybe they were. But I think they wanted to be someplace where they could be . . . good to each other. I used to be like you. I used to think men like Alex and Mike just took whatever they wanted. But Mike and Alex tried to *build* something together. And I have no choice but to respect that."

She turned to face him, looking genuinely astonished by this speech. "And how exactly are you respecting that, young man? It sounds like you're the one who broke up their little marriage."

"I've never had a sexual thought about another man. You just assumed that, and I let you because apparently you can't understand that anyone would care about your son without wanting to fuck him."

"That's a lie," she whispered.

"Good. Then pick up that phone right there and call the Hanrock County Sheriff's Department and tell them that you have been having sex with Captain Ray Duncan." Her open hand caught him across the jaw. She went to pinwheel her other arm but he managed to grab her wrist in his left hand and hold up his cast for protection. They stumbled backward for a few steps like dancing partners that had knocked into another couple. Then John's butt hit the edge of a table and stopped their momentum enough for him to get his balance back.

"How long?'" John asked her. For a while she didn't answer, just struggled to catch her breath, then swept her bangs back from her forehead. "How long have you been sleeping with Ray Duncan?"

"I kept it away from the house!" she shouted. "Alex shit in our own backyard, but I kept it away from the house!"

A *long time* he realized—long enough that revealing the affair to anyone would jeopardize her standing in her mother-in-law's will, make her seem like a hypocrite in front of her only son, to say nothing of the Sisters of Light charity luncheon the following morning, which could go on without a hitch if everyone believed Charlotte's only son had willfully left his mother's positive influence years before and wandered down a deviant path.

"You have an obligation to tell the Hanrock County Sheriff's Department about your affair."

"I have an obligation to *my life*! The life I built on my back under men who couldn't remember my name. Henry had his women. They usually worked for him, and I never *asked* for their names. And no matter what hell Alex chooses to put himself through, he will never have to make the sacrifices I did to get us *here*." She threw her arms out to indicate not just their opulent surroundings but also the entire town. "He thinks he is so strong, and so brave, to have held up under the weight of my disapproval. That's because he has never had to face anything worse than disapproval in his entire life!"

"He's facing it now!" John shouted. "He's out there, on the run, alone, while you're standing here making speeches about a fucking beach community, lady!"

She shook her head violently, waved both hands in front of her face. "My obligation to my son was fulfilled long ago. He walked away from everything I gave him. Everything!" He let the after-effects of her fury linger in the room. When she heard them, she seemed to weaken. She went for the nearest chair, then held its back in one hand, as if sitting down in it would have been an unacceptable form of surrender.

"Does Ray know about the life insurance policy?"

For a while she just stared at him, shaking her head slightly, her eyes full of tears. "This is a fantasy," she whispered. "Ray's not capable of any of this. You've brought me a fantasy, and you're trying to ruin my life with it. You don't even know me, and you aren't fucking my son. Why would you do this to me?"

"Does Ray know about the fifteen million dollars?"

This time the question hit closer to the target. She covered her face in her hands, sagged against the back of the chair. A show for his benefit? He didn't know. He didn't care. What he knew was that he needed to take decisive action, and cutting through this woman's layers of self-serving bullshit would take him another decade. She knew the truth and she wouldn't divulge it, and she was rich enough to float high above men like John on a magic carpet of influence and first-rate legal representation.

Charlotte stopped her piteous sobs when she saw that John was headed for the host stand. Then he put his hand on the phone, and she let out something between a shriek and a groan. She lunged at him, but he managed to grab the collar of her raincoat in his left hand before she made impact. He shoved her backward, and she almost fell over before grabbing the chair she had been holding earlier for support. Her eyes were huge, as if the threat of violence offered some sort of unexpected reprieve from her own self-loathing.

John called the prepaid cell phone Patsy was carrying. She answered after the first ring. "Get out of town. Now. Go back to where we came from and stay there." He hung up on her, as she started shouting.

Then he dialed 911. When the dispatcher answered, he said, "My name is John Houck. The police will be able to find me on the lawn below the Alhambra Hotel in Cathedral Beach. My right arm is in a cast and I'll be wearing a black raincoat. I'm not armed and I would like to turn myself in."

"What are you turning yourself in for, sir?"

"The murder of Mike Bowers."

He hung up on her. Charlotte let out a short startled breath. He nodded at her and started for the stairs. She was behind him in an instant. "What the hell is this?" she said. "Are you trying to teach me a lesson? Is that it?" She stopped at the top step as he started down the stairs to the seventh-floor hallway. "Oh, so you're a regular martyr, is that it? What does that make me, John Houck? *Answer me,* you white-trash piece of shit!"

At the bottom of the stairs, he stopped where he was and turned to look up at her. Her head had been turned into a silhouette by the chandelier directly overhead. "Lady, there are too many words for what you are, and not enough for what you don't have."

She didn't follow him any farther, and as he moved down the seventh-floor hallway to the staircase Franklin had brought him up an hour before, he heard the low, distant thumping of an approaching helicopter.

By the time he reached the lawn below the hotel, sirens were wailing in the distance and a searchlight was traveling toward him through the veils of mist that still hung over the cove. Then he was blinded by its halo as the San Diego PD helicopter banked hard and started circling above him. The first officers to leap from their cars did so with revolvers drawn, and as they moved in on him he looked up to see the police helicopter's searchlight strobe the plate-glass windows of the Soledad Room.

Charlotte Martin looked down on the entire scene like just another hotel guest who had been awakened by a roar in the middle of the night.

16

The small motorcade went north on the 5, pursued by several news helicopters. Their searchlights blazed through the interior of the car every few minutes, turning the two cops in the front seat into ghostly silhouettes. Five cars in all, two in front and two in back of the one John rode in. Their bridge lights were on but their sirens were silent.

He had spent three hours in the Cathedral Beach sheriff's station. He had been read his rights, but no one had questioned him. No one had even spoken to him or engaged him in a way that had required him to play the role of cold-blooded killer. Silence and an interrogation room, until a deputy had informed him that he was being transported to Boswell.

Two more news helicopters joined the swarm as they rode

through Los Angeles, then fell away just north of Santa Clarita as they traveled up into the mountainous section of the 5 known as the Grapevine. John felt fear for the first time, as if the sudden darkness of the surrounding landscape were a great sea and he was being pulled farther from shore, away from the courage of his convictions and closer to Captain Ray Duncan.

In the hours before dawn, the city of Boswell was desolate, a tiny cluster of stubby concrete-and-glass high-rises surrounded by the uninterrupted night darkness of the San Joaquin Valley. Somewhere to the west were the mountains that cradled Owensville, but there was no making them out at this hour of the night, and this dusty, scorched industrial town seemed to bear no relation to that woodsy idyll.

He was fighting to stay awake when a heavyset man came into the interrogation room alone and introduced himself as Detective Barkin. A uniformed sheriff's deputy had already been in to set up a small camcorder and tripod. Barkin took a seat right next to it so he was safely out of the frame and John was the star. The detective was about one hundred pounds overweight, his immense girth splitting his denim, silver-buttoned long-sleeved shirt. His bushy salt-and-pepper mustache matched the fringe of hair around his bald head.

"Where's Ray Duncan?" John asked.

"I'm sorry. You were expecting him to be here?"

"I owe him an apology," John answered. "The night I killed Mike, I tried to convince him that someone else had done it, and he believed me. He even let me go without charging me with anything. I figure if I'm coming clean about everything . . ." He allowed himself to trail off, lifted his eyes from the table to the detective. "I'm sorry. Were you not aware that Ray Duncan questioned me that night?"

The detective gave him a weak smile, flipped back some sheets on his yellow legal pad, and studied chicken scratch notes. He could clearly sense that John was baiting him, and he was in no mood for it. "Let's roll it back a bit, shall we?"

So John did just that. Staring down at the table as if he were working to remember each event he described, he told the detective how he had driven to Mike's house in Owensville that night to give him a gift for having saved his life in combat and having been one of the best Marines he had ever met. He described how he had been forced to ask for directions, described the female gas station attendant in detail, and saw the detective listen more intently as he did so. Then he described how he found the driveway to the house and walked up it. He described how he went to one of the front windows, peered through, and saw something that sickened him to the point of rage.

John paused for effect.

"What did you see, John?"

"At first I couldn't tell what it was. But I kept looking in, and that's when I saw—Bowers was on his back on the couch, and this other guy—Alex—"

"Did you know that at the time?"

"Know what?"

"That it was Alex Martin."

"Hell, no. I'd never seen Alex before in my life."

Barkin nodded and gestured for him to continue. "They were fucking. He was just fucking him in the ass, right there on the living-room couch—" He forced himself to see the scene he had confronted when he walked into his younger brother's room that day: Oster's freckled, hairy ass, and his brother's legs spread in the man's hands. He forced himself to forget what he had learned about this scene and drew it back to him just as it had played out in his mind for almost a decade. A rape, a violation. "I couldn't believe it. It was . . . it didn't look human."

Barkin grunted slightly—almost sympathetically, it seemed.

Then he described how he sneaked inside the house after Mike went upstairs to the bathroom to clean up. He described how his first plan had been to murder Alex for violating his buddy. Then he described how he watched Alex discover a plastic bottle of something on the kitchen counter, how he smelled it and jerked it away from his face and hid it in a lower cabinet. He described how he waited for Alex to leave the room, and went for the bottle, realized it was GHB, which he had once taken during a wild weekend. He described how he poured some into Alex's drink, knowing full well the combination of liquor and the drug would knock Alex flat in a few minutes, leaving him alone with Mike without having to get his hands bloody first.

He described how he hid in one of the back rooms after he spiked Alex's drink, listened to the sounds of the two men passing each other on the stairway, waiting until he heard the thud of Alex collapsing in the living room. Then he described how he went for the stairs just as the sound of Alex collapsing drew Mike from the master bedroom.

"He was coming out of the bedroom when I got him," John said, staring at a spot on the wall just past Barkin's right shoulder.

The memory of what he had actually seen in that messy bedroom collided with the fictional version he was trying to sell, and he fell silent, trying to drive down any genuine emotion that might come into his voice, drive it down where he could harden it into something that sounded merciless and cold.

His eyes on the table, he described how he had panicked as the blood from Mike's chest had poured down his naked torso, how he came out of his rage and realized what he had done. Then he scrambled to get the body out of the house, wrapped it in the sheets that were on the bed and carried it to a woodshed he had spotted next to the gravel path that led to the house. He wanted to make sure he cleaned the scene down as best as he could before he loaded everything into his truck and left. He went back to the house and was barely finished wiping up the bedroom when he heard Alex at the bottom of the stairs. He'd awakened much earlier than John had expected him to, so John flipped out and pulled the gun on him, chased him out into the woods, and was planning on killing him as soon as he caught up with him, but he didn't want to start popping off shots that would draw the attention of the neighbors.

He described how they fought in the creek, then on the slope, how Alex begged for his life, kept asking for Mike, kept asking where Mike was. He described how he lost his nerve at that moment, described how he realized Alex didn't have the slightest idea what John had done.

When he realized he had cleaned the scene, he saw a way out. He saw a way to try to make it better, so he marched Alex back to the house, harassed him as if he were guilty of Mike's murder, claiming ignorance as to who Alex truly was. Then the rest of what he described was what had actually happened, how Alex had showed him the photographs on the wall of Mike sitting in the middle of a gay bar. He described how Duncan had brought him in for questioning and then released him to his own vehicle. At best, his account made Duncan sound like a sloppy small-town cop who didn't want any inconvenience in his town.

When John stopped, when enough silence passed between the two men that the detective realized that John was finished with his version of the story, Barkin rocked back in his chair, tapped his pen against the pad, and chewed his lower lip.

"So you drive all the way to your buddy's house in the middle of the night just to give him a present," Barkin said carefully. "Then when you see him and Alex going at it, you stand there and watch the whole thing. How long did you stand there?"

"I don't know," John said, purposefully sounding annoyed. He hadn't expected this part of the story to be believed—that was part of his plan.

"Yeah, well, me neither. 'Cause, see, what I'm sitting here thinking is that you weren't acting like a guy who was just mad, John. You were acting like a guy who was jealous. Now, who you were jealous of, I'm not quite sure. Are you?"

"Jealous?" John asked, as if he had never heard the word before, as if it had no place in the story he had just told. He shot a nervous glance at the camcorder, intended to convey the anxiety of someone who had just realized that a half truth wasn't going to be enough.

"Yeah, John. *Jealous*. Jealous like maybe you wanted to be doing what you saw those two doing on the living-room couch."

"Bullshit!" John hissed through clenched teeth, but he was staring at the table, sucking breaths through his nostrils, doing his best to look cornered and terrified.

"See, I'm thinking the reason you were at that house in the middle of the night is 'cause—well, you thought someone was lying to you. Isn't that why we show up places after hours? I mean, it's not like I'd blame you, John. There've been times when I've left the house and waited just down the street for a few minutes just to make sure my wife was really going to the grocery store like she said she was. Right? I mean, everybody's real big on trust when it's not someone they actually care about, when it's not someone they're afraid to lose, right?"

John was determined to tell a story that would send the homicide detectives in the direction of the truth, a story that didn't put one false word in Alex's mouth, a story they could tell Alex in a room down the hall and probably have him believing it if they were convincing enough, because it didn't contain anything that contradicted Alex's experience. He could think of no other way to protect the man for the time being, but to do that he had to drag Mike's name down into the mud with his own. So finally he had arrived at a decision. That repaying his debt to Mike meant protecting Alex no matter the cost.

Forgive me, Bowers, he prayed. *Please forgive me, but I can't see a way out of this without dragging your name through the goddamn mud. But I'm doing it for what I think you would have wanted. I'm doing it for what you tried to build for yourself.*

He looked up at the detective with the most pathetic expression he could muster, and the man furrowed his brow and cocked his head slightly to one side in a false pose of sympathy. John whispered, "He said he was waiting for the money."

"Who was waiting for the money?"

"Mike."

"Whose money, John?"

"He told me he didn't love him," John muttered. "He told me that he knew something Alex didn't. Alex thought his family had cut him off, but it turned out his grandmother had named him as the second beneficiary in her life insurance policy."

"How did Mike find this out if Alex didn't know?"

"Alex wouldn't go back to visit his grandmother because he didn't want to have to deal with his mom. But one time his grandmother called the house, when she first got sick, and she told Mike about her policy, because she thought it would get Alex to come."

It was the first lie he told that involved anyone besides a corpse, but it didn't matter if Charlotte disputed it, because this lie would lead the detectives to a paper trail that was closer to the truth than the bullshit story he had used to get into their custody.

The detective said, "Did it, John?"

"No."

"How come?"

"Because Mike never told him. Mike never told him he was about to become a millionaire."

"But he told you, didn't he?" Barkin asked. John pretended to hesitate, stared down at his lap. "John?"

"He said if he could get his hands on that money, we could be together."

"But you didn't believe him?"

John shook his head, stared down at the table, tried to force tears but they weren't fast in coming, so he gave up lest he should betray his true motives. "No, I didn't. I had to see them together. I had to see the way Mike acted around him."

"And you saw a lot that night, didn't you?"

"Yes. I did. I saw they were in love."

It was the only true sentiment he had expressed since he had sat down, and the detective reacted to the power in it by wiping at his lips with one hand and allowing a silence to pass. "Why didn't you kill Alex first?"

John pretended to need a few moments to summon his answer. Then he met the detective's eyes. "Because he likes Marines, that's why." The detective didn't get it, so John helped him along. "And after what Mike had put me through, I thought I should get paid."

"I don't follow, John."

"When I realized Alex hadn't seen the body, I saw that I could use it all to convince him that he needed me to protect him. I just had to pretend like I was straight so he wouldn't suspect anything about me and Mike. And if that worked, if he really thought he needed me, if I did my best to protect him against Mike's *killer*— well, then I might just get paid for all the pain Mike caused me."

The detective nodded gravely, like a sympathetic teacher. He got to his feet, asked John if he wanted anything to drink. John declined, and he left the room. John prayed he was going to check on the specifics of Alex's grandmother's life insurance policy.

He had no idea how much time had passed before a different

man entered the room. This one had a deeply lined face and a shaggy toupee and rheumy blue eyes. He set his plastic coffee cup down on the table, out of John's reach, and said, "How's it going, Sergeant Sodom?"

John averted his eyes as if this were an actual insult. "So, you're a real bona fide pansy-ass faggot, are yah? Tell me. What size anal beads do you prefer? Large, extra-large, or Big Gulp?"

John looked to the camcorder. "Is that thing on?"

"Hey, I've weathered my fair share of discrimination suits in my day, son. But I must say that those suits involved people who were actually members of the minority they accused me of discriminating against. You, on the other hand, have cooked up some cock-and-bull story—pardon the pun—for reasons I can't comprehend. So I'm going to take a different approach with you, Mr. Houck. We're going to start by talking about where you dumped the body."

A silence fell. "I'm sorry," John said. "I didn't hear the question."

"Where did you dump the body?"

He met the detective's stare, saw the cash box he had dug from the sand, saw the red ruby ring and the limp fingers of Bowers's right hand. John was confident Duncan knew that at some point the body would surface, and one missing hand would be a strange detail that wouldn't fit with a frame job.

"I thought you'd be more interested in hearing why I cut off his hands and feet."

No response from the detective other than a small shift in the set of his mouth. It was enough. But the detective wasn't willing to give any more away, wasn't willing to take the bait John had offered him.

"My original question still stands, Mr. Houck."

"I want a lawyer."

A thin smile this time. "That's real good timing, mister. If I were in the midst of screwing up a major homicide investigation with a false confession, I would want a lawyer, too."

Another few minutes of his unnerving stare, and the detective left the room.

✕

His cell was a good ways down the hall from the drunk tank, with an empty cell on either side. He figured they wanted to keep him isolated so he wouldn't say anything to another prisoner that might leak to the media, who had been camped outside the sheriff's station in full force when they had brought him in early that morning.

John lay flat on his back, staring at the ceiling with the vacant gaze he assumed a remorseless killer might use. Two sets of footsteps approached the cell. He listened to their arrival, then listened to one of them depart. He didn't make any move to acknowledge the person standing outside the bars.

Ray Duncan said, "They know you're covering for him. I told them Bowers saved your life in Iraq, so they think Alex got something over on you. Maybe introduced some kind of *sexual confusion* that changed your definition of loyalty. They thought it last night when they got word you turned yourself in, and they're thinking it now. So you would have had to do some real good work in there to convince them otherwise."

John said, "Well, they haven't told you what I've said, so I'd say that's a bad sign for you, Duncan."

"How's that, John?"

"See, I told them I hid Mike's body in the woodshed while I wiped down the scene, which means they probably asked you if you did a search of the area after your deputies arrested me and you would have had to tell them you didn't, which was a fuckup on your part, which doesn't give them anything to disprove my story with." He fought the urge to sit up and look at the man because he knew all he would see was Bowers's hand resting in that cash box. "I think you've been cut out of the investigation, Duncan. Is that right?"

A brittle silence. Then, "You haven't thought this through, John. Don't pretend otherwise."

"And you have?"

"Yes, sir. I have. That's my job." Not quite a confession, just an inch to the right of one. "There's still time to set this thing straight, son. Hell, I'll even back you up. Tell them what you told me about how Mike saved your life."

"I bet you would, Duncan."

"Call me Ray, John. It'll let me know you're really hearing me."

John rose to a seated position, swung his legs to the floor, and looked up at Duncan. Everything about the man seemed calm and settled if you didn't notice the details. The way he held on to the bar in his right hand in a tense grip, the tension in his upper lip, and the fact that he had rolled the sleeves of his uniform shirt three-quarters of the way up his arms.

After a long silence John said, "Are you waiting for me to blink?"

Duncan said, "You know I used to be an actor?"

"I didn't."

He nodded and smiled, as if they had just met at a cocktail party. "I never made much of anything at it, but the first time I ever wore a cop's uniform was on the set of a TV show. I was just some guy in the background, but people told me I was good. They told me I never broke character. Not for one minute." John nodded at this threat but said nothing. "I went to one acting coach when I first started who told me that acting is *reacting* to the stimuli we are presented with. Does that make sense?" John nodded. "But really, that's life now, isn't it? Because we are not a product of where we came from or what was done to us. We are what we choose to be in every situation that God delivers. And that's why when a thing of beauty enters my life, I rise to the occasion with everything I have. Some people are humbled by beautiful things, John. I'm not. I'm *inspired*. I go after them with everything I have. *Everything*."

John took a few minutes to pretend that he was digesting this speech. Then he nodded respectfully. "Here's what I think happened, Ray. I think she let you start boning her because her husband dragged her up to that cabin every other weekend and she didn't want to go because it was too far from her nice clothing stores and her charity lunches and her hair salon. And I think maybe you showed her some things she'd never seen before, so she let you hang in there.

"But I think after a while you started to want more, and she always had an excuse. She started with the obvious one: her husband. Her marriage. Then he was out of the picture and you thought maybe that was your shot. But then she had another excuse, just as good, if not better: her mother-in-law's will. She couldn't jeopardize her inheritance. But then—and this was the kicker, Ray—this is what I think really got to you: when her mother-in-law started to get sick, she sprang a big surprise on you. She wasn't first in line for the life insurance. Alex was and, well, you couldn't support her in the lifestyle to which she had become accustomed. I guess it counts for something that you couldn't bring yourself just to kill him. He is her only son, after all.

"But this is where I get confused. Maybe you did it because you thought she would actually be with you once she got that money. Or maybe—and this is the part that really fucking scares me—maybe you just did it to find out whether she was feeding you a load of shit. Maybe you just did it to find out, once and for all, if you're really just some dumb pony she likes to ride when she's done buying new shoes."

Duncan's laugh didn't get past his throat, and his strained breaths flared his nostrils. "Is that what you told them in there?" he asked. His voice was thin and reedy.

"Wouldn't you like to know," John said. "But just for the record, Duncan, I think it's 'cause she thinks you're a dumb pony she likes to ride when she's done buying shoes."

Duncan turned on one heel and started walking away from the cell. John rose and moved to the bars, "Hey, Duncan. Has she called?" Duncan kept walking. "'Cause I talked to her last night and I thought she might have called you."

Duncan turned, started back toward the cell. His mouth opened, but he licked his lips instead of giving voice to his fear. John said, "I told her Alex was going to try to kill you. Are you sure she didn't call to warn you?" The answer was on Duncan's face. "That's a shame," John added.

"I'll fucking roll over you. Do you understand me? I will *roll over* you, son."

"Do it right now. You want me to go down for this, then tell me what I need to tell them when they ask me what condition I left the body in. Tell me everything I need to know to convince them I did this."

"Why the hell would you want to do that?"

"Because the longer I'm in here, the more time Alex has to reconsider blowing your fucking head off. And in my book that is a good thing. It is the *only* good thing. Because I care about you about as much as you cared about Mike Bowers." Even as the words poured from him effortlessly, he wasn't sure he believed them. What he wanted was a confession. "Tell me what I need to know to take the fall for this."

For a long time they stared at each other through the bars.

Then Duncan glanced around him, looked down at the cracked cement floor, and cleared his throat. "The body was found in a dry streambed that feeds into Nesbit Creek. The area is accessed down about twenty yards of a rocky slope, near the intersection of Nesbit Road and Old Holloway Drive." John held on to the bars in front of him for support, worked to steady his breath as he tried to memorize all the details he would need to know to issue a complete false confession. "Facedown, arms spread on either side. Hands and feet severed by a circular saw, not left at the scene." As Duncan delivered these details, his quiet voice took on a breathy, high-pitched quality. "Various contusions indicate he was kept inside an industrial-size freezer for several days following his murder. Contusions to the face and chest indicate that he was dragged down the slope for several yards."

His vision of Duncan blurred and shifted. He blinked back tears, spoke to chase away the uncontrollable wave of emotion that had just swept through him. "You haven't even read the fucking coroner's report, have you? You just know all this is going be in there."

"Pretty good for some dumb pony," Duncan whispered.

"You're never going to have her. She believed me, Duncan. That's why she didn't call you. She believed me."

Duncan brought his face right to John's and whispered, "Let me tell you what wasn't in the coroner's report. When Marines get cut, they don't sound like Marines at all."

Duncan had already withdrawn by the time John lunged at the bars and spit at his face. John thought he had missed; then he saw Duncan wipe his cheek with the back of his right hand as he walked off in the direction of the central holding cell. Nevertheless, this small burst of inadequate violence left John feeling pathetic and childlike, as if he had spit into a fan.

17

When he saw that the metal door he was being led toward was marked "Visiting Room," his heart leaped at the thought that Patsy might be waiting for him on the other side. Maybe once he had left the picture the police hadn't been all that interested in her. But when the guard opened the door, he revealed a long, empty well of a room divided by a giant metal wall that cut the room into two sections and held large viewing windows. The wall stopped about six feet short of the ceiling so that guards stationed at the top of each metal staircase could look down into the entire area below.

No visitor was waiting for him. Indeed, it seemed the room had been cleared out. But a guard deposited him on the stool in the middle of the row, seating him in front of a Plexiglas panel that offered nothing more than a view of the empty stool on the other side and the metal-clad wall behind it. Instead of the telephones you saw on television, the panel had a vent of thumbnail-size holes at mouth level.

He looked up and was surprised to see that only one guard was still with him. Maybe the other had gone to fetch John's secret admirer. The guard reached down and uncuffed him, then gave John a hard warning look. He could interpret it in only one way: the guy thought John was getting away with something, and he didn't approve of this strange, silent proceeding. Then the guard moved back up the metal staircase they had just descended and stepped out the door. John saw part of his hulking back blocking the door's viewing window.

For what felt like several minutes, John was completely alone. Then, on the other side of the wall, at the top of a metal staircase opposite the one John had been brought down, the door opened and a different guard stepped through. Charlotte Martin was behind him. The guard allowed her to descend the stairs unaccompanied, holding his ground just inside the door at the top. She wore a black pantsuit with a white silk shirt that had an almost metallic sheen to it. He wondered whom she had already gone into mourning for; then he reminded himself that she was the type of woman who mourned damaged reputations and lost opportunities, not human beings.

Carefully, she took a seat on the other side of the Plexiglas, reaching back to make sure the hem of her coat didn't catch under her butt, even as she maintained unblinking eye contact with him. Then her eyes cut past him and he realized she was looking on his side of the wall at the top of the staircase, which was empty, but she could still see the guard's back through the wire-reinforced glass window.

"I didn't realize you had this much influence around here," John said.

"They brought me in for questioning. Of course, they didn't tell me what you told them. But I could tell from the nature of their questions it was quite a yarn."

"What are you doing here?"

She smiled thinly, then looked down the length of her shirt, as if she were checking it for a stain. "There are two things you need to know before we go any further."

"Open your eyes, Mrs. Martin. I'm not going anywhere."

"Indeed. First thing. My husband changed his will without my knowledge. I had no idea he was leaving Alex the place in Owensville, and I never would have allowed it if I had known. Not because I am driven by a desire to punish my son, mind you, but because I never would have allowed my son to get that close to Ray."

"Right. 'Cause you kept it away from the house."

"Second."

"I'm listening."

"There's a tape recorder taped to my waist and a microphone hidden in the lapel of this jacket. It's not a wire, mind you. No one's listening in right now. Apparently it would have taken a day or two to get that kind of technology. So it's just a plain old tape, and when we're done here, Detectives Barkin and Lewis are expecting to listen to it and discover that I have somehow led you to admit that your confession is bogus."

He just stared at her, wondering if his exhaustion was causing auditory hallucinations. When she said nothing to refute what she had just told him, he leaned forward to get a better look at her. "Are you kidding me?"

"No."

"And you're telling me this?"

"I just told you. Yes."

"So there's no chance of that happening now, is there, Charlotte?"

"No. There isn't."

He was about to suggest that she leave, when she broke the silence with "I'm a very competitive woman, John. And as much as I am loath to admit it, you impressed me last night. But you're out of your mind if you think I'm going to let you take the fall for this."

"You don't want me to show you up?"

"No, I don't."

"Good. Then tell the detectives about your relationship with Ray Duncan."

"I won't need to," she said with a smile. "Ray will be here soon enough."

John waited for her to elaborate. When she did no such thing, he opened his mouth, but she cut him off with, "And soon, I assume the affair will be public knowledge, given the enormous number of reporters your false confession has drawn to this building. If she lives long enough, my mother-in-law will gladly cut me out of her will altogether, and I—"

"What do you mean Ray will be here *soon enough*?"

She smiled broadly at the sound of fearful anticipation in his voice. "John, you could say I have been *inspired* by your hatred of me. After you left in handcuffs last night, I took a good, hard look at myself. At my accomplishments." Her eyes glazed over at this word, as if she knew it wasn't quite adequate but couldn't find a suitable replacement. "I wasn't proud."

"You knew," John said quietly. "You knew what he was going to do."

"I most certainly did not!" Her anger was clear and unguarded. She took a minute to catch her breath. Then in a cooler tone she said, "I thought he kept asking me to marry him because he felt some kind of duty. I thought he believed that because I was a woman, I couldn't just keep going to bed with him the way I had for years. I thought by putting him off again and again, that I was doing him a favor. Freeing him from what he saw as an obligation—an obligation to my sanctity as a woman. That's a favorite word of yours, isn't it, John? *Obligation?*"

"Charlotte, what did you mean when you said Ray would be here soon enough?"

"Oh, for Christ's sake," she whispered, rocking back in her seat, smoothing invisible pieces of lint from her thighs. "He was practically throwing himself against the door to the interrogation room the entire time they were questioning me. I thought he was going to try to come in through a vent. It's just a matter of time before he figures out they've brought me in here. With you."

"All right. And just what the hell are you doing in here? Now that you've blown your own cover."

"Explaining myself, John. What does it sound like I'm doing?"

"Explain yourself to Barkin and Lewis."

"How is that even possible, John, now that you've poisoned the waters with all of your lies? Those poor men can't tell heads from tails in there. Don't you see you haven't left me with many choices when it comes to redeeming myself? Believe me, you've made it very clear that I am in desperate need of redemption. So what other choice do I have?"

Slowly she slid her right hand backward across the table, revealing the sharp point of a wooden stick the diameter of a human finger. She had taken the handle of a wooden spoon and sharpened it into a slender stake. He figured she had taped it to the inside of her leg to get it through security. "I'm told that a man like you knows a thousand different ways to kill. Teach me one of them, John. Teach me quick."

"This is insane," he whispered.

"You're sitting in jail right now because you confessed to a crime you didn't commit, to protect a man you don't love. I'm not sure of many things right now, but I am sure that you have not been asked to determine the true definition of the word *sanity.*"

"If you tell them the truth, I'll change my story. I'll tell them what happened last night."

"So I'll be in league with a liar as my life is *destroyed* in the public eye. No, thank you, Mr. Houck. I have decided how this should be taken care of. You're either going to help me or you won't."

At the top of the staircase on his side of the metal wall, John saw the guard move away from the glass window in the door. He listened, trying to recognize the voices shouting at each other on the other side. He couldn't make out the words or who was delivering them.

"He's coming in, John," Charlotte whispered. "One way or another, he's coming into this room. You can help me make sure he never leaves."

Against his will, his eyes went to the barely concealed weapon resting under her fingers. With so pathetic a weapon, her best option would be a downward strike to the area just above Duncan's collarbone, aiming for the subclavian artery. Immediate internal bleeding would result if the tip went deep enough, and death would follow quickly. But there were too many variables. The tip would probably break on impact, screwing her aim. Three inches off and the stake would snap against his collarbone. It infuriated him that he would even entertain these thoughts, but they were reflexive.

"I'm disappointed, John. You had such *passion.* Such *convictions.* But you're too young for them. You get frightened when the concepts you toss about with such abandon actually take root and become reality. And that's exactly what's about to happen, John. I'm about to show you what you believe in. You'll have to decide how it looks once I'm done."

"I asked you to do something to take care of your son. To honor the fact that you're his mother. You do this, and it's about your ego. It's not about a damn thing I said last night."

"*Honor* is a word that teenage boys use to make their vanity and their ego sound like things they shouldn't live in fear of."

"They'll gun you down before you can even make a flesh wound."

On her side of the metal wall, the door atop the staircase flew open and the guard whirled around just as Ray Duncan stepped onto the landing, one hand raised to hold the guard back. At first John thought Duncan was holding a weapon, but then he saw it was a key ring. There was also someone behind him. The older man had silver hair and patrician features and wore a Sheriff's Department uniform that matched the one Duncan was currently sweating bullets in. John recognized him from the photo that was hanging on the wall at the entrance to the station. He was the sheriff of Hanrock County.

Duncan turned and looked down at them. "This is exactly what I told you!" he shouted. "I told you they were up to something. You want to tell me what the hell these two are doing in here together, and why the room had to be shut down for them to do it?"

Dumbfounded, the sheriff stared down at them as Duncan descended the steps two at a time. "John," Charlotte whispered.

He met her eyes but kept his mouth shut.

"Will you ever believe that I did this for my son?" she asked him.

"No. I won't."

"Fair enough. Then you should probably warn him now."

Duncan's voice boomed, amplified by the metal-clad walls, which were clearly intended to make conversations between prisoners and visitors more audible to the guards above. "Mrs. Martin, if you could come with me. The sheriff and I are going to try to straighten this whole thing out. Clearly something highly unorthodox has been—"

As soon as his hand touched her right shoulder, Charlotte was on her feet. It happened so fast that the stake she held in her right hand was in the air and covered in blood before John realized she had struck the first blow. Duncan let out a series of yelps, both hands pressed to his eyes, blood pouring from between his fingers. Shouts rang out from overhead. The sheriff had drawn his revolver, was shouting warnings for Charlotte to stop where she was. Instead, Charlotte took another step forward, her lips pursed in concentration, and went for the second most obvious target: she drove the stake into the side of Duncan's neck just before he collapsed against the far wall.

Then Charlotte's right shoulder exploded, shooting tufts of fine fabric, and the Plexiglas panel in front of John splintered and he went to the floor. He hit the floor as the metal walls amplified the second and third gunshots, turning them into a single unearthly roar. But he wasn't there anymore. Acrid black smoke had swallowed him, and his skin was aflame from tiny pieces of shrapnel, and for the first time he could hear the words Mike Bowers had whispered into his ear in that moment. *Easy, brotha. Easy easy easy.*

When the hands of the living finally pulled him from the cement floor of the visitation room, he tried to take solace in the fact that the horrors of war could sometimes protect him from the agony of the present.

18

The attorney introduced himself as Eric Reynard, but John recognized him from the news, defending celebrity clients who had been accused of various murders. He had a lantern jaw and a long, almost lipless mouth that gave him a blank and unreadable expression as he listened to John's story. Patsy sat next to John, holding his uninjured left hand in both of her own. She had probably taken out mortgages on her home and her bar to afford the lawyer sitting across from them.

When John was finished, Patsy let out a long sigh, held his hand against her stomach as she blinked at the floor. As if silence of any kind made him uncomfortable, Reynard flipped pages on his legal pad. "Ray Duncan died of blood loss at the scene. Charlotte Martin just got out of about nine hours of surgery and is still in critical condition."

In a timid voice, Patsy said, "Earlier, you said he had options—"

"All of this depends on who they decide to make an example out of. You or Ray Duncan. They've already turned up some interesting things on Duncan, and someone in the department is leaking them to the media, which tells me that someone at Hanrock County Sheriff's Department wants to be done with the guy. And that's good news for you, because if they hit you with anything hard, and I fight them, then Ray Duncan goes on trial, too. And embarrassment doesn't even begin to describe what this has already brought to the department. Detectives Barkin and Lewis have already been suspended for the stunt they pulled with you and Charlotte Martin, and that's just the beginning. My guess is their careers are over. The public-information officer is already grumbling things to the press about how they weren't used to conducting investigations under that kind of media pressure."

"What have they found on Duncan?"

"He bought a commercial-grade freezer the day after your little surprise late-night visit to Owensville. It wasn't in his house when they searched it, but they did find an area in his cellar that has stains that might have come from the freezer's drain port. He also ran an extra electrical wire to the nearest socket, which gave it about the amps it would need to keep a commercial-grade freezer running. Did a bad job, too. Like he needed to do it himself because he didn't want anyone to know what was down there."

Patsy said, "So they might not charge John with anything."

"Oh, no," the lawyer said. "They'll absolutely charge him with something. They have to, given the rather spectacular manner in which he turned himself in. The question is, How severe will the charges be? An obstruction of justice conviction sentence can run from a year or more of prison time to several months of confinement—more commonly known as house arrest."

A knock at the door startled Patsy so badly she jumped. The guard outside cracked the door, and John saw a well-dressed woman in an expensive suit. Reynard excused himself, rose from his chair, and slipped outside. Patsy got up and followed him to the door, remained standing there after he was gone. She held one hand to her mouth, as if he were a lover who had just told her he was going back to his wife.

Finally she lowered her hand from her mouth. "Where is he, John?" she whispered. "He could verify everything you're telling them. Where the hell is he? Duncan's dead. The least he could have done is send you some goddamn flowers." He didn't need her to say it to know that she was talking about Alex.

Just then, the door opened. Reynard took a step inside and stopped in his tracks, as if he needed sufficient space between himself and the two of them before he spoke. "Charlotte Martin died of a pulmonary embolism about an hour ago."

They were struck silent. Reynard left without any discernible change in expression or feeling. Once again, John saw the look of quiet, almost serene concentration that had appeared on the woman's face as she had stabbed her lover to death, as if all of her real emotions had retreated to a place deep inside of her at the first sign of murderous intent, never to return from the hiding places they found in the last seconds of her life.

Patsy said, "The cops had surveillance on my bar, but they pulled it after you turned yourself in. He could have called there. He could have tried to reach me, but he didn't. Anyone with a TV knows you're in here. He knows better than anyone that you're in here for him. Maybe it's time for him to do something for you."

"I did this to keep him from killing Duncan. That's been accomplished."

"Do you really believe that, John?"

He looked up into her eyes, but his instinctive response was lost to him. Maybe it was fatigue or maybe it was the genuine fear in his sister's eyes, as if his own convictions were about to push him past the reach of the last family member he had left. "Why is it so hard for you to believe, Patsy? Why is it so hard for you to believe that I would take that kind of risk for someone else?"

Her eyes watered and she withdrew from the table and turned her back to him while she steadied herself. "Because I don't want you to be that good anymore. I want you to come back, John."

"From where?"

"Iraq. Dean's room. Baton Rouge. Take your pick. But if you're going to do that, you're going to have stop being so noble all the time. You're going to be just another person. Please tell me you'll consider it."

After a while he said, "Let's see what they charge me with first."

"Asshole," she whispered, but he saw she was hiding a smile with the hand she had been using to hold back tears.

×

This time the interrogation room had a giant mirror on one wall. This time both detectives were sitting across from him at once. They had introduced themselves as Benay and Aaronson, and they were younger and less battle-scarred than the two detectives whose stunt had resulted in the death of two deceitful lovers. This time they were joined by the district attorney, Sam Colby, a sandy-haired man with beady eyes, and his petite blond ADA with slanted green eyes and a gravelly voice that made it sound like she smoked three packs a day.

No one played good cop or bad cop. They listened to John recount a truthful and unedited account of the past week with an almost prayerful silence.

When he was finished, John expected the detective to pepper him with questions, but it was the DA who cleared his throat and sat forward. To the detectives investigating Ray Duncan, John was simply another piece of potential evidence.

"You maintain that the only reason you gave a false confession was to prevent Alex Martin from making an attempt on Ray Duncan's life," Colby said quietly.

"That's correct, sir."

"So, it was not your intent to deliberately mislead the detectives?"

Reynard raised a hand, but John spoke anyway. "The opposite. I gave them a story with specific details regarding Alex Martin's inheritance, details I thought were the basis of Ray Duncan's motive for killing Mike Bowers."

"A story that did not include any mention of Ray Duncan committing this murder?"

"That's correct."

"Why is that? You thought it would be best to get inside before you started to work your magic on this investigation?"

"Kind of like a suicide bomber," one of the detectives grumbled.

John said, "Having seen their work firsthand I would say that title belongs to Ray Duncan, sir." The detective reddened but nobody said anything, a silent consensus that it was the detective who had spoken out of turn.

Colby leaned back in his chair and gave Reynard a long stare. "This is sounding an awful lot like obstruction to me, Mr. Reynard."

"I'm sorry. Was there a flourishing investigation of Captain Ray Duncan under way that John somehow derailed? He wasn't even on your radar screen for this."

"It has not been established that Duncan murdered Mike Bowers," Colby said quietly.

"No, that burden will fall on me if you decide to put Mr. Houck on trial. And I'm highly confident that as soon as that freezer's found, while you all rush around trying to plug the leaks in your department, I won't have a very hard time of it."

"That sounds like a threat," the ADA said quietly.

"My job description is threatening to you, Sam? I don't even know where to begin with that."

Colby barked with laughter. The ADA looked to her lap, probably to avoid rolling her eyes, John thought. Once silence settled, the DA leaned forward, placed his elbows on the table, and studied John with squinted eyes and his hands clasped against his lips as if he were praying. "What is it you Marines say to each other when you want to shoot from the hip? 'Permission to speak freely'? Something like that?"

"Marines don't say that, sir. We're encouraged to think critically and to give even commanding officers our point of view if we think it's important to the mission's success."

"I see," Colby said. "Does it bother you in the slightest that this guy already knew how to shoot? You took him all the way out to Arizona to train him how to *defend himself* and it turned out he already knew how to fire a gun. Does that bother you at all?"

John hesitated long enough to raise the interest of everyone in the room. Finally he said, "Maybe he just wanted practice."

"Or he wanted you to believe he didn't know how to shoot," the DA said. "First he pulls the gun on Duncan in your trailer and his grip is so bad you think he's going to blow his own head off. Then he chases Duncan out of the trailer park but never fires a shot. Then, miracle of miracles, you're out in Arizona and he's shooting cans off a rock well enough to scare you silly when he finally points the gun at your face."

Reynard said, "I wasn't aware Alex Martin was being charged with a crime here."

"Oh, calm down, Eric. I'm not charging anyone with anything yet. I'm just asking some pretty obvious questions about the one guy who should be here but isn't. Where do you think he is, John? Did you teach him how to survive in the woods?"

"I did not, sir. And I don't understand what you're implying."

Colby said, "Can you not see that he wanted more from you than to learn how to shoot? Can you not see that he played the victim, played to your guilt, so you would be his protector? And now that you've done the job, he's nowhere to be found. You don't feel used at all, John?"

When Reynard placed a hand on his knee, John realized that everyone in the room seemed to have sensed the riot of emotions within him. Maybe Colby was shooting for some kind of outburst.

Just as Reynard began to make some comment about getting back to the business at hand, John said, "I did what I did so that I would feel better about what Mike did for me. That's all. I don't need a medal, or flowers, or a card. But if you think for one moment that Alex Martin was responsible for the murder of Mike Bowers, you are wrong, and I will testify to that from my own prison cell if I have to."

After several minutes of silence that almost seemed respectful, the DA and his blond sidekick excused themselves. The detectives followed them out of the room without a formal good-bye. Once they were alone John said, "Are they really going to accuse Alex of murdering Mike?"

"I doubt it," Reynard said. "But they may charge you with excessive integrity."

×

They finally charged him with making false statements in a criminal investigation and sentenced him to a year of probation. It was the lesser charge, and Reynard was so overjoyed, John felt guilty for not being able to match his enthusiasm.

As they left the building, the reporters amassed outside erupted with questions. Patsy held him by one shoulder and led him toward a sand-kissed Ford Explorer driven by one of her female bartenders. But before they were inside the car, John heard one reporter, a pretty Asian woman whose perfect hair and designer suit suggested she was from L.A., shout a question loud enough to be heard above the rest, "What's going to happen to Mike's body?"

As they pulled away from the curb, Patsy said, "His parents. They won't claim it."

John thought, *If that won't bring Alex out of hiding, nothing will.*

19

From the guest bedroom in his sister's house, John could see the necklace of headlights on Highway 62 and the pay phone he had called Patsy from, breaking a ten-year silence. Now he stared at the pay phone from afar like a dog awaiting the return of its owner. It was a place Alex could return to, a spot on the map they had made together in such a short time.

The rising sun had started to set the mountainous gates of Joshua Tree State Park aglow, and he hadn't slept a wink. The night before he had spoken to Philip, who hadn't heard a word from Alex, but who answered John's questions without any of the sarcasm or anger John had come to expect from the guy. As the night wore on, John couldn't help but contemplate the possibility that by depriving Alex of his opportunity for vengeance, he had effectively stolen the only thing Alex had to live for, the only purpose he had left. But now, as pale light washed the desert outside, he saw this as another grandiose fantasy. The truth was he needed Alex to answer the questions the DA had raised, but he had no idea where to find him.

Before the sun was fully up, he dressed hurriedly and slipped silently out of the back door. If Patsy heard him starting Eddie's truck, she didn't come rushing out of the house to stop him. The police hadn't located her Jeep Grand Cherokee, which Alex was either still using or had dumped somewhere.

As morning broke, John drove west on I-10, and about an hour and a half after leaving his sister's house, John was parked outside of a redbrick tract home on the northern edge of the city of Redlands. This was the address he had been given for a man named Charles Keaton, formerly known as Danny Oster.

He had brought Dean's suicide note with him. He was about to read it again, to further delay the inevitable, when a short, chubby woman with a cap of steel gray hair walked up to Oster's mailbox and unloaded its sizable contents. Her arms full, she turned on her heel and walked down the sidewalk.

When John called out to her, she spun and dropped several envelopes of coupons. He forced a smile and extended his hand before she could have time to recognize him from television. "My name's John," he said. "I was looking for Charles. Is he around right now?"

"I know who you are," she said quietly. "I saw you on the news. Why are you looking for my brother?"

"I need to discuss something with him."

She winced and blinked. He couldn't tell if it was out of fear or anger or both. "You seem to have a lot of things going on in your life right now. Why don't you just leave my brother alone? He already left the country because of you."

Because he was unprepared for her candor, he said, "Your brother left the country because of what *he* did."

"No!" she whispered. "*Your* brother was doing exactly what he wanted to until you caught him doing it."

John could think of only one good way to end this, so he started for his truck. She must have assumed he was leaving, because she shouted after him, "He knows you were following him!" By then he had pulled Dean's suicide note off the front seat of his truck and was crossing the street again toward her.

"I wasn't following him," he said.

"Someone was. Taking pictures of him outside the house. He figured it was you. That you knew he was back."

John didn't see the point of telling her that her brother had been followed by a PI someone had hired on his behalf but without his knowledge. Instead he handed her his brother's suicide note. If she could meet him toe-to-toe about it without so much as a formal introduction, he figured she could handle reading his brother's last words.

"What do you want?" she asked as soon as he was finished.

"I have to talk to your brother."

"To show him *this*?" she said, pointing at the note. "*You* are the only one who didn't know this!"

"Then let me tell him that I know now."

"Stay right here," she ordered him. She shuffled off down the sidewalk while she pulled her cell phone from the pocket of her khaki shorts. John politely turned away, as if she were about to take a pee against one of the trees, looked back after a few minutes, and saw she had walked all the way to the corner to place this call.

After what felt like an eternity, she walked back toward him, sandals slapping the pavement as she went. She said, "You ever heard of a town called Crafton?"

267

✕

Crafton. Another mountain town, only this one was in the Sierras and at a higher elevation than Owensville. Fresh snow clung determinedly to its soaring pine trees and blanketed the winding highway that led into town. He'd read the advisory signs on the way up the mountain and pulled off at a service station to buy chains for his tires, keeping his sunglasses on and his baseball cap shoved down over his forehead the entire time. From what he'd been able to tell, no one had recognized him. By way of his sister, Danny Oster had asked John to meet him at a diner called Crane's on the highway's pass through town. John didn't know if the place was named for someone with the last name Crane or if the owner was just fond of the bird. It turned out to be the former.

John's heart was a steady hammer when he pulled into a parking lot next to the shiny Airstream trailer the diner was housed in. Inside, an elderly couple in matching plaid parkas whispered to each other over steaming cups of coffee. They were tended to by a heavyset waitress with a long black ponytail.

Danny Oster sat in a booth the farthest from the front door. He wore a black baseball cap and a black waffle print hunter's vest over his plaid long-sleeve shirt. As John approached, Oster managed to keep eye contact, wetting his fat lips nervously with the tip of his tongue. But at the last minute, his eyes cut to the table, as if he thought John were about to strike him across the back of the head and he was prepared for the blow. Instead, John set Dean's suicide note on the table in front of Oster, then took a seat across from the man.

Oster read intently, his wide eyes welling with tears. The waitress came, and John ordered coffee in the quietest voice he could manage. "You all right, Charles?" the waitress asked Oster when she saw his worsening condition. He gave her a polite smile and nodded emphatically, even as tears slipped down his cheeks. The waitress gave John an icy glare. Maybe she recognized him, or maybe she just blamed him for Danny's little breakdown and no one in this town was fond of breakdowns. After she departed and Danny returned to reading, John stared out the window, which offered a view of more pine-shrouded mountains dusted white.

When he was finished, Danny Oster placed the note carefully on the table in front of him, as if it were written on old parchment that might come apart like a wet tissue. He used his napkin to wipe his eyes and blow his nose. And part of John wanted this to be it, wanted to just get up and leave and let this be as okay as things we're ever going to get between them.

"Why did you come back?" John asked.

Oster steeled himself, studied John as he blinked the tears into submission. In a high-pitched nasal voice that took John back ten years, Danny Oster said, "Statute of limitations on statutory rape in California is ten years. That was the only crime I committed that day. What I did was wrong, but it wasn't rape. And I didn't run away because I was afraid of you, John Houck. I ran away because I knew what I had done was wrong."

John didn't argue. "You two were going to move away together? To West Hollywood?"

"You didn't believe that part?"

"Maybe you were leading him on. Telling him what he wanted to hear."

"I told him what I thought would make him feel safe. That's always what he wanted—to feel safe."

"So we didn't keep him safe? Is that it?"

"No," Oster said in almost a moan. "I said it was what he *wanted,* not what he needed. What we want and what we need are two different things." He went silent, as if waiting for John to

strike at this cliché, but when John kept silent, too, Oster smiled and continued, "You know, I tried to read this book once. It was about physics, something about how everything in the universe is really a string and if it vibrates enough it turns from one thing to another. That's how I used to think of your brother. He was like this string that was always about to vibrate out of this universe."

Not even Patsy, or himself, had managed to speak of their brother with the same genuine affection Oster had just used. John felt a tremble in his chest, as if his throat were about to close up. "You expect me to believe you weren't afraid of me at all? That you just ran away because you knew what you did was wrong?"

"I'm still afraid of you, John. But that was only part of it. I loved him, but I did something terrible to him. I convinced him that I could save him from everything he felt. And he felt so many things, all the time, that I should have known I never could have done that for him. I did know, really. I knew."

He had not heard a more accurate description of his brother, and the fact that it was coming out of the man he had almost killed cleaved something inside of him. The best he could do was close his eyes and draw some deep breaths until the prospect of crying in front of Danny Oster became too humiliating for him to give in to.

When he found his voice, John said, "I knew he was gay. But I never acted like it was a real thing because I thought I could change it. I thought *he* could change it."

"You were jealous of him," Oster whispered.

"What did you say?"

"You thought he was getting away with something."

"You're saying I wanted to do what he was doing with you that day?"

"Hell, no," Oster said, voice steady but eyes wide with fear at John's growing anger. "Your brother did other things."

"Yeah. Drugs."

"No, back then."

"What, Danny? What did he do?" Just as John had hoped, Oster winced at the sound of his real name, but after a deep breath he steadied himself, lifted his eyes to John so John could see they were drained of fear.

"He cried. He cried for your mom and dad every day. He said he never saw you cry for them once."

Nothing he thought to say in response to this made him feel anything other than sick to his stomach, so he said nothing.

The idea that he envied Dean's grief seemed too insane for John to comprehend, especially when he considered that Dean's wild emotions—his vibrations, as Oster had dubbed them—had led him down a path of relentless self-destruction. How could John envy *that*? And the deaths of their parents now seemed to be buried beneath so many other losses that John could barely brush his fingertips up against any of the feelings associated with them. But maybe this was how epiphanies really came to a man—not with a burning bush or a lightning strike, but with a seemingly obvious and simplistic statement that forces him to look at the ground at his feet instead of the distant horizon he has been searching for most of his life.

For a long while, neither man spoke. John knew he didn't have much more in him. It was almost three-thirty in the afternoon, and he'd been driving since the crack of dawn. He couldn't bring himself to say good-bye because he didn't know how you said good-bye to a man who had occupied so many different positions in your life. He felt more tired than he had ever been in his life. So he excused himself and said he would be back in a few minutes. He told Oster he was going to use the pay phone outside, which was the truth, but he didn't tell him this was just an excuse to say a hurried good-bye once he came back, without sitting down, without extending his hands, without doing any other neat gesture a therapist might recommend to achieve "closure."

Outside, the cold air hit him with force. He'd left the house in a T-shirt and jeans and had picked up a cheap sweatshirt with the word *Yosemite* written on it in multicolored cursive letters. As he listened to the phone ring, he realized he wasn't sure he wanted to tell Patsy what he had just done. He just wanted to make sure she wasn't worrying about him. She answered breathlessly, as if she had run for the phone.

"I don't believe this. Where the hell are you?"

"Doesn't matter. I'm coming back soon."

"Hurry."

"Why?"

"Because I was just sitting in front of my computer looking at a wire article that says they found my car." She gave it a second to sink in, but it didn't register. "My car! The Jeep! Christ, *Alex's* car. The one he stole in Sedona."

"Where?"

"Hold on," she said, and he could hear her footsteps on the tile floor, a clack of keys on the keyboard as she scrolled through the article. "The Sierras. They found it crashed off the side of Highway 129." John turned slightly and stared out at the highway next to the phone booth, saw without needing to look for it, the giant sign that labeled it Highway 129. Patsy read aloud, "'Believed to be vehicle that was being used by fugitive Alex Martin, who is still wanted for questioning in . . .' Here you go, 'some hikers found it this morning about ten miles west of . . .' some town I've never heard of."

"What town?"

"Crafton."

He hung up on her. He couldn't see Oster from where he stood, and that was a good thing, because he knew the expression on his face would betray the rage and confusion inside him. When the pay phone rang he jumped and started away from it, back toward the diner, convinced now that Oster was hiding something monumental.

When he opened the door to the diner, he found Oster sitting in the exact same spot, his hands laid flat on the table in front of him. He had politely folded the suicide note shut, and as John approached the table a second time, he was surprised to see the man crack a weak smile.

Because it seemed likely the only option available, John took a seat for a second time and said, "Do you have family here?"

"My mother retired here."

"You're staying with your mother?" John asked, but Oster's attention was focused on Dean's suicide note, which he slid across the table toward John.

"My mother died three years ago," he said. "My sister and I have been trying to sell her place, but we haven't had much luck." But there was a tense edge in his voice now, which suggested he had noticed the change in John. When John looked up, Danny Oster, aka Charles Keaton, blinked rapidly and cleared his throat. Then he said, "Well, I need to get going." He stood up and started to leave.

And John said, "I'll walk you to your car."

And John saw a shiver go through Oster, saw the man glance at John over his shoulder with pursed lips and a crease above the bridge of his nose, then continue toward the entrance to the diner without another word. Behind him, John matched him step for step, even as Oster quickened his pace. With his left hand he reached up and undid the knot in the sling that held his cast close to his chest. As the two of them stepped out the door one after the other, he let the sling slip free and fall to the pavement behind him.

Outside, Oster started walking toward the spot where John had parked Eddie's truck. Alongside it was a blue Econoline van and a battered maroon Honda Accord. "Which one's yours?" John asked. But Oster didn't answer, just kept walking toward the cars, pretending to be oblivious that John was barely a foot behind him the whole way.

"The van," Oster finally said without looking back.

"Gotcha."

And Oster went for the driver-side door. When John saw that they were out of sight of the diner, he swung his cast out from his body and delivered a blow to the back of Oster's head. Oster slammed face-first into the side of the van, but that's when John saw his hand had dipped inside his vest before the blow had been struck. The pain sang through John's body, and as he took a step back, preparing to deliver another blow, Oster rolled over onto his back, hit the asphalt ass-first, and raised the pistol he had pulled from his vest.

"It's not what you think," Oster said, gasping.

"Maybe this time it is!" John replied.

Oster shook his head madly, blinked rapidly, desperately trying to clear the effects of the blow to his brain cavity. "No, John. No!"

"What then? What? What was Alex Martin doing up here? Why did they find the car he was driving ten miles down the road?"

Oster gasped for breath, but he held the pistol steady. "Anything I say you're going to think is a lie."

"Yeah. So where the fuck does that leave us?"

"Start walking. I'm done talking. I've got something to show you."

20

The milky cloud cover that had moved in while they were inside the diner started to shed frail snowflakes that looked like ash. Oster ordered John to walk several yards in front of him, left arm at his side. They came to a narrow asphalt road that curved up a pine-covered slope.

"Your sister said you thought someone was following you," John finally said, loud enough to be heard without turning around. He had no idea how far behind him Oster was. Far enough, he assumed, to have a good aim, and far enough to run if he missed. "She said you thought it was me. Did you?"

"Keep walking," came Oster's response.

John did, but he kept talking as well. "You know what I think? I think you started following *me*."

"Left up the driveway," Oster said. John did as he was told, even though the driveway snaked uphill through dense woods.

John said, "I think you were following us for most of the time. You must have followed us to Arizona, and then when he left, when he went off on his own, you . . ."

Now that he had arrived at this point, he had trouble getting the words out. Oster must have sensed the rage building inside John because he ordered him to place his left hand on the back of his head. "What a stupid fucking move, Oster. You wanted to get back at *me* and you killed someone just like you."

Behind him Oster barked with laughter that had a tinge of madness in it. "Like me, huh?" he gasped. "How's that? A *rapist*? A *child molester*? Your fucking punching bag when you couldn't accept who your brother was?"

John could see they were approaching a house up ahead—a dark green cabin that stood on stilts twenty feet above the slope, so that its front porch had a view across the treetops. The stilts were painted the color of bark, as if the entire house were meant to be camouflaged by the woods. The staircase that climbed all the way to the front porch had high railings and made two turns. As he made the second turn, paused on the landing for a few seconds holding his cast in front of him to keep his balance, he saw that Oster was making the first turn twenty steps below him, keeping more than a safe distance.

John stopped at the top step, tried to gauge how many steps it was to the front door. But Oster ordered him to move forward. John practically had his nose to the front door when heard something hit the porch floor and slide toward him. A key ring bumped against his right shoe.

"Open the door," Oster said in a trembling voice.

John dared a glance back, saw Oster holding the pistol on him in a two-handed grip that looked steady and sure. Behind him, the snowcapped trees descended the horizon until they lost their definition inside the fast-moving white clouds that had blown in over the entire mountain. "Promise me that if you shoot me, you won't do it in the back," John said.

Oster groaned and screwed his eyes shut, as if John were a stubborn child. "Open the goddamn door, take ten steps, and then turn to your right."

Twice he almost dropped the keys because the cast forced him to use his left hand. Then the key slipped in the lock. He turned it, then released it so he could turn the knob. Inside he saw cheap Oriental rugs, wooden French country furniture that looked like it could be snapped into kindling without much effort. Just as Oster had ordered him to, he took ten steps and turned to his right, found himself facing a closed door. He looked back and saw Oster standing in the front door to the cabin, pistol still raised. John opened the door.

The room had once been a home office. A small secretary was pushed against one wall, its top shelf stuffed with tattered paperbacks. The window had a lace curtain and a view across snowy treetops, and on an air mattress on the floor, Alex Martin lay wrapped in a plaid comforter, sleeping with his mouth open, his nose still swollen and bruised from their last fight, his chest rising with breaths that sounded pained. The floor next to him was a veritable nurse's station: rolls of Ace bandages, cold compresses, a few prescription medicine bottles.

"I told him you were coming," Oster said. "He said you were probably going to try to hurt me. He told me not to meet with you, told me to wait until he was back on his feet so he could be the one to tell you."

John waited for Oster to elaborate on the preposterous statements he'd just made, but instead Oster turned to the secretary and opened his fist on the desk, keeping his hand in place so the six bullets he released onto its surface didn't roll to the floor. John assumed he had taken them out of the pistol he had used to subdue him.

"He followed me from Redlands up the mountain, three days ago," Oster said. "But he didn't have chains on his tires, and it was snowing hard. He went off the road. I almost called the police, but I went back for him first because I was sure he was hurt. Then I saw who it was—his face was all over the news by then. He begged me not to take him to the hospital, but I think he broke a rib. The pain pills are my mother's, from an old surgery. But they're almost out, and I'm not about to try to refill a dead woman's prescription. Not with my history."

"Why did he come up here?"

"Ask him," Oster said.

"Does he know anything about what happened? Has he seen the news?"

"No," Oster whispered. "I wouldn't show it to him, and when he asked me, I lied. I thought if he knew, he would be too afraid to go to the hospital. A lot of good that did."

John sank down next to the mattress and laid a hand on Alex's shoulder. It took a light shake to wake him, and when Alex saw who had pulled him from his stupor, he screwed his eyes shut. Tears spilled from them. John assumed it was physical pain, drew the comforter down, and then pulled up Alex's T-shirt. The bruise looked like a bag of ink that had burst around his lower rib and then been driven up the right side of his body by a powerful wind.

"What are you doing here?" John asked.

"You can't rape a man on his back, John." At first, John assumed it was the medication talking. But after a deep breath, Alex continued, "It's not possible unless he's tied up. And your brother wasn't tied up. You didn't see what you thought you saw that day. I thought if I found Ost—if I found Danny, I mean, I could find out what really happened. I could make you understand. I thought what happened to your brother was the reason you hated Mike."

"I never hated Mike."

"Maybe not. But I wanted you to accept him. And I thought you would do that if you knew what really happened to your brother."

He took a moment to digest this. Then he said, "You knew how to shoot. You didn't need me to teach you how to defend yourself."

"No," he said. "Mike taught me when we moved into the cabin. I needed . . ." He lost hold of his words, clenched his teeth, and looked to the ceiling, as if the exertion of his honesty and the physical pain he was fighting were too much in combination. "You were right, John. I was the reason you never came to our house." He gave John a moment to process this. "He asked me if he could invite you, and I told him I would leave him, because I was afraid of you. I was afraid of what you could make him do."

It was the very accusation John had leveled against Alex back in Arizona a few nights earlier, and looking back now, he could see how the truth in it had sent Alex off the rails.

Alex continued, "I didn't know I was taking away his last chance to show you who he truly was. And I can never take that back, but I thought if I could make you accept him then it would be okay."

John sat back, brought his knees to his chest, and tried to get control of his breathing. Since their first meeting, John had assumed that Alex's only real desire was to punish him for his own failings. But now he could see that Alex had been driven by a need to repay a debt to Mike Bowers that exceeded the one John owed.

"He knew, John," Alex said. "He knew why you screwed up that day. You told him, but he pretended to be asleep so you wouldn't have to deal with it. He knew and he understood."

John turned his head away from Alex so the guy couldn't see his tears, but Alex reached out across the carpet and laid his fingers gently on one of John's knees. "I know you won't give up until someone tells you your mission is done. It's done, John. Mike was right. He used to say about you, 'There is a hero wherever he walks—he just don't know it yet.'"

"He said that?"

Alex nodded.

John turned his face away from Alex so the man wouldn't see the emotions he could no longer control. Alex had just given him permission to grieve Mike as he would a brother. "And where are you going? Now that I'm *done,*" John asked.

"When I start to feel better, I'm going to go away for a while. Danny—I'm sorry, *Charles*—is going to show me how. He has experience. And friends. Maybe I'll go to Mexico just like he did."

John had to remind himself that Alex had not seen the news for the past three days, didn't know that both his mother and Ray Duncan were dead, had no idea that he was about to inherit millions of dollars that had almost been stolen from him. For all Alex knew, Duncan and men just like him walked the world with impunity.

"My mission is not done," John said. "Everyone knows what Ray Duncan did. It's over, Alex. But Mike's body is lying in the Hanrock County morgue because his parents won't claim it. That means you have to do it. That means I have to see that you do it. We don't leave our dead behind. After you claim his body, you can set me free all you want. But not until then, okay?"

He gave Alex several minutes to process this, expected more questions, but none came. "Can you walk?" he asked him.

"I walked some yesterday," he said.

"Good. That's good."

As if to prove himself, Alex sat up slowly, wincing slightly before he shifted his weight onto the left side of his body. He stopped and took several deep breaths, then looked up into John's eyes and he saw that John was intently watching his every move. Then he asked for a little while to get ready, as if he had simply been roused from a nap.

×

Danny Oster was leaning against the rail of the front porch, smoking a cigarette and watching the parade of snow clouds move over the treetops. "You're going to drive me back to my truck," John said.

"What are you going to do?"

"He has something he needs to take care of."

"He needs to go to the hospital."

"He's needed that for days!" John snapped. Just this tiny outburst had them both staring at their feet, a small but potent reminder of the violence that had flown between them in the past. "He needs to claim Mike's body before his parents have a change of heart. They're big-time Bible thumpers, but the longer they look like assholes on television, the better the chances they might reconsider. If they claim that body, Alex will never get to pay his last respects."

Five minutes later, they were pulling into the diner's parking lot in Oster's Cadillac Seville, inherited from his mother. John gripped the door handle, then felt the words coming up out of him, too fast to stop. "You're not to blame for everything my brother did to himself, but you had no business with him. No, it wasn't rape, but it wasn't love, either. Maybe inside you were the same age as him back then. But I hope you're older now, Danny. I really do."

He looked at Oster, saw him staring dead ahead with a defiant set to his jaw and both hands holding the steering wheel. John got inside his truck, and they both drove back to the house. They were pulling into the driveway when John saw that Alex had walked halfway down the steps by himself, but the half grimace on his face and the flush in his cheeks suggested that he had been halted by pain. John parked his truck as Oster mounted the steps five at a time and began leading Alex down the rest of the way, with one arm wrapped tightly around the guy's lower back.

Alex was loaded into the passenger seat, and John was about to step behind the wheel when Oster called out to him. John looked up, saw Oster was ten steps from the bottom, a safe distance between them once again. "Where is he buried, John?"

He wanted to break the guy's nose again. But he was learning not to trust these full-body reactions to short sentences. Hiding the location of his brother's grave felt akin to hiding the fact of his death. So instead he told Oster the name of the cemetery in Cherry Valley that had been emblazoned on his memory ever since his sister had mailed it to him upon his return home from Iraq.

John had just turned onto Highway 129 when Alex said, "Where did you think I was?"

"I didn't know. I tried to find you. I thought you were hiding."

"Why?"

"I thought you were going to kill Ray Duncan."

Alex turned to look at him without lifting his head from where it was resting against the window. "Why, John?"

"Because if I had been through what you'd been through, it's what I would have done."

×

Four hours later, they reached Boswell. As they approached the squat stone building that housed the Hanrock County morgue,

John saw that Patsy had followed his instructions to alert every television station in the state of their imminent arrival. When the shouting reporters moved in on their truck like a tide, Alex gave John a fearful look, but in such a short time John had become so accustomed to crowds of reporters that he knew he could lead Alex through the crowd without fail.

With his left arm wrapped around Alex's lower back for support, John walked them toward the glass doors to the building's lobby. Patsy was already inside, standing before several uniformed sheriff's deputies who didn't seem happy to see her, the reporters outside, or the two new arrivals who had become the center of the storm. He had instructed Alex not to respond to any questions, which left him to do the talking.

Why were they there today? What were they trying to do?

John shouted over the reporters' questions, "We are here to claim the body of Michael Bowers, former captain in the United States Marine Corps. His body has been in the morgue for three days now, like a John Doe, due to the bigotry of his family members. He should be released to the man he shared his life and his home with, and that man is Alex Martin." He tried to ignore the reporters angling their tape recorders at his mouth and the hot glare of the news cameras blocking their path.

It took them fifteen minutes to reach the front doors of the building. Several times Alex almost lost his footing, winced in pain when John's attempt to readjust him brushed up against his injured side. If two of the deputies hadn't come out of the lobby to guide them through, they might not ever have made it inside.

Patsy made no move to welcome either of them. Her pale, wide-eyed expression suggested that the cops had threatened to beat her with their nightsticks before John and Alex showed up. The cold look she gave Alex was for show; she had cried when John had told her where he finally found the man and how he had ended up there. The miniphalanx included the white-haired sheriff, whom John had not seen since those frozen seconds before Charlotte Martin had been fatally shot.

For a few seconds they all stood there, frozen, listening to the clamor of reporters outside. Finally the sheriff said, "This was not the way to go about this, Mr. Houck."

"Has anyone claimed the body of Mike Bowers?"

"Mr. Martin," the sheriff said, ignoring John altogether, "there are some questions we need—"

"*After* he sees the body," John interjected.

The sheriff glared at him fiercely. "No bodies will be changing hands today," he said quietly. "Is that understood?"

"Fine. But I don't see why he can't pay his respects."

"And I don't really care what you think, Mr. Houck."

"I know you don't. But you care what *they* think," John said, nodding his head at the reporters behind them.

With a schoolteacher's condescension, the sheriff said, "An appropriate time will come for Mr. Martin to pay his respects, but for now we need to—"

"You're standing on the wrong side of this one, and you know it. Step aside," John said.

The sheriff said, "Now, if I could ask you folks to please clear—"

"Step aside!"

One of the deputies reached for his gun holster. Patsy whispered John's name under her breath. The sheriff went stone still; then his Adam's apple jerked and his eyes focused on the melee outside the glass doors. In a careful voice he said, "Mr. Martin, after you pay your respects, there are some questions my detectives will need to ask of you. Given the circumstances, you can rest assured *I* won't be asking them, but someone will. And they'll be waiting for you outside the morgue."

The implication of the sheriff's last statement was lost on Alex. John still hadn't told him that his mother was dead, much less dead by the sheriff's gun. Several reporters had shouted questions at Alex about Charlotte's death, but Alex hadn't been able to hear them. Alex offered a meek thank-you that betrayed no confusion. There was a moment's hesitation as the deputies looked at each other like dancers who had forgotten their steps. Then the sheriff waved them aside. "Your first right," the sheriff said.

John and Alex moved to the head of the small formation. He heard Patsy's footsteps right behind him, felt her hand squeeze his shoulder as they continued forward. John glanced back, saw the sheriff and three of his deputies following them from a distance of several yards. At the end of the hallway was a set of double doors beneath a sign for the morgue. When Alex saw them, he took a sharp breath. Then his legs seemed to go out from under him. He pulled John down with him until Alex was on his knees and John was crouching in front of him, Alex's arm still wrapped halfway around his back.

Behind them, the assemblage had stopped. Patsy brought one hand to her mouth, as if she were terrified that any show of weakness by Alex would have the sheriff and his men rushing forward to end this moment once and for all. Alex struggled to gain control of his breathing. He was trying to speak, but sobs were threatening to break from him, and John couldn't see a way to break them for him.

When he finally caught his breath, Alex whispered, "I don't think I can do this. I'm sorry, John. You picked the wrong man for this mission."

"I didn't pick you for this one. Mike did."

Alex looked up into his eyes and went still. Then he gently placed his hands on either side of John's face and kissed him on his forehead. Before this moment could become anything other than skin brushing against skin, Alex got to his feet once again and curved his arm around John's back.

John walked Alex toward the double doors at the end of the hallway and the blaze of fluorescent light on the other side. John walked toward a scene of death with the confidence that there would be more life waiting for him on the other side of it. The forgiveness he had sought had come to him in a form he would have found repugnant just days before, a gentle kiss that had neither turned his stomach nor greased his palms.

He had hoped for many things in his life. Had they already arrived in forms he couldn't recognize or refused to accept? Forgiveness had been his only goal, but he had also been granted a stranger's eyes. Those eyes had glimpsed John's past and seen the true story John had not been able to see, a story that released John from a brother who had never wanted to be saved.

At the moment John and Alex slipped through the doors to the morgue, he heard one of the deputies ask Patsy if she was all right, but he couldn't make out her answer, and he figured she was crying.

Later, when he asked her what she had said, Patsy answered, "I told them I was never happier. I told them my brother was home."

ACKNOWLEDGMENTS

I've found a wonderful new family at Scribner, starting with my editor, Mitchell Ivers, and including Nan Graham, Susan Moldow, Rosalind Lippel, Louise Burke, and the divine Carolyn Reidy. Endless thanks to Lynn Nesbit for getting me there.

My research assistant, Sherry Merryman, was invaluable, although I was pretty sure she was going to quit if I asked her to send me one more map of one more California mountain town. Kurt Troxler answered all of my questions about firearms and how *not* to use them, by e-mail, mostly from locations in the Middle East he couldn't disclose. As with all research, I could use only about 10 percent of it, and any errors belong to me alone. Additional thanks go to Josh McNey and Gregg Hurwitz.

I probably wouldn't have written this novel if I hadn't read the following three books. One was *Twentynine Palms: A Tale of Murder, Marines, and the Mojave* by Deanne Stillman, which introduced me to the high desert and the women who try to make a life there. As of this writing, it's out of print; it shouldn't be.

Another was *Generation Kill: Devil Dogs, Iceman, Captain America, and the New Face of American War* by Evan Wright. When I was unsure of what to write after my last book, Evan Wright and two of the Marines featured in his book appeared at a book festival I was attending. Their presentation introduced me to Force Recon and the uneasy place it occupies in an increasingly unpopular war that continues as of this writing.

The last book was *One Bullet Away: The Making of a Marine Officer* by Nathaniel Fick, which articulated Marine Corps philosophy from a perspective I could relate to. These three books are nonfiction. Mine is fiction. There's a big difference. But it's my hope that John Houck and Mike Bowers share some of the core values with the better men depicted in the last two.

I am also indebted to *Los Angeles Times* staff writer David Zucchino for his series of articles on medical conditions in Iraq and long-term care for our war wounded.

Profound gratitude also goes to the usual support system that makes each book possible: Sue Tebbe, Beckett Ghiotto, Sandra LaSalle, the Quiet Riot 2 Boys, Rich Green at CAA, and, of course, my mother.

Last, several Marines helped me with the writing of this book. But they're gay, so I can't mention them by name or else they might be discharged. Some of them were in Iraq as I wrote this. Like everyone who serves, straight and gay, they are in my prayers.

ABOUT THE AUTHOR

At twenty-nine, Christopher Rice is the author of three *New York Times* bestselling novels and is a regular columnist for *Advocate* magazine. His first novel, *A Density of Souls,* was published when the author was twenty-two years old and to a landslide of media attention, most of it due to the fact that Christopher is the son of bestselling vampire novelist Anne Rice. He followed up with a second *New York Times* bestselling thriller, *The Snow Garden,* a dark tale of infidelity and art history set on a New England college campus. (*The Snow Garden* received a Lambda Literary Award.) His third *New York Times* bestseller, *Light Before Day,* was selected as the first annual summer reading book by *Frontiers* magazine and hailed as a "book of the year" by bestselling, critically acclaimed thriller writer Lee Child.

A native of California but a Southerner by blood, Christopher returned to the West Coast four years ago. He lives in West Hollywood. He was recently a visiting faculty member in the graduate writing program at Otis College of Art and Design.